BILL FOR THE USE OF A BODY

DENNIS WHEATLEY

DENNIS WHEATLEY

BILL FOR
THE USE OF A BODY

Frontispiece Portrait by
MARK GERSON

Original Illustrations by
GARY REES

Distributed by
HERON BOOKS

Published by arrangement with
Hutchinson and Co. (Publishers) Ltd.

For

SHEILA

and for all those who showed such
gracious hospitality to my wife and
myself while we were in the Far
East.

CONTENTS

THE PAST CATCHES UP WITH
MR. HAYASHI

MR. INOSUKE HAYASHI's lined face remained impassive as he looked down into the square wooden box that contained the bloody severed head of his only son. But his apparent calm did not deceive Police Chief for External Affairs, Okabe. A little vein pulsing in the bereaved father's forehead told him that if Hayashi could get his hands on his son's murderer there would be another murder done.

The box had been sent from Macao, the Portuguese colony on the coast of China, and addressed to Mr. Hayashi at his home in Kyoto. It had been opened by the Customs who had despatched it to Police Headquarters Tokyo, and Hayashi had been summoned to the capital. There, Okabe had broken to him the news of the grisly present he had been sent and asked him if he could identify the blotchy, mortifying features of the head in the box.

There was no clue to the sender and Hayashi could throw no light on the affair. He could say only that his son, a man of thirty, had gone a fortnight before to Hong Kong on business connected with a line of coastal trading ships of which his family were the principal shareholders.

Although Okabe had never been able to secure evidence against the Hayashis, he had good grounds for believing that a considerable part of their wealth came from using these small ships for dope smuggling. In consequence, had there been no other factors in the case he would have assumed that the younger Hayashi had become the victim of a rival organization, and that his head had been sent to his father as a warning to cease operating in their territory.

But that seemed unlikely, because this was not the first severed head in a box that had arrived in the same way on the Police Chief's desk. Since 1952 four others had come in at long intervals and, as far as he had been able to find out, none of these previous victims had been in any way connected with criminal activities.

The first, Otoya Matsuko, had been the representative of a big firm of radio manufacturers; the second, Yasunari Kido, a doctor who had gone to Hong Kong to attend a medical conference; the third, Kayno Nakayama, an engineer who had hoped to secure a contract connected with the improvement of Hong Kong's water supply; and the fourth, Zosho Iwanami, a traveller in Japanese cultured pearls. All four had disappeared after being for upwards of a week in Hong Kong and their heads had been despatched from Macao. One thing only linked the four victims: they had all served in the 230th Infantry Regiment, commanded by Colonel Shoji when it had been part of the Army that had invaded and conquered Hong Kong in December 1942. But the best endeavours of the Japanese Police, with the willing co-operation of the Hong Kong and Macao Police, had failed to provide any indication as to when, where and why these men had been murdered.

Having given Hayashi such particulars as he could of these previous crimes, Okabe went on, 'While our enquiries revealed no circumstances in their previous lives for anyone wishing to bring about their deaths, it will not have escaped my honourable visitor's astute mind that a common motive may have inspired their untimely end. However unwillingly, we must admit between ourselves that during the conquest of Hong Kong some of our troops,

2

elated by their splendid victory, got out of hand and committed acts of a discreditable nature. It is therefore not unreasonable to assume that someone in Hong Kong who suffered at the hands of men of the 230th Regiment is systematically revenging himself upon the men of that unit whenever opportunity offers. Your honourable son, would, of course, have been too young to have participated in the war; but it has occurred to me that your honourable self, perhaps . . .'

He knew the answer before Hayashi gave it. The small, elderly man inclined his head and replied gravely, 'The assumption of the honourable Chief of Police is correct. Before the war I spent much of my time in Europe. I speak English fluently and also acquired some small understanding of the curious and frequently illogical mentality of the English. In 1940, thinking it probable that the exalted Son of Heaven would decide to extend his Empire at the expense of the British, I naturally offered my humble services to our country and was accepted into the Intelligence Corps. My poor abilities received recognition beyond their deserts and I was rapidly promoted. By December 1941 I had become a Colonel, and Chief Intelligence Officer to the 38th Division. The 230th Infantry Regiment was a part of that Division and with it I entered Hong Kong. There were, of course, certain regrettable incidents and from what has gone before it seems highly probable that the shrewd deduction of my honourable friend provides the motive for this abominable crime.'

Hayashi did not add that after the war he had been tried as a War Criminal and served a ten-year sentence for atrocities for which he had been responsible. But Okabe knew that too. He merely nodded, sucked his prominent teeth and said:

'That being so, perhaps my honourable visitor can recall some specific incident of which he was a witness: a British officer who was badly beaten up, or something of

3

that kind. If so we might trace the man and find him to be the murderer of your son.'

With a slight shake of his nearly bald head Hayashi replied, 'There were a number of incidents. Our men had fought hard. It was natural that in the hour of their triumph they should wish to see the insolent English grovelling at their feet. But it is all so long ago. The names of such officers as I chanced to have dealings with have passed out of my memory.'

The bespectacled Police Chief shrugged his plump shoulders. 'In that case we can do no more than proceed with routine enquiries. Now that you have identified the victim as your son the police in both Hong Kong and Macao will do their utmost to trace his last movements and investigate any persons with whom he was known to have associated during his stay on the island. But in view of their lack of success with regard to the earlier victims I cannot hold out any great hope that your honourable desire to see justice done will be satisfied.'

The small dark eyes in Hayashi's wrinkled face narrowed to slits, and in a venomous whisper that was almost a hiss he said, 'In that, honourable sir, you are mistaken. You cannot refuse me the fullest possible particulars of those earlier victims, their families, business associates and so on. With that information, and by an exhaustive enquiry into my son's activities while in Hong Kong, I shall succeed in hunting down this English pig who has become an assassin. Yes, if it costs me my last hundred yen I'll see to it that he pays in full for his abominable crime. And when I get him I shall not call on the law to provide him with a relatively painless execution.'

The Police Chief rarely felt sympathy for any of the many criminals with whom his work brought him into contact and he had none at all for Hayashi, except as a father who had just lost his only son, for he knew him to be a man who had brought disgrace on his country, and had good reason to believe that he had amassed his big

4

fortune mainly in ways that had brought misery to great numbers of people.

Okabe also knew that Hayashi had contacts in every port in the China Seas, and the wealth to employ scores of unscrupulous hirelings who would use methods barred to the police to extort the truth from people; so there was quite a possibility that, sooner or later, he would get his man. He had spoken with such cold, malevolent determination that, at the thought that he might succeed, even the hardened Police Chief felt a sudden surge of pity as he envisaged the ghastly death in some secret hide-out that Hayashi would inflict on the Englishman who it was presumed had killed his son.

CHAPTER II

HELL IN A SEA-GIRT PARADISE

JULIAN DAY was sitting on the grass, in the warm February sunshine, near the flagstaff on the Peak of Hong Kong. The Peak is so often mentioned as a main feature of the beautiful island that many people who have never been there are apt to visualize it as a somewhat larger Gibraltar: a solitary mountain rising out of the sea. But that is far from being the case. The Peak is only the highest of nine mountains in the eleven-mile-long island, and the island itself only the second largest of an archipelago which, together with Kowloon on the mainland and the New Territories, goes to make up the three hundred and sixty square miles of the Colony.

Even from where Julian was sitting, eighteen hundred feet up, other peaks to the south and east, outlined against a cloudless blue sky, cut off his view of many of the beautiful bays with their beaches of golden sand. But looking northward he saw a magnificent panorama spread before him. The ground sloped almost sheer to the splendid city of Victoria, nearly three miles long and half a mile deep, curving along the nearer shore of the enormous harbour.

Riding at anchor in the harbour, gaily dressed with flags but looking like toys at that distance, lay a part of the Western Allies' Far Eastern Fleet—three aircraft carriers, four cruisers and eight or ten destroyers. Fringing the docks were a score of merchant ships and liners.

6

Resembling water-beetles, the big ferries that carried a hundred thousand people a day scuttled back and forth between Victoria and her twin city of Kowloon on the peninsula opposite. From the peninsula's eastern side the great causeway of the Kai Tak Airport projected like a pointing finger out into the sea, and every few minutes an aircraft owned by one of a dozen nations was either landing or taking off from it. Beyond the sprawling city the land broadened out into hills and fertile valleys, then in the distance there rose range after range of mountains, merging some twenty miles away into Red China.

As Julian's gaze roved over the massed roofs down on the sea-shore he marvelled at the way in which Hong Kong had grown since he had last been there. The city had not only spread both to east and west as far as the eye could see, but a score of skyscrapers now towered up from it and another dozen dwarfed the biggest older buildings in Kowloon. The airport too had formerly had only two short runways, whereas now, by a great feat of underwater engineering, it had been extended for a mile and a half out into the sea, so that the largest jet aircraft could land there.

But the feature which more than any other showed the growth of the two cities was that in a hundred places where there had previously been areas of mean streets or waste land there were now great blocks of modern flats; while further out in the suburbs there were whole groups of these blocks. Yet even those that Julian could see with his bird's-eye view he knew to be only a small part of the amazing feat that the Government of the Colony had achieved to cope with the enormous influx of refugees from Red China. At Choi Hung they had erected eight blocks all twenty storeys high with forty flats on each floor. That estate alone accommodated some fifteen thousand people; and to care for the children they were opening a new school for a thousand pupils every ten

7

days. As he thought of that, Julian wished that the anti-colonial Americans and the Blacks, Browns and Yellows who so consistently abused Britain in their parrot-house, the United Nations, could be forced to come to Hong Kong and see what the old British Raj, at its best, could do.

He knew, though, that although this herculean labour for humanity was mainly due to the able planning and administration of selfless and devoted British civil servants, it could not have been achieved without the wholehearted co-operation of the Chinese, who made up nine-tenths of the Colony's population.

Before the war Hong Kong's prosperity had arisen from the fact that it was the entry port for the great Chinese city of Canton that lay some sixty miles away to the west up the great island-spattered estuary. With the triumph of Communism in China the door had suddenly been slammed, cutting off the multi-million trade between Europe and China. For a while it had looked as though Hong Kong must wither and become bankrupt. But during the years of strife on the mainland great numbers of wealthy Chinese had seen the red light, got their money out in time and emigrated to Hong Kong. With British encouragement these highly intelligent men had revolutionized the status of the Colony. It had originally been mainly a channel for supplying China with goods from the Western world, but by building over 5,000 factories, large and small, and establishing a great variety of new enterprises, they had made the Colony not only self-supporting, but, with the one exception of Japan, the greatest centre of industry in the Far East.

To that had to be added the contribution of the million Chinese who, mostly penniless, had sought refuge in the Colony. Thrifty, cheerful and industrious by nature, they were gluttons for work. They were no believers in short hours, let alone wildcat strikes. Their one aim in life was

8

to be able to support their families in comfort and have a little money put by in case of misfortune. Three hundred thousand of them had been settled on farms, to start with in wooden shacks, but now great numbers of them were living in pleasant bungalows with radios, refrigerators and washing machines. Hundreds of thousands of others who, at first, teemed like ants in squalid shanty towns had since earned enough to furnish and live well in the flats on the great housing estates that the Government let to them at a nominal rent.

As Julian's eyes again swept the seventeen square miles of blue water that formed the almost land-locked harbour, they came to rest on Stonecutter's Island. It lay close to and on the west side of the Kowloon peninsula. On a Christmas night twenty-two years earlier he had taken his life in his hands and, fully clothed, swum the two miles out to it. Even when, utterly exhausted, he had floundered ashore, and for many hours afterwards, he had still been in deadly peril; for the whole area was swarming with Japanese. At 3.15 that afternoon Hong Kong had surrendered, but the bestial Japs were still butchering any stray British soldiers they came upon, and only the fact that Julian knew a few sentences of Japanese had later saved him.

That he knew any Japanese at all was due to the extraordinary flair of the Service departments for posting square pegs in round holes. Julian had joined up in Cairo early in the war. As he could speak most of the Mediterranean languages, including Arabic, Russell Pasha had, with his usual good sense, secured him a commission in the Interpreter Corps. In that capacity he had fought with the New Zealanders during General Wavell's brilliant campaign in Libya and later in the disastrous expedition to Greece. After the evacuation of what remained of the British force to Egypt he had been seconded to Intelligence and for some weeks employed in Cairo translating Arabic documents. Then it had been decided to increase the

Headquarters Staff in Singapore; upon which, although Julian knew nothing about the Far East or any of its languages, some dunderhead had had him posted there as an extra Intelligence Officer.

As he had a flair for languages, after some months of tuition he picked up enough Japanese and Chinese to get the general sense of printed or typed documents, but no-one pressed him to exert himself. The convinced opinion of the General Staff was that the Japanese had no intention of entering the war against Britain. It was said that they still had plenty on their plate in China and that they would be fools to imperil the seaborne trade out of which they were making so much money. For a young subaltern Singapore offered many delightful distractions; so, with an untroubled conscience, Julian had spent a minimum of time in his office and had happily given himself up to the joys of tennis, bathing, cocktail parties and good dinners with pretty girls.

But this pleasant existence was not destined to last. In September 1941 the energetic Major-General Christopher Maltby was nominated to succeed General Grassett as G.O.C. British Troops in Hong Kong; and with him, as one of his Staff Officers, he took Julian.

On arriving there they found the same state of complacency as had existed in Singapore, and Julian discovered that the island in the China Seas offered a personable bachelor who had ample private means even more distractions; so for some weeks, although his new Chief worked him considerably harder, his leisure was most happily filled by participating in the peacetime activities of the Colony.

Nevertheless, he was aware that his General and the Governor, Sir Mark Young, also newly appointed, were extremely worried men. Neither of them concealed from his Staff the anxiety he felt about the poor state in which he found Hong Kong's defences.

The mobile military garrison consisted of only four

battalions: the 2nd Royal Scots, the 1st Middlesex, the 5/7th Rajputs and the 2/4th Punjabis, and all were under strength owing to the prevalence of malaria and venereal disease. At the last moment they were reinforced by two Canadian battalions: the Winnipeg Grenadiers and the Royal Rifles of Canada; but these troops, gallant as many of them proved when they found themselves with their backs to the wall, were raw, ill-disciplined and quite unfitted to be put into a line of battle before they had had several months' intensive training. To these could be added seven companies of the Hong Kong Volunteer Defence Corps, many of whom were middle-aged and, again, were unsuited to being thrown into a battle. With this force, totalling some six thousand men, half of whom could not be deployed, Maltby was expected to hold a line on the mainland laid down by some past military pundit that extended for ten and a half miles against—as it later transpired—thirty thousand battle-hardened Japanese.

The prospect of having to defend the island would not have appeared quite so grim if Maltby had had adequate sea and air forces to support his troops on the mainland and, when they were forced to withdraw, to prevent the island being invaded. But the Navy could muster only two old destroyers and six motor torpedo boats, while the pitiful air force consisted of four Vickers Wildebeeste torpedo bombers and three Walrus amphibians, none of which had a maximum speed of more than one hundred miles per hour.

Still more perturbing, the garrison's munitions had been most scandalously allowed to run down. Shells for the gunners would have to be so strictly rationed that it would be impossible for them to put up barrages lasting for more than a few minutes; ammunition for the mortars was so limited that the whole lot would be blazed off in a single day's intensive fighting; effective training had to be curtailed because little small-arms ammunition could

11

be spared for it; the supply of drugs and other hospital requirements was hopelessly inadequate and the four torpedo bombers had not a single torpedo.

Yet in the winter sunshine the social life of the Colony continued unabated. There were dances at the Peninsula Hotel, water picnics in Gindrinkers Bay, golf tournaments on the fine course in the south of the island, and every Saturday the race course in Happy Valley was thronged with huge crowds that afterwards dispersed to form hundreds of jolly parties in private houses.

It was not until Sunday December the 7th that Maltby knew definitely that his testing time could not now be long delayed. He was attending a Church Parade that had all the glamour of a peacetime military ceremony. He had just finished reading the first Lesson when an officer came in to whisper to him the disquieting news that the Punjabis had reported a threatening concentration of Japanese troops to be massing on their front north of Fan Ling. The General and his senior officers quietly slipped away and back to his Headquarters. But there was little that he could do. The Royal Scots, the Rajputs and the Punjabis were already thinly spread out along the preordained front line. The Middlesex and the Canadians were held in reserve on the island. All units were alerted and the Hong Kong Volunteer Defence Corps swiftly mobilized to take up their war stations.

It was at ten to five on the following morning that Julian was roused from the deep healthy sleep of the young by his Chief, Major Charles Boxer, the senior Intelligence Officer on the General's staff. Boxer had been sitting up all night listening to the broadcast from Tokyo. At 4.45 an announcer who had been giving particulars of the programme for the coming evening was suddenly replaced by another, who had harshly declared that Japan was now at war with Britain and the United States of America.

From that moment there were no more picnics or

12

parties for Julian. Life became grim and somewhat more than earnest. By five past eight a squadron of Japanese dive bombers had utterly obliterated Kai Tak Airport and soon afterwards the skill in evasive manœuvres of gallant, one-armed Lieutenant-Commander John Boldero was being exerted to the utmost to keep his old destroyer, H.M.S. *Cicala*, from being sunk.

For close on forty-eight hours the line on the mainland held. The Punjabis and the Rajputs, with absolute faith in their British officers, behaved magnificently, carrying out every order without a moment's hesitation and inflicting terrific casualties on the enemy. But the Royal Scots, made flabby from too many months of indolence, too much cheap liquor and too many willing Chinese women, failed to show the fighting qualities that are the proud tradition of that famous regiment. On the night of the 9th/10th they allowed themselves to be surprised and driven from the strong Shingmun Redoubt, the holding of which was vital to the retention of the line. They fell back on Golden Hill, but were so demoralized that they also failed to hold that position. By midday on the 11th General Maltby realized that he was left with no alternative than to withdraw all Imperial Forces from the mainland.

The night was moonless and, in the Stygian darkness, conditions at the Kowloon ferry were chaotic. For four days without sleep the three battalions had been pitted against two divisions of fanatical Japanese, yet they had inflicted infinitely more casualties than they had sustained. Lost, punch-drunk and bewildered, the greater part of them somehow found their way to the waterfront. Somehow the handful of naval officers organized a miniature Dunkirk and got them away to the island.

By the 13th the Japanese had brought up their heavy guns and had begun the bombardment of Hong Kong Island. Even up to a few days before the outbreak of this new war there had been scores of Japanese agents in the city, working as barbers, waiters and electricians. Extraordinary to record, for the past year a Colonel Suzki of the Japanese Intelligence had been permitted to reside there on the excuse that he was learning English, and it was not until the end of November that he had blandly taken leave of the many trusting residents who had entertained him. In consequence the Japanese had registered the exact position of every fort and strong point, which led to the shelling, and the bombing by their aircraft, proving terrifyingly effective.

At 9.15 on the evening of the 15th the enemy sought to probe the strength of the island's defences by sending across two companies of infantry. The operation was suicidal. Caught in the glare of the searchlights the small invading force was completely annihilated while still in the water. As the attempt was made on a sector of the shore held by the Canadians, it was a heartening experience for these raw troops to defeat it utterly. But the success proved a most misleading curtain raiser.

On the 17th the Japanese Commander, General Ito Takeo, sent across, under a flag of truce, a peace mission. As Governor and Commander-in-Chief, Sir Mark Young replied that he declined absolutely to enter into any negotiations for surrender and that he was not prepared to receive any further communications on the subject. That afternoon the bombardment was renewed with greater intensity; but on the morning of the 18th the Japanese guns fell ominously silent. With tensed nerves everyone knew then that they would shortly be called on to face an all-out attack by the enemy.

General Takeo had used only two of his divisions in the fighting on the mainland. He had kept the third in reserve for an assault on Hong Kong. At 10 p.m. on the 18th its three regiments—the 228th, commanded by Colonel Doi, the 229th by Colonel Tanaka and the 230th by Colonel Shoji—made their landings between North Point and Lyemun. To add to the difficulties of the defence the night was very dark, it was raining and a strong wind was blowing; so that dense clouds of smoke from the oil tanks at North Point, which Japanese shells had set alight, rendered visibility near zero along the greater part of the north coast. The result was that several units received no warning that the enemy had landed, and were taken by surprise.

That was the case with the 5th Anti-Aircraft Battery of the Hong Kong Volunteers. The twenty-nine men occupying Lyemun Fort found themselves surrounded by a horde of Japanese before they were even aware that the enemy had got ashore. What followed remains as an indelible record of shame on the Japanese Army. Hopelessly outnumbered, the Hong Kong Volunteers saw no option but to accept from the Japanese Commander the promise of their lives if they surrendered. Told to lay down their arms and come outside with their hands up, they did as they were ordered—to receive in turn a bayonet in the stomach from the hilariously laughing Japanese soldiers, while their officer stood there showing his teeth in a delighted grin. But that was only a foretaste of what was in store for the garrison of Hong Kong.

At 7 a.m. on the 19th the medical orderlies at the Salesian Mission, which had been turned into an advance dressing station, were about to have their breakfast when a company of Japanese suddenly appeared on the scene. The post was flying the Red Cross and, as it was a non-combatant unit, the senior doctor naturally offered no opposition. On his surrender the orderlies, cooks and ambulance drivers were ordered out of the building, made to strip to their undergarments, then lined up some way off with their backs to their captors. A Japanese officer gave an order; screaming *Banzis*, his men surged forward at the charge and bayoneted every one of the prisoners in the base of the spine.

D Company of the 5/7th Rajputs, although outnumbered

15

ten to one, put up a splendid stand until their gallant Commander, Captain Bob Newton, was killed and the survivors, thirty mostly wounded men, realized that their position was hopeless. With ferocious glee the Japanese butchered the lot.

In scores of desperate engagements no wounded were taken prisoner but were bayoneted where they lay; and such prisoners as were taken were trussed like turkeys, with their wrists and ankles tight together in the small of their backs. With their spines arched to near breaking point they were left to lie in agony for hours on end. Then, when they were at last untied and marched to a cage, every one of them was beaten about the body or head with rifle butts. Several lost the sight of an eye and many of them had their teeth smashed in.

So it went on for five ghastly days. Post after post was surrounded and overwhelmed by swarms of Japanese. Yet never have Imperial troops fought with greater tenacity and been more deserving of imperishable glory. The Royal Scots, determined to atone for their precipitate retreat on the mainland, displayed stubborn courage equalling that of their predecessors, the 'Old Contemptibles' at Mons. The ever-cheerful Cockneys of the Middlesex made the enemy pay a terrible price for every foot of ground he gained. The Indian troops, born fighting men and trained to the last degree of perfection, showed incredible bravery, in many cases holding their positions for many hours after their officers had been killed. The Canadians, raw troops though they were, showed the same mettle as had their fathers at Vimy Ridge, while the Hong Kong Volunteers performed feats of valour that are still a legend on the island. Both the Portuguese and Eurasian companies held their positions to the end, and a platoon of British veterans repelled continuous assaults on the Power House for over two days. Most of them were in their sixties ánd some over seventy, yet when they were at last driven from the Power House the survivors continued their battle from an overturned bus without hope of relief. But it was all of no avail.

By the third night after the landing fighting was taking place in every bay along the coast, the Japanese had driven the defenders from several of the island's crests and communications between Headquarters and a number of major units had been cut. The battle thereby having become chaotic and unmanageable, there was little of any value that a junior Intelligence Officer could do; so Julian asked his General's permission to go out and fight, and it was readily granted.

Not knowing when he would have a chance even to lie down again, he had the good sense to get a last night's good sleep in the fortress; then early on the morning of the 22nd he went down into the city. The bombing and shelling had led to its becoming a scene of indescribable confusion, but down at the docks he found a young Captain who had already been wounded collecting together a miscellaneous body of men. There were half a dozen sailors from the *Cicala* which, with four out of six of the motor torpedo boats, had been sunk, and some Canadian stragglers; the rest were not soldiers in the true sense but details from the Base Ordnance Corps and the R.A.S.C., clerks, cooks and storekeepers. Many of them had never before handled a rifle, but they were all game to fight. Julian joined them and they set off past Happy Valley up into the hills.

That afternoon they had their first engagement with the Japanese. For thirty-eight hours, though gradually dwindling in numbers, they managed to hold their position against a series of attacks; but at dawn on the twenty-fourth they were forced to withdraw from it in disorder. Julian got away with six men down a steep gully; but for the twenty-four hours that followed he felt himself to be living through a nightmare. In whichever direction the little party made its way they found themselves heading towards parties of Japs.

17

During the day they engaged in a dozen skirmishes and each time had to beat another retreat. Two of the party were killed, another was shot through the wrist and Julian had a wound in his left forearm. By nightfall they had run out of ammunition, were hungry, thirsty, looking like scarecrows and almost asleep on their feet.

Their first position had been on Mount Cameron; but the series of zigzags they had made during the day had brought them round on to the lower slopes of Mount Butler, not far from the eastern suburbs of the city, and Julian decided that their best hope now lay in getting down to it. But shortly afterwards they came upon a cave and they were all so weary that he thought it best that they should first rest there for a few hours.

At midnight, limping and stumbling in the dark, they set off along a narrow track that led downwards. Ten minutes later, at a junction of the track, they ran head-on into a Japanese patrol. The nearest man jabbed at Julian with his bayonet. He side-stepped and clubbed the man in the face with his pistol. As he jumped back he heard the Canadian who had been following him shout:

'We've no ammunition left! We surrender!' But the Japanese ignored his cry and several of them dashed past Julian. Next moment he heard the screams of his companions as sharp cold steel was plunged into their bodies.

Realizing that if he remained where he was his life was not worth a moment's purchase, he took a pace forward and threw himself over the cliff. Although steep, it was not sheer and was covered with coarse grass. He bounced twice, rolled over and over for a hundred feet and came to rest caught up by a good-sized bush.

For a while he lay there half stunned; then he pulled himself together, wriggled free of the bush and, sitting on the steep slope with his head in his hands, tried to think what was now the best thing to do. If he continued his progress while it was still dark he might go over a real precipice or, perhaps, run into another patrol of Japs. Deciding that he would stand a better chance of getting down to the city in safety if he postponed his attempt until it was light, he fell into an uneasy doze.

When dawn came he roused himself and, lying on his stomach, scrambled his way down the lower part of the slope to the cover of a group of small houses. His wound was not serious but, fearing that if he did not get it dressed it might become gangrenous, he was anxious to have it attended to. There were no Japanese to be seen, so it did not look as though they had yet penetrated the city. His strength renewed by his hours of rest in the cave and on the slope, he set off through the streets, already filled with scared and bewildered Chinese, towards St. Stephen's Hospital. By half past six he was within five hundred yards of it. Suddenly he noticed that the streets were no longer teeming with frightened crowds but almost deserted. As he halted in his tracks a Corporal of the Middlesex with a bloody handkerchief round his head stepped out from a nearby doorway and asked in a husky voice:

'Where yer goin', sir?'

When Julian told him, the Corporal said, 'Fer Gawd's sake don't, sir. The Japs is there. Them little yellow bastards'll jab a bayonet in yer guts fer certain. 'Alf an 'our back I got art of a scullery winder. But I seen enough ter know the form. Ole Doc' Black, what's the big shot there, tried to prevent 'em comin' in; but they just laughed an' gave 'im the works on the doorstep. Then them swine set abart the wounded. Bayoneted the poor sods in their beds. That's what they did. Then them swine set abart raping the nurses, may they rot in 'ell.'

Julian closed his eyes and a shudder of horror ran through him. Opening them again, he said thickly, 'Thanks for stopping me, Corporal. It's too ghastly to think about. I'm afraid we've had it. What a Christmas morning! It's every man for himself now and I doubt if many of us will see in the New Year.'

'That's it, sir,' the Corporal agreed. 'Sell our lives dearly. That's the drill. Like my Brigadier. I were on 'is 'Eadquarters Staff these lars' few days while 'e were commanding the western sector. It were my luck to be sent art to try to mend a telephone wire so when I gets back I saw what 'appened while lying in the bushes. The 'Eadquarters was surrounded. 'Ole area just swarmin' with them little yellow 'orrors. Then art comes Brigadier Lawson wiv a pistol in each 'and. 'E gives it to 'em right an' left an' took six of the misbegotten bastards wiv 'im. When the rest of the Staff come art wiv their 'ands up they was tied up in bundles of three, then stuck again and again, just as though they was 'ay sacks in a bayonet practice. Gawd, it were awful! Me stomach turned over at their yellin'. I was sick as a dog, an' pissin' meself that the Japs 'd spot me. But they didn't, an' when it fell dark I crawled away. The Brigadier 'ad the right idea though.'

Julian nodded. 'He certainly did. And when we have won the war we ought to castrate every Japanese who has set foot on this island.' After a moment he added, 'I think I'll make for the Jockey Club, as the best chance of getting my wound dressed. It's been turned into a temporary hospital. What about coming with me and having your head attended to?'

'No, thanks, sir,' the Corporal replied. 'My Chinese girl friend lives in a room upstairs. Those sons of bitches won't make do with them few nurses fer long. I give 'em no more 'n an 'our and they'll be darn 'ere 'unting fer wimmen in the tarn. I mean ter stick around. And Gawd 'elp the first few bloody little sods who get the idea that they'd like ter play their filthy games on 'er.'

They wished one another luck, then Julian turned his steps towards Happy Valley. When he reached the Jockey Club he found every bed in it occupied and the landings and passages crowded with other wounded men. Some were dying as they lay or crouched in corridors. After an hour he managed to get a nurse to look at his arm. Having given it a cursory glance she said, 'That's not serious, and I've far more urgent cases to attend to.'

'I'm sure you have,' he agreed, 'but if it's not sterilized I may lose my arm.'

She gave a quick nod. 'All right, go into that ward on the left and wait there. As soon as I can I'll come and attend to you.'

Just inside the ward he found a group of other lightly wounded men waiting to be patched up. To get free of the crowd he walked down between the beds to the window at the far end of the ward and perched himself on the sill. He had been sitting there for about twenty minutes when he caught the sound of shouts and curses coming from the corridor. A moment later the door burst open and a score of Japanese streamed into the ward.

They were obviously drunk on looted liquor. Yelling like scalded hell cats, they proceeded to lay about them with demoniac fury. In a matter of seconds the group of lightly wounded near the door had been reduced to a bloody shambles. Every one of them had gone down. Half disembowelled or with frightful neck wounds, they lay writhing and screaming on the floor.

Julian had turned, flung up the window and scrambled out on to the fire escape. While hesitating whether to run up or down it he gave a quick glance in through the window. The Japanese were swarming down the centre of the ward, pausing only at each bed to bayonet the wounded man in it. Riveted with horror, he stared in at this ghastly spectacle for another thirty seconds. During them the nurse to whom he had spoken, in a heroic endeavour to protect one of her patients, threw herself face down on top of him. With a fiendish grin the nearest Japanese raised his rifle sideways, then plunged his bayonet into the middle of her bottom.

The girl's piercing scream did something to Julian's stomach. Overcome by nausea, he choked and vomited. As he leaned forward to spew he caught sight of several Japanese outside the building, below him. Seeing that his only hope lay in endeavouring to hide in one of the rooms in an upper storey, he shinned up the fire escape and entered a window on the top floor.

The room was a fairly large one. It was furnished as a lounge, with two settees, several armchairs, a bookcase and a writing desk. As he stumbled into it he saw that criss-crossing the ceiling there hung several paper chains, and that on a square table in the centre stood a group of jugs, glasses, dishes and open boxes of such items as preserved fruit and chocolates. The decorations brought home to him again with a sudden pang that this, of all days, was Christmas Day. It seemed probable that he was in the nurses' off-duty room and that the goodies, left only partly arranged on the table, had been hastily abandoned by someone preparing a Christmas spread for them.

He had not eaten for many hours, so he grabbed up some biscuits. As he munched them he decided that to remain there could only postpone his capture and death, for it seemed certain that the drunken Japanese would break into every room in the building in search of other women to violate. Above him, along the middle of the ceiling, ran a wide, two-sided skylight, evidently to give the room more air during the great heat in summer. It had curtains to keep out the sun, but it was now shut and these were only partly drawn. From the skylight his mind flashed to the roof. There was at least a chance that the Japs would not search it, so he would be safer up there.

Seizing a jug of lemonade, he gulped down half its contents, then crammed his pockets full of biscuits and sugared almonds. Within three minutes he was back at the window. He had climbed out and was already a few steps up the fire escape when he caught the sound behind him of the door of the room being flung open and running feet. With his heart pounding he quickly tiptoed the rest of the way up to the roof, praying that his legs had not been seen by the Japs who had burst into the room.

Once on the roof he remained standing there for a few moments, from fear that if he advanced the tread of his heavy boots on the lead walkway would attract the attention of the men below. As he had noticed some bottles of port and sherry on a side table, he thought it probable that they would not leave the room until they had drunk them. To make certain that they were still there, he got down on his knees and crawled forward a few feet so that he could look down into the room through one of the panes of the skylight over which the curtain had not been drawn. He saw then that it was not the Japs who had burst in but a V.A.D., and she was dragging the writing desk across the door with the evident intention of barricading herself in.

Kneeling there by the skylight he found that it was not, as he had supposed, completely shut, so he lifted one of the sections and called down to her: 'Hi, there!'

With a start she turned and looked up at him. Her uniform was bloodstained, her cap awry and her features distorted by frantic terror. Yet at the first glance he realized that she was a lovely young creature. The wisps of hair that had escaped from beneath her cap were pale gold, her eyes a bright blue, her features regular and her flushed face was the colour of milk and roses. Giving a gasp, she shouted up to him:

'Oh, save me; save me! Those fiends downstairs are raping all the women. I won't be raped! I won't! Come down and help me make a barricade.'

Julian gave a quick shake of his head, but before he could speak she hurried on hysterically. 'You must. Oh,

23

for God's sake. I'm not strong enough to do this alone. I won't be raped. I'm a virgin. I'd sooner die first.'

'Don't be a fool,' Julian shouted back. 'No barricade we could make will keep those devils out. You'll stand a better chance if you come up here.'

At that moment the door handle rattled, then there came loud shouts from outside and the sound of heavy blows on the door. The girl's terrified eyes turned towards it, then up to Julian. 'They're here!' she gasped. 'But I won't let them get me. Shoot me! Shoot me while there's still time. I'd rather die.'

She was standing just below Julian; so had he had any ammunition for his pistol and been able to nerve himself for such a terrible act, he could easily have put a bullet through her head. Instead of wasting words to tell her that he couldn't, he cried, 'Do as I say! Come up to me. Not by the window. Get up on the table and I'll pull you up. That will be quicker.'

With sudden resolution the girl put one foot on a chair and the other on the table. But in her haste she slipped, lost her balance and measured her length on the floor. As she did so Julian subconsciously registered the fact that she was much taller than he had thought when looking down on her, and a strong, well-built young woman with long shapely legs. Next moment she had regained her feet and scrambled up on to the table.

She had locked the door before dragging the writing desk across it, but the howling Japanese outside had just fired a burst that had shot the lock away. As the desk was not a very heavy one there was not a moment to be lost. The girl held her arms high and went up on her toes. Reaching down, Julian found that he could get a comfortable grasp on her wrists. Next moment, as he took the strain, he realized that when he had told her to let him pull her up he had both forgotten the wound in his forearm and greatly underestimated the dead weight of such a big girl's body. Tensing his shoulders, he heaved to draw her upwards. A sharp pain shot through his arm and blood from the reopened wound began to flow down to his wrist. Only by gritting his teeth and exerting his utmost strength was he able to lift her clear of the table.

Staring up into his face, the girl sensed his sudden doubt of his ability to drag her through the skylight. Her bright blue eyes wide with terror, she yelled at him, 'Pull me up! Don't let them get me! Pull me up. For Christ's sake pull me up!'

For an agonizing two minutes that seemed an eternity Julian strove to raise her further. His muscles hurt intolerably and big beads of perspiration had broken out on his forehead, but he could not raise her even another few inches.

The sound of cracking wood now mingled with that of the blows from rifle butts on the door. The girl cast a swift glance over her shoulder. She saw that the writing desk had been forced back and that the Japs now had the door a little open. Frantically, she screamed at Julian, 'You bloody fool! If you hadn't the strength to pull me up you should have let me go out through the window. Oh, make an effort! Save me from them! Save me!'

Sweat was running into Julian's eyes, his heart felt as though it was about to burst, but she seemed to weigh a ton and it was all he could do to hold her dangling there.

With a yell of triumph the leading Jap forced his small body through the partly open door. In two springs he had reached the table and seized the girl by the legs. As she tried to kick herself free she gave a last despairing wail. 'Drop me! Drop me and shoot me!'

Julian did not wilfully let go her wrists. The extra strain of the Jap pulling at her legs and her kicking out tore them from his grasp. She fell with a crash among the crockery on the table but slid off it on to her feet. Too utterly distressed and horrified at the failure of his attempt to get her out, Julian temporarily forgot that he was exposed to a bullet and continued to stare down through the open skylight.

Three more Japs had charged into the room, their yellow faces sweaty from their exertions and the alcohol they had drunk. One of them struck the girl in the eye with his fist. With a moan she went over backwards on to the sofa. Almost as she fell the whole pack was on her. One of them ripped her blouse down from the neck, exposing one of her fine breasts; another put his foot on her stomach and, grasping her skirt with both hands, tore a large strip of it away, revealing her long slender legs.

Still impervious to his own danger, Julian shouted, 'Stop that, you swine! Stop that!'

For a moment they let go the girl to turn and stare up at him. The last to enter the room was still holding his machine pistol. He raised it to fire a burst but, just in time, Julian threw himself backwards.

Picking himself up he turned and ran, fearful now that one of them would come up after him and shoot him in the back. But he need not have worried and by the time he had concealed himself behind a chimney stack at the far end of the roof he realized that they had taken far too fine a prize in the girl to leave for the pleasure of shooting him.

Never before had he experienced such utter depths of misery as weighed upon him that afternoon. Still apprehensive that a Jap might come up on the roof and spot him, he spent the time crouched behind the chimney stack; but he could not keep his mind off what the girl must be going through and bitterly reproached himself with the thought that had he not overestimated his own strength she might have got away through the window and be up there with him. He could only pray that she had become unconscious or gone out of her mind early in her ordeal; but he thought that unlikely because her strong young body was just the type that could stand up to almost any amount of physical endurance before final exhaustion set in. And there was another factor that would make things even worse for her. The Japanese had a chip on their shoulder about being small men, and he knew from what he had heard in the past week that they took a special delight in inflicting pain and humiliation on the taller of their prisoners; what they might do to a tall, blonde English girl simply did not bear thinking about.

The long hours of the afternoon dragged by. Soon after darkness fell he cautiously made his way down a fire escape at the far end of the building. As the electric power on Hong Kong had failed during the battle, the city was in darkness, except for the glimmer of oil lamps and candles behind windows here and there. The sound of drunken singing told him that the Japanese were still in the hospital, but there were no sentries outside it, and as he slipped from one patch of shadow to another he did not encounter any of the enemy.

From mid afternoon, apart from the occasional crack of a rifle all firing had ceased, so he guessed that Hong Kong must have surrendered. Later he learned that the Japanese having penetrated the capital in several places and the situation having become beyond all hope, the capitulation had been made at 3.15 p.m.

Sir Mark Young and General Maltby had defended the Colony for seventeen days with an inadequate garrison, mainly obsolete weapons and a crippling shortage of munitions of war. No leaders, or the men under them, could have done more. It stands to their eternal glory that over five thousand men of the Imperial Forces were killed or severely wounded before they laid down their arms, and that as the price of victory they made the Japanese pay with thirteen thousand well-trained troops.

Two hours after Julian left the hospital his furtive progress through the darkened streets brought him to the waterfront of West Victoria. He had set off in that direction with the vague hope of being able to get hold of a sampan. But evidently all the boats had already been used by their owners to escape, or had been collected by the Japanese. As there were none to be seen, he was forced to face up to a major decision. Should he wait about until he was caught by the Japanese or risk his life in an attempt to reach the mainland? If he let himself be captured the best he could hope for was internment in a Japanese prisoner-of-war camp. He had always believed that in the end Britain would win the war; and now that, owing to the treacherous attack on Pearl Harbour, the United States had come in, he had no doubt at all that Britain, the Soviet Union and America would defeat Germany and Japan. But it might be years before they could liberate prisoners taken in the Far East. And it was quite on the cards that instead of taking him prisoner the first Japanese patrols he met would slaughter him out of hand. Summoning up his resolution to risk death sooner by drowning, he decided to swim for it; then, having taken off his boots and tied them round his neck, he entered the water.

It was a long hard swim and towards the end he began to fear that he would not survive it, but at length his feet touched bottom. Gasping for breath and half frozen he staggered ashore on Stonecutter's Island and for some time lay there exhausted. But he knew that if he were to escape capture he must get much further afield before morning. Pulling himself together, he made his way inland towards the north-east bay, which he knew to be a junk harbour. When he reached it he saw that a line of unlit junks was tied up against the quay. But as he stood in the deep shadow cast by a godown he caught the tramp of heavy boots. Then, by the faint light of the new moon, he saw a Japanese sentry patrolling the wharf, evidently for the purpose of preventing anyone escaping in one of the junks.

Unarmed as Julian was, it would have been suicidal to attack the sentry openly; so he resorted to a stratagem.

Crouching down beside the warehouse, next time the sentry was about to pass it he emitted loud groans. The sentry halted in his tracks, then came over to him.

Having chosen his words carefully from his small stock of Japanese, Julian moaned in that language, 'Help, honourable comrade; help. I have been knifed by a filthy Chinese.'

In the darkness the soldier could not see that he was a European and bent down towards him. Julian's right hand shot out and seized him by the throat; with his left he grabbed the man's automatic rifle. As Julian was much the stronger, the struggle was brief. When he had throttled the small yellow man into insensibility he hoisted him over his shoulder, carried him to the dockside and threw him into the water.

Since his first days in Egypt, Julian had always worn a money belt with a considerable sum in banknotes in it and some fifty gold coins. He also now had the Jap's weapon and he meant either to bribe or force the owner of the last junk in the line to set sail and put to sea. When he had gone aboard and roused the man it transpired that neither bribery nor threats were necessary. The Chinese skipper and his family, who made up the crew, all hated the Japanese like poison and, now that they no longer ran the risk of being immediately boarded and shot up, they were only too eager to get away from Hong Kong. It was thus that Julian had escaped death, or years of semi-starvation as a prisoner, at the hands of the Japanese.

As he sat now, on a lovely sunny morning near the flagstaff up on Victoria Peak gazing down at the prosperous city and Stonecutter's Island, those were some of the memories that drifted through his mind. The fears and horror that he had felt on that terrible Christmas Day twenty-two years ago were difficult to recapture, but he knew that he would never forget the ghastly blunder he had made while trying to save the young V.A.D.

Hearing the sound of voices behind him, he turned his head. A man and a girl were approaching and within a dozen yards of him. On the instant he decided that the girl was one of the loveliest he had ever seen.

CHAPTER III

LOVE AT FIRST SIGHT

WITH his first glance at the approaching couple Julian took in the fact that the man was young, on the short side, dark and tanned; then his eyes became riveted on the girl, almost to the point of rudeness. She obviously had Eastern blood, but he felt sure that she was an Eurasian; for it is only by the union of a European with a Chinese that such flower-like faces are produced—and this one was absolute perfection.

Her abundant, carefully dressed hair was dark with reddish lights in it; her face was wide and flattish, with a good straight nose, a large beautifully modelled mouth and a firm jaw line. Her cheek bones were high, the outer ends of her dark eyebrows slanted slightly upwards and her flawless skin was a pale gold; but these evidences of her Chinese blood were offset by a pair of magnificent grey eyes. She was wearing a blue silk blouse with open sleeves that displayed her slender arms, and a short kilted skirt showing a pair of legs that any girl might have envied.

She returned his gaze with unruffled calmness, for she was accustomed to such tributes to her beauty and had put him down at once as an Englishman of the kind she usually liked. The hearty, bovine types who, without the least encouragement, swiftly became amorous were a bore to deal with. But the slim, well-built ones with their quiet expensive clothes and ease of manner strongly appealed to her, provided that on acquaintance they proved intelligent and had a sense of humour. This one, she

31

decided promptly, might be a top-line business executive, but more probably held a high post in Government Service. That he was very much older than herself did not lessen her interest in him, as from his bronzed, strong-featured face she judged him to be as fit as a fiddle and the fact that his thick, dark hair had gone grey at the temples gave him an air of considerable distinction.

Suddenly conscious that he was staring at her, Julian looked quickly away. The couple passed behind him to the far side of the flagstaff and sat down on the grass some forty feet from where he was sitting. Covertly he watched them, while speculating about their relationship and wondering if he could manage to scrape acquaintance with the lovely girl. It was quite on the cards that they might be lovers. If so, any attempt to join them was certain to be resented and short-lived. But it was a considerable time since any woman had seriously attracted Julian and his one long look at this one had made him suddenly feel as though he were again in his twenties.

As he watched them he saw that the girl was doing nearly all the talking, and that she was pointing out various places of interest to her companion. Deciding to risk a rebuff, he stood up and strolled over to them. At his approach the girl gave him a charming smile. Returning it, he said:

'I hope you will forgive my butting in, but I wondered if you could tell me if one can see Macao from here?'

She shook her head. 'No. It lies behind us to the south-west, forty-five miles away. But even on a clear day it would not be possible to glimpse it because the mountains on Lan Tao Island cut off the view in that direction.'

Casually he followed up with, 'Lan Tao is the biggest of the islands, isn't it?'

'Yes; it is bigger than Hong Kong. But not many people live there because there is very little water on it.'

'Water is quite a problem in Hong Kong, I gather,' Julian remarked.

'Yes; there are many reservoirs and more are being built. But we are mainly dependent on the rains for our supply, and if in the spring they are late in arriving it causes great inconvenience.' She then went on to name all the reservoirs and gave the figures of their capacity.

Smiling down at her, Julian said, 'It surprises me that anyone like yourself should have all these statistics at your finger tips.'

'It is part of my job,' she laughed. 'Although they must forget them next moment, American visitors are insatiable in their demand for figures and I am a professional guide working for the Hong Kong Tourist Association.'

'Not all Americans,' remarked the young man on her other side. 'I'm just happy to sit around and listen to you talk. And perhaps now you'll get back to where we were. You were about to give me the history of the Colony.'

His tone made it clear that he resented Julian's intrusion. But now Julian was aware that the girl was in his company only as a professional guide he felt no scruples about making a third in the party. Calmly sitting down beside her, he said, 'History has always fascinated me and I should very much like to hear, Miss . . . Miss . . . ?'

He caught a twinkle in the girl's grey eyes as she responded, 'Sang; Merri Sang. And this gentleman is Mr. Bill Urata.'

Julian gave a slight bow. 'My name is Julian Day and I am delighted to meet you both.'

'It's good to know you,' said Mr. Urata, although he obviously did not mean it.

Meanwhile Julian had taken stock of him. Seen closer to, he also obviously had Eastern blood. He looked about twenty-four, was about five foot seven, broad-shouldered and had strong, square, practical hands. His hair was crew-cut, his eyes very black, his face sallow and, apart from his teeth seeming over-large, he was decidedly good-looking. The gaudy check shirt he was wearing was open at the neck and not tucked into his grey trousers.

Two cameras and a range-finder were slung round his body. After a moment Julian remarked to him:

'You implied just now that you are an American, but from your name and, if I may say so, your appearance I should have taken you for a Japanese.'

'My folks are Japanese and I was born in Japan,' replied Urata laconically. 'But since I was old enough to make high school I have lived in the U.S.; so I've gotten to think of myself as more than half American.'

'Mr. Urata is the son of a big ship-owner in Osaka,' Miss Merri Sang volunteered. 'Having completed his education at Berkeley University in California, he is going into his father's business, and he is combining pleasure with business by using Hong Kong as a base from which to visit other ports in the Orient.'

Julian only raised an eyebrow, but Urata caught his thought and said aggressively, 'Any objection?'

'Not in the least. Where you choose to take a holiday is no affair of mine. But since you raise the point, I shouldn't have thought you could expect to find a very warm welcome in Hong Kong, in view of the way your countrymen behaved here when they captured the island.'

Urata shrugged. 'Some of them got high on looted whisky and behaved pretty rough, I'm told; but the Germans did plenty worse and no-one kicks them for that these days. When I took my vacation in Europe last summer they were rubber-necking all over France, Italy and Greece. What happened twenty years ago, either there or here, doesn't stop the locals from being civil. Most all of them think about is how much dough they can take off sucker tourists. Besides, come to that, part of my family was on your side. The uncle I lived with in the States had become an American citizen before the war and fought against the Germans in Italy.'

Julian nodded. 'How interesting. Well, anyway, I'm glad to hear that you are enjoying your stay here.'

'I certainly am. Now that's settled let's hear Merri tell us about the island.'

'With pleasure,' smiled the ravishing Miss Sang. 'I will say my short piece telling how, from an island that one hundred and thirty-two years ago was inhabited only by a few poor fisherfolk, Hong Kong has become a great metropolis with a population of over three million.

'You must know that it all started because the English took a great liking to tea. By the early years of Queen Victoria's reign it had become very popular and they could not get enough of it. But it had to be paid for in silver because the Chinese Emperor maintained that China had everything she wanted and no need or wish to trade with the outside world.

'As tea drinking increased, the British Government became more and more annoyed at having to send money instead of goods to China, so they hatched a most unscrupulous plot to stop the drain on their silver. Over a hundred years before this the British East India Company had established a post in Canton to buy silks, Chinese porcelain and other things for which Europeans were willing to pay a high price. The Company's representatives had a far from happy time there. They were not allowed to take their wives to Canton, or to mix with the Chinese or learn their language. They were forbidden to have weapons or ride in a rickshaw or go out after dark; and they had to do all their business through a corporation of Chinese merchants that was called a *Hong*. But at least they had their foot in the door and they determined to use the *Hong* for their wicked ends.

'In India the Company grew opium on a very large scale and sold it to the people there at a big profit. But it happened that in the 1830s they had a large surplus of the evil drug on their hands. In those days opium was hardly known in China, except for medicinal purposes, so the British said, "Let us encourage the Chinese to smoke it, then we will kill two birds with one stone. We will have made a market for our surplus stock and pay for the tea with that instead of with silver."

'The *Hong* merchants were just as unscrupulous as the British and willingly agreed to market the drug. During the next few years thousands of chests were imported and tens of thousands of unfortunate Chinese became drug addicts. Greatly distressed by this, in 1839 the Emperor issued an edict sternly forbidding all further traffic in the drug.

'The British Government were greatly upset by this; but they soon found a way round it. The Company, as the Government's agents, stopped importing opium into China; instead they sold it to big trading houses such as those of Mr. Matheson and Mr. Dent, who were quite willing to smuggle it in, and the *Hong*, anxious not to lose its big profits, continued to distribute it almost openly.

'This resulted in the Emperor sending a Mandarin named Lin Tse-hsu as Viceroy to Canton to put a stop to the smuggling. That caused the smugglers no uneasiness because they assumed that all that would happen was that they would have to give away a small fraction of their huge profits to the *Hong* so that it could give the new Viceroy a somewhat bigger squeeze than it had been paying the old one, and that by putting up the price of opium in a few months time they would soon get their money back.

'But things did not turn out at all like that. Viceroy Lin proved an upright man. Far from proving bribable, he threatened the merchants of the *Hong* with death if they did not surrender their stores of opium, and ordered the British merchants to disgorge theirs as well. To save themselves the Chinese sent in a thousand chests, but the British stood firm and Captain Elliot of the Royal Navy had the Union Jack run up over the trading post in Canton. Viceroy Lin retaliated by withdrawing all Chinese labour and surrounding the post with troops.

'Captain Elliot had only one sloop of eighteen guns

under him and that was down river, so rather than risk their all being killed he told the smugglers that they must give up their opium. Furious but helpless, they handed over two million pounds' worth of it and the honourable Lin had the satisfaction of employing five hundred coolies to mix it with salt and lime then throw it into the river.

'Trade having come to a complete standstill in Canton the disgruntled British retired to the Portuguese colony of Macao. They had hardly had time to settle in before fresh trouble arose. Some of their ships were lying in the bay here. A party of sailors came ashore, got drunk and started a fight with some of the Chinese fisherfolk, one of whom was killed. Captain Elliot punished the men severely and compensated the bereaved family. But that did not satisfy Viceroy Lin. He demanded that one of the British sailors should be handed over for execution. Captain Elliot refused, so Lin attempted to blockade Hong Kong harbour and forced an approaching supply ship to unload her cargo. For Captain Elliot that proved the last straw and he retaliated by ordering one of his ships to open fire on some Chinese war junks. By November 1839 Britain and China were officially at war and, as you both must know, China got the worst of it.

'Britain sent sixteen men-of-war from India and four thousand troops. The fleet sailed up the Yang-tse and occupied the island of Fing-hai. The Chinese could offer little resistance to modern European weapons. An expeditionary force advanced eight hundred miles. When they were within one hundred miles of Pekin the Emperor sent his Grand Secretary, the Mandarin Kishen, to gain a respite by entering into negotiations. Elliot, annoyed by Kishen's procrastination, forced his hand by seizing all the forts round Canton. On that Kishen agreed to surrender and signed a treaty with Elliot permitting the reopening of trade in Canton and ceding Hong Kong to Britain.

'But matters did not end there. The British Government felt that Elliot had not driven a hard enough bargain to compensate them for the trouble to which they had been put; and, on his side, the Emperor, furious with poor Kishen for having given away anything at all to the barbarians, had him brought to Pekin in chains, sentenced him to death and repudiated the treaty. So the war was renewed and Sir Charles Pottinger was sent out to take charge of the situation. He arrived in the summer of 1841. Several more Chinese cities were taken and when Nankin was surrounded the Emperor threw in his hand. By the treaty of Nankin, in August 1842, he not only confirmed Britain in her possession of Hong Kong but agreed to open the five ports of Canton, Amoy, Foochow, Ningpo and Shanghai to trade, and made restitution for the two million pounds' worth of opium destroyed by Lin.

'This terrible trade was resumed and prospered, so that by 1850 India was shipping the drug to China at the rate of fifty-two thousand chests a year. In vain the Emperor tried to protect his subjects by punishing those caught selling the drug. In 1858, by another war, the British forced the Chinese to make legal the sale of opium, and in 1860 to cede to them the Peninsula of Kowloon.

'Meanwhile the original Colony had passed through many ups and downs. For a long time the Governors sent out from England were men who knew nothing of the Far East and were always at loggerheads with the trader tycoons. In the early days, too, the merchants had visualized Hong Kong as a warehouse that would in time supply China with the greater part of the goods she would buy from the outer world, and when the Government put up for sale the land along the waterfront high prices were paid for all the plots. But a few years after the treaty by which China agreed to receive goods through five ports, each of which began to prove a rival to Hong Kong, property here became as valueless as shares in the South Sea Bubble. A plot for which a Mr. McKnight had paid ten thousand Hong Kong dollars was auctioned in December 1849 and knocked down for twenty dollars.

'The merchants were in despair and the island had acquired a most evil reputation. It was said to be the haunt of vice, piracy, pestilence and fever and the British Government was urged to give it up. It even became a saying, 'Oh, go to Hong Kong', instead of 'Go to Hell'. But a new Governor arrived, Sir George Bonham. He was a very different type of man from his predecessors. Instead of despising the wealthy merchants he invited them to Government House and sought their advice on ways to better the Colony. They offered him the funds with which to drain Happy Valley and transform it from a mosquito-infested swamp into a healthy suburb and helped him to improve conditions in many other ways. A local aristocracy, led by the Jardines, the Mathesons and the Dents, came into being. They fathered the Hong Kong Club, the Jockey Club, the Cricket Club and amateur theatrical and operatic societies. By their efforts Hong Kong at last began to prosper and the first tourists arrived. Relations with China improved and in 1898 she leased the New Territories to Britain for ninety-nine years, so that the Colony should have more land to supply itself with agricultural produce.'

Julian had already been aware of most of the facts that she had given in her obviously well-rehearsed speech, but that did not lessen his enjoyment of watching her mobile young face as she told the story of the island; and he remained enraptured, almost as though hypnotized, while gazing at her profile as she went on for a further quarter of an hour to tell of the great typhoon of 1906, the conquest of the island by the Japanese, the fears of bankruptcy when in 1949 Mao had bolted the door to Red China, the amazing way in which Hong Kong had saved itself to become more prosperous than ever before, and the wonderful work that was being done to rehabilitate the refugees.

39

When she had done, Urata said, 'Thanks a lot, Merri. You've certainly given us a good picture of how the place has grown. But, as you know, I'm in shipping and you've said nothing about pirates. It's said they are still pretty active in these parts. Would that be so?'

Merri gave a slow nod. 'Yes; piracy still goes on. But not in a form that should worry you. As far back as anyone can remember there have been bad men sailing these seas who attack small coastal vessels and rob them of their cargoes. If, too, they find a passenger on board whom they know to be wealthy they take him prisoner and hold him to ransom. But in these days they would never dare to attack anything larger than a junk.'

'How about the drug traffic?' Julian enquired.

'That, too, continues, in spite of all efforts to prevent it. In 1917 the British Government agreed to stop importing opium into China, but after nearly a hundred years the habit of smoking it had become ingrained in the Chinese people, and for a long time past they had taken to growing it for themselves. Today China is not an importer but an exporter of the drug and it is largely from there that the addicts in Hong Kong receive their supplies.'

'Are there many addicts here?'

'Alas, yes. It is a terrible problem, and has become much more difficult to deal with since the practice started of converting opium into heroin. That greatly reduces the bulk of the drug so makes it much easier to smuggle.'

'In the States they're doing a big job reclaiming addicts', Urata put in. 'Are they doing anything of that kind here?'

'Oh, yes,' Merri informed him. 'Out at Tai Lam we have a special prison for the treatment of addicts who have been convicted, and at the new hospital at Castle Peak there is a special ward set aside for addicts willing to submit voluntarily to a course of treatment. My mother works for the Hong Kong Advisory Committee on Narcotics, in a special section of the Customs employed in preventing the smuggling of drugs, so I could tell you a lot about such matters. She wanted me to work in her office, but I would not like such a life, and as I have never travelled I greatly enjoy talking to people who come from all parts of the world. That is why I asked Major Stanley, who is the head of the Hong Kong Tourist Association, to take me as one of his private guides.'

'Are you very booked up?' Julian enquired casually.

'I expect to be free after tomorrow,' she replied. 'I have been taking Mr. Urata round for the past few days, but on Wednesday he is leaving for Manila.'

'In that case I wonder if you would care to act as guide for me? I arrived only yesterday and it's over twenty years since I was in Hong Kong, so there are lots of places that I would like you to take me to.'

Producing a card from her bag she handed it to him and said, 'It would be a pleasure, Mr. Day, if my office has not already booked me for another engagement. Here is the address. Please check with them. Where are you staying?'

'At the Repulse Bay.'

'You are wise. It is much more pleasant out there than at the hotels in the town. If all is well, then, I'll call for you with a car at half past nine on Wednesday morning.'

Urata got to his feet and said with more geniality than he had previously displayed, 'You're a lucky guy to be staying on here, if you get Merri for a guide. But now it's about time that we got back to the city for lunch. Merri's car is parked down where the road ends. Can we give you a lift back?'

Julian was more than satisfied at having achieved such a promising opening to his acquaintance with the beautiful Miss Sang; so he resisted the temptation to deprive Urata further of having her to himself, and said, 'Thanks, but I think I'll walk. It was good of you to let me join you.'

Seating himself again, he watched them go down

the steps in the grassy slope. Ten minutes later he followed. A mile's walk brought him to the highest station of the cable railway that serves the many fine private properties scattered about the seaward slope of the Peak. In one of its cars he made the precipitous descent to the city. There he took a rickshaw to the office of the Tourist Association. To his relief he learned that Miss Sang would be free on Wednesday morning, so he booked her services from then for the remainder of the week, then he lunched at the Parisian Grill. When he had finished his meal he began to wonder how to while away the afternoon.

Filling in time was Julian Day's perpetual problem. For years he had drifted round the world doing little else. He had a fine house in Gloucestershire, but since he had inherited it he had never been there. With it he had inherited a baronetcy, and his real name was Hugo Julian du Crow Fernhurst; but he never used it. As a product of Eton and Oxford he should have been able to come to Hong Kong with a sheaf of introductions to some of the most interesting people, to sign his name in the book at Government House and to be made a temporary member of the Hong Kong Club; but none of these things was for him, because his real name might have aroused in people's minds a most discreditable affair of the past in which he had been the principal figure.

The fact was that he was absurdly oversensitive about the folly which had ruined his career when young, and underestimated both the shortness of people's memories and the fact that few of them took the view that a youthful indiscretion damned a man for life. His dread of being recognized and ostracized was so great that for years he had avoided mixing with English people of his own class and for company made friends with foreigners or casual acquaintances met on liners or in hotel bars.

Any thought of marriage he had long since ruled out as impossible, because he was by nature fastidious, and the only sort of woman he would have cared to make his wife was of the kind who moved in the circles from which he was debarred.

Now, a new thought stirred in his mind. To ask any English or American girl, or a foreigner who would at times wish to go to London, and so risk sharing the shame to which he was liable to be exposed, was out of the question. But that would not apply to an Eurasian with whom he could make a home in Hong Kong. They need never go to England or mix with the Government House set. He was so utterly weary of drifting from place to place, living in hotels and on liners, or taking furnished flats. How wonderful it would be to settle down at last with a home of his own and a wife who was intelligent, amusing and unbelievably beautiful.

Before he left the restaurant he had made up his mind to marry Merri Sang.

CHAPTER IV

SET A KILLER TO CATCH
A KILLER

AT THE moment when Julian Day's mind was illuminated by the thought that if only he could persuade Merri
Sang to marry him his long lonely years of restlessness,
roaming the world like the Wandering Jew, would be
forever behind him, and that his life would begin anew
following a pattern of tranquil bliss, some fourteen hundred miles away in Japan Mr. Inosuke Hayashi was
conferring with one Udo Nagi, his right-hand man for
conducting his nefarious enterprises.

It was December when Hayashi had been interviewed
by Police Chief for External Affairs Okabe, in Tokyo.
Okabe had been only too glad to see him depart, carrying
his son's head in its box; for from the head there emanated
a most unpleasant smell, even when the box had been
rewrapped in good thick brown paper.

Snow had been falling outside and it was bitterly cold.
Not knowing the reason for which he had been asked to
come to Tokyo, Hayashi had planned to spend the night
in a comfortable suite at the Imperial Hotel. But now,
his agile mind seething with rage and venom, he decided
to go straight home; so that he might the sooner set to
work the network of agents that he controlled in the Far
East on the job of enabling him to exact vengeance on
his son's murderer.

At the hotel he enquired about trains and collected his
suitcase, then went to the station. Such is the efficiency of
the Japanese railways that, having shown his ticket to a

44

porter who told him where he should stand on the platform, when the train came in the coach in which he had reserved a seat drew up immediately in front of him.

It was a very long coach with a walkway down the centre and on either side pairs of seats similar to those in air-liners, so that each occupant could adjust his and lie back to sleep if he wished. But Hayashi's agitated brain was in no state for sleep. Like the other passengers, he took off his shoes and sat with his small feet on the foot-rest.

The train remained two minutes exactly, neither more nor less, in the station then it shushed out, soon to attain a speed of a hundred miles an hour as it hurtled through the vast areas of shanties that house the greater part of Tokyo's ten million population and make it the largest, ugliest and most depressing city in the world.

Hayashi was duly offered fruit, soft drinks, ices, sweets and other stopgaps to hunger from an aluminium trolley wheeled ceaselessly up and down the walkway of the coach by an obsequious attendant. But, with an impassive nod of the head, he declined these amenities and, presently, walked through to the restaurant car.

There, unlike the sad little menus on British Railways, he was offered a choice of four set meals, ranging from soup, fish and fruit at the equivalent of seven shillings and sixpence, to a six-course dinner including a steak at the equivalent of thirty-five shillings. But Hayashi felt that he had no appetite for European-style food, so he ordered the Japanese dinner. Even when that came he found that he could do no more than toy with some delectable morsels of raw fish. But when in Europe as a younger man he had acquired a taste for wine; so he ordered a bottle of the best champagne, regardless of the fact that it cost him the equivalent of twelve pounds sterling.

The train accomplished its six-hundred-mile run to Kyoto in the scheduled six hours and arrived punctually to the minute. He had telephoned for his Mercedes to be at the station to meet him, so in another fifteen minutes he was home and had sent for Udo Nagi.

Since then Hayashi had received a number of progress reports from Nagi. Now on this afternoon of the 18th of February he was conning over the summary of the results of the investigation that he had ordered to be made.

Nagi was a big man for a Japanese. As a youth he had been a professional wrestler, but while still young he had come to the conclusion that life could be more pleasant living on the immoral earnings of women than by participating in gruelling bouts in the ring. His size and fearsome reputation soon led to his becoming the protector of a score of girls whom he exploited most profitably in depleting the dollar rolls of the American Occupying Forces. Then he discovered that even more money could be made out of peddling dope. Early in his new activities he came into conflict with the strong-arm men of Hayashi's organization. Their ultimatum had been 'become one of our agents or become a corpse'.

To begin with he had felt very sour at losing his independence but the drop in his income led to his working very much harder, so he received promotion. Later he was blindfolded one night and taken to Hayashi's house. While still blindfolded he had a long interview with Hayashi, who reached the conclusion that Udo Nagi had not only brawn but brains. In the years that followed he had been given increasingly more important parts to play in the organization, although it was not until 1956 that he had actually seen Hayashi face to face. For the past three years he had been Hayashi's Chief of Staff.

During the past three months Udo Nagi's agents had investigated thoroughly the families and pasts of the four men whose heads in boxes had preceded that of Hayashi's son to Police Headquarters in Tokyo. His agents had also tirelessly pursued every clue to the way these men, and the younger Hayashi, had spent their time while in Hong Kong, and had also made exhaustive enquiries in Macao.

46

The result was a dossier of over a hundred pages on each of them. To summarize their contents:

The radio salesman, Otoya Matsuko, had gone to Hong Kong in September 1952, to solicit stocking-up orders for the winter season. He was unmarried and said to be much addicted to women. He had stayed for five nights at the Broadway, one of the less expensive hotels in Kowloon. A number of his customers recalled the police enquiries that followed his disappearance, and a few of them remembered him personally as a small, bespectacled, pleasant-mannered man; but after a lapse of eleven years no-one at the hotel could give any information about him.

Dr. Yasunari Kido was a lung specialist and had gone to Hong Kong to attend a conference on tuberculosis in April 1956. He was married but known to frequent a well-known geisha house in Yokohama, his home city. He was a man of some means and had stayed at the de-luxe Peninsula Hotel. Such doctors as had attended the conference and who could be traced spoke of him as a jolly fellow and something of a *bon vivant*. Two of them had enjoyed good dinners with him and said that he had not appeared to have a trouble in the world. They had not even heard of his disappearance, because he had remained in Hong Kong for the full week of the conference, then left his hotel in a normal manner. However, as it happened, the doctor had a livid scar on his right cheek from an old war wound; so two of the staff at the Peninsula remembered him.

One was a night porter whom he had asked to tell him of a night spot where there was a good selection of Chinese girls, ready to accommodate visitors in comfortable quarters, and the man had recommended him to a house in Hong Kong named the Moon Garden. In the early hours of the morning he had returned to his hotel, and told the porter that he had had a good time; so obviously he had come to no harm there. The other was a

47

waiter who had seen him one evening in the lounge of the hotel standing drinks to a good-looking blonde. She was not a regular habitué of the hotel and the waiter remembered the incident only because Dr. Kido had given him an exceptionally generous tip, probably with a view to impressing his companion.

The engineer, Kayno Nakayama, was another bachelor, but he kept a regular mistress in a flat in Tokyo. He had gone to Hong Kong in August 1957 and with him he had taken his assistant, a young man named Araki. They had stayed at the Victoria Hotel in Queens Road. Araki had at the time been engaged to a girl of good family whom he had shortly afterwards married; so from fear that he might be called on to give evidence in court which could wreck his marriage prospects, he had refrained from giving the police a full account of how he and Nakayama had spent their time while in Hong Kong. But Udo Nagi's agents had unearthed the fact that one night during their stay the two men had not occupied their beds at the Victoria. Informed that he might become the victim of an unpleasant accident unless he came clean, Araki had supplied the following information.

After a week in Hong Kong he had felt the urge for a little feminine entertainment and, having heard of a house called the Moon Garden, he had suggested that Naka-yama should go with him to it. Nakayama had at first demurred, as he was a man of fifty and perfectly content with his mistress in Tokyo. But Araki had persuaded him and he had thoroughly enjoyed his night there. Evidently this departure from a normal humdrum fidelity had stimulated his sexual appetite, for three days later he told Araki that he had become acquainted with a beautiful English woman and was going with her to Macao for the week-end. Hardly able to contain himself at this amazing piece of luck, he had departed, but had never been seen again.

The dealer in cultured pearls, Zosho Iwanami, had

gone to Hong Kong in January 1960. He was married but living apart from his wife, who had stated without beating about the bush that he was an inveterate woman-izer. He had stayed at the Golden Gate Hotel in Austin Road and the manager there remembered him on account of the police enquiries subsequent to his disappearance, and because on one occasion he had had to be prevented from taking a prostitute to his room. On three nights out of the nine he had spent there he had slept out, presumably with a woman. But no-one who had been questioned could throw further light on his doings while in Hong Kong.

The younger Hayashi had gone to Hong Kong in the previous November. Being a rich man, he had stayed at the fabulous Marco Polo in Kowloon. His disappear-ance having occurred only a few months ago, several of the staff there remembered him perfectly well; but they could give little information of any value. On two nights out of the seven that he had stayed there he had not come in until the small hours of the morning and, knowing his tastes, his father had no doubt that on those nights he had gone with some woman. However, on leaving the Marco Polo he had asked that his room should be made available again to him two days later, as he was only going on a forty-eight-hour trip to Macao.

Boiled down this added up to: Three of the men had definitely sought sexual entertainment while in Hong Kong and there was good reason to suppose that the other two had also done so. Two of them had visited the Moon Garden Night Club. One of them had been seen in the company of a blonde girl and another had said that he had made the acquaintance of a beautiful English woman, who was, possibly, the same person. Nakayama had told Araki that he was going to Macao with his new acquaint-ance for the week-end, and Hayashi had also left Hong Kong to spend forty-eight hours in the Portuguese colony. It therefore seemed a possibility that a blonde English girl had been employed to lure all five men to Macao and their deaths.

Nagi had gone personally to Hong Kong to investigate the Moon Garden. He found it to be one of the best houses and run by a Chinese named Mok Kwai. But no European girls were employed there and Mok Kwai had assured Nagi that none ever had been. Neither, Mok Kwai informed Nagi regretfully, could he supply one on call, much as he would have liked to earn a good fee for so doing. Therefore it did not appear that the blonde had any connection with the Moon Garden, and it might well be no more than a coincidence that both Dr. Kido and Nakayama had visited the same establishment.

But then Nagi had had a lucky break. One of his agents who was making enquiries at Macao had spent several days questioning the officers and crew of the ferry steamer that plied between Macao and Hong Kong. As a great number of visiting Westerners made the trip and the boats were always crowded, the hope of identifying a fair woman who had crossed in the company of a Japanese several months before was slender. But it happened that an elderly steward had noticed such a couple. His reason for doing so was that back in the 1940s, before he had had the misfortune to become bankrupt, he had frequented a high-class brothel owned by a Mr. Lo Kung, and he had felt certain that the woman was Mrs. Lo.

Nagi had promptly crossed to Macao and made enquiries at the brothel. There he learned that Lo Kung had died at least ten years before and that after continuing to run the place for a while Mrs. Lo had sold it. Since then it had changed hands several times and all its old staff had been dispersed. But an advertisement in the local paper had brought forward an old crone who had worked there in Lo Kung's time. To Nagi's delight she produced a really valuable piece of information. After selling the brothel Mrs. Lo had bought herself a pretty little villa on the sea-shore, and she was able to give Nagi the address.

Enquiries at the villa of an elderly couple who occupied the place as caretaker servants elicited the fact that Mrs. Lo came there very seldom. They were under the impression that she was very rich and spent most of her time travelling, but they had been in her employ only two months and had not even seen her. Their money was sent to them monthly through the post from a bank in Hong Kong.

Another advertisement produced two couples who had earlier acted as caretakers at Mrs. Lo's villa. The first couple had been there from May 1956 until August 1957, the second from January 1960 until the previous December. Both, for a handsome remuneration, had the same story to tell. They had seen Mrs. Lo only once and on each occasion she had brought a Japanese gentleman to the villa. They assumed that she intended to sleep with him, but did not wish them to know about that, as in both cases after they had served a good dinner she had given them money, telling them that she wished them to go to an hotel for the night and not return to the villa until the following evening. When they had returned neither she nor the Japanese was there, so they cleared up and thought no more about it. Then a few weeks later they had been given three months' pay and told that their services were no longer required.

It was in April 1956 that Dr. Kido had disappeared and Hayashi had done so the previous November. In consequence Nagi swiftly came to the conclusion that each time Mrs. Lo lured a victim to her villa, and either handed him over to be killed by her associates or killed him herself, she shortly afterwards engaged a new couple as caretakers, so that no enquiry at the villa would disclose that she had ever brought a Japanese there.

Nagi then took strong action. Having mustered his thugs, he went to the villa at night, had the caretaker couple tied up and searched it. In a locked inner cellar he found the remains of five headless bodies in varying stages of disintegration from having been covered with quicklime. After relocking the cellar so that his captives should remain in ignorance of what he had found there, it occurred to him, as they had said that they had never seen Mrs. Lo, to question them about who had engaged them. Sweating with terror, they had described a tall middle-aged Chinese named Ti Cheng, who had aggressive features and a slight squint. To Nagi's intense satisfaction the description fitted Mok Kwai of the Moon Garden.

Returning to Hong Kong, he set his people to keep Mok Kwai under observation. He had feared that if Mrs. Lo did spend most of her time travelling he would either have to wait a long time for results or kidnap the brothel keeper one night and take him to pieces. But he did not wish to risk trouble with the exceedingly efficient Hong Kong police; so he decided to give Mok Kwai ten days, and on the eighth day Mok Kwai led his shadowers to the quarry.

Now, with pardonable pride, Udo Nagi revealed to his master the final result of his investigation. They were seated cross-legged facing one another on mats in a room that was bare of furniture except for one long low table, and lacked all decoration except for one vase of carefully arranged flowers that stood in a corner.

Having said his piece, Nagi remarked, 'Since it is clear, Honourable Master, that the woman has sought to revenge herself on officers and men of the 230th Regiment for at least the past thirteen years I find it surprising that she has claimed only five victims.'

Hayashi gave a sign of disagreement. 'You must remember that, although the 230th Regiment numbered several thousand men, the great majority of them were either peasants or low-paid workers who, if they survived the war, would not have had the money to leave Japan again. But that is beside the point. We now know the name under which the woman who either murdered my son, or was responsible for his death, is living in Hong Kong. I mean to make her pay a price. Go now and arrange matters so that she should come here and grovel to me.'

Nagi slowly shook his head. 'Honourable Master, that will be far from easy, because this woman is very clever and will not readily fall into a trap. But it may be that I shall find means to persuade her to pay a visit to Japan.'

CHAPTER V

A GENTLE WOOING

AT SIX O'CLOCK on the Wednesday morning Julian awoke in his bedroom in the west wing of the Repulse Bay Hotel. When he had been young he had slept his head off. During the war, if he had to go on early duty, in order to rouse him it was not enough for his soldier servant to wake him with a cup of tea; he had to be propped up and the hot tea poured into his mouth. But now, unless he went to bed well after midnight, he always woke between half past five and half past six.

That did not worry him because, while dozing comfortably between six and eight, he had the opportunity to con over in advance any pleasures the coming day had to offer; and on this Wednesday he woke to the knowledge that for him this was the Day of Days. For the whole of it, and for as many days afterwards as he liked to pay for her services, he could explore the personality and bask in the smiles of Merri Sang—the loveliest human being he had ever set eyes on.

At 7.30 he roused himself to take in again the splendid room of which he was the occupant. The Repulse Bay had been built long before actuaries had worked out for financiers the minimum number of cubic inches that rich tourists would accept as living space in London, New York or Hong Kong. Either side of the door there was a closet six feet by eight for hanging clothes and keeping baggage. The main part of the room was thirty feet long by twenty wide with a lofty ceiling. At the far end there was a spacious bathroom, and an alcove with table, armchairs and a writing desk, from which one could look out on the blue waters of the bay.

He rang for the Chinese boy and ordered breakfast—pawpaw, mangoes, coffee and croissants. Then, in his dressing gown, he took his time to enjoy it at the table near the big window. By the time he had had a leisurely bath and dressed it was getting on for nine o'clock. Impatient now for this happy day to begin, he made his way to the entrance of the hotel and stood there for a while watching other people who were staying there boarding the little bus that took those who wished across the pass to the city or back every half-hour.

Soon after half past nine Merri Sang arrived in her car. Today, as it was somewhat colder, she was wearing a coat and skirt of grey Thai silk; and Julian thought that, if anything, she looked more delectable than ever. She greeted him gaily and asked him where he would like her to take him. On his replying that he would leave it to her, she said, 'Then we will spend our first day making a tour of the island.'

Had Julian not known himself to be in the Orient, for much of the next few hours he might have supposed that he was in the South of France; for the roads strongly resembled the Corniche, winding round cliff after cliff to open new prospects of lovely bays down below. Heading south-east they drove down to Stanley where, long ago, the British population of the island had suffered from semi-starvation and great hardship as prisoners of the Japanese. After running out along the Tai Tam peninsula they turned north to Red Hill, came south again to Aguilar Peak, then down to the bathing resort of Sheko. From there they had to turn inland and run through the mountainous country to the town of Sau Ki Wan on the north-east point of the island. By midday they had completed over half the circuit and reached Victoria.

When they came opposite Starr Ferry, Julian said,

'It's time to think about lunch before we go any further. You can park the car here and we'll go over to the other side. I'm told Gaddi's restaurant at the Peninsula is one of the best in the island, so I though we'd go there.'

'Oh, I find my own lunch,' she protested. 'But I'll drop you here and pick you up again at any time you wish.'

'You don't find your own lunch when you are with me,' he laughed. 'It's part of your job as a guide to accompany me to restaurants and advise me on the best things to eat.'

The big ferry boats ran every few minutes to cope with the huge crowds constantly passing from shore to shore, and half an hour later they were at the Peninsula Hotel. But it was Julian who advised on the things they had to eat and he saw to it that the meal was an extremely good one.

By half past three they were back on Hong Kong and heading through Victoria to the western end of the island. After circling the Peak and Mount Davis, they drove south-east to Aberdeen, the oldest settlement on Hong Kong, with its great floating town of junks and sampans in which for many generations tens of thousands of Chinese have been born and died. Circling Brick Hill, they passed the Golf Club on the shore of Deep Water Bay and were back at the Repulse at five o'clock.

As Julian got out of the car he looked across the massed beds and pots of flowers below the hotel terrace to the line of bathing tents down on the beach and remarked, 'What a pity that the water is not warm enough for us to bathe.'

She smiled at him. 'I should not find it too cold, and quite a number of people have started bathing at Sheko. But if you like swimming in warm water there is a fine indoor pool at the New Ritz Hotel.'

'Let's go there tomorrow, then.'

'If you like. We could do the city first, then have a swim before lunch.'

Having refused to come in for a drink, Merri waved him good-bye and drove off. He had not pressed her to stay, and during the day he had been careful not to rush his fences; for he was only too well aware that Merri Sang must regard him as of another generation. But she seemed to have a passion for knowledge of the world outside Hong Kong, so he had been able to entertain her with accounts of the many places he had visited during his wanderings. And he was quite content with the progress he had made, for she had proved a charming companion and, at his suggestion, now called him Julian instead of Mr. Day.

Next morning in Victoria they parked the car and, having pointed out the great banks and office blocks in Des Voeux Road, she took him to see the famous ladder streets. They were steep narrow canyons, hung with brightly coloured banners, lined with shops and swarming with Chinese, that lack of space has led to extending the city up the slope of its dominating mountain. Then they visited the fascinating Thieves Market. By midday they were at the New Ritz, laughing together in the swimming pool. Merri had brought a pale blue bikini that concealed very little of her lovely lithe body and, as she swam for minutes at a time under water, she looked like a magnificent golden fish. At the sight of her Julian felt his heart turn over.

After they had lunched on the sun terrace she suggested taking him to the Tiger Balm garden, but he shook his head. 'No, thanks; I looked in there on my first day here and it's more like a stonemason's yard than a garden.'

'I know,' Merri agreed. 'All real gardeners, like my mother, think it awful. She is a great gardener and, as she rarely goes out except to her office, she spends a lot of time looking after her flowers.'

Seizing on this possible opening to meet her mother, Julian said, 'Perhaps, then, you'd be kind enough some time to take me to see your mother's garden.'

Merri shrugged. 'Perhaps. We'll see. Unfortunately mother is something of a recluse, and does not encourage visitors. What would you like to do this afternoon?'

'Sleep,' he replied with a smile. 'I usually do in the afternoon.'

She nodded. 'Lots of older people seem to find that necessary. Then you won't be wanting me any more today.'

Her reference to older people gave him a nasty jar; but he said at once, 'Oh, yes, I shall. I thought we might go somewhere to dine and dance this evening.'

'That's not in my contract,' she demurred. 'Except when I'm on special trips, I'm supposed to finish at five o'clock.'

'Then count this as a special trip. Please, I'll willingly pay you overtime.'

'Oh, I don't want that. It's . . . well, I don't often accept such invitations from men I scarcely know.'

Leaning forward, he held her gaze and said, 'But surely, Merri, you've seen enough of me now to know that I'm not the sort of chap who would try to pull a fast one on you on the way home. Be a darling and rescue me from another lonely evening.'

'All right, then. But I must be home by half past eleven. Mother insists on that.'

That night they dined at the Marco Polo and for the first time Julian saw Merri in a dress called by the Chinese a *cheongsam*. It is a one-piece dress, skin tight, buttoned up to the neck and slit up the side to well above the knee. Its bronze flowered satin formed a perfect mould for Merri's sylph-like figure and it set off her dark beauty to perfection.

In his youth Julian had been a good dancer, but it was a long time since he had danced except occasionally; so, to his annoyance, he found that he could do no more than move round the floor rather sedately. Merri, who danced beautifully, was disappointed in him but had the good manners not to show it; and, by and large, they both enjoyed their evening.

On the Friday they went across in the car ferry to Kowloon and she drove him out along the beautiful Pearl River to see the New Territories. They visited the old walled village of Kam Tin—the last outpost of resistance when the British had had to enforce their rule on the inhabitants of the mainland—then went to the carpet factory at Tai Po. The factory had been in existence for only a few years but it had already made for the Queen one of the largest carpets at Windsor Castle, and now employed nearly a thousand hands. The industry was one of the many started by the Kadoorie brothers in their wonderful campaign to make the refugees from Red China self-supporting. They had devoted a great part of their fabulous wealth to buying land, stocking it with cattle, pigs and poultry, and giving it to the refugees free of rent, so that they could start small farms, many thousands of which were now flourishing; and they had initiated many other enterprises. Later Merri drove Julian to the Kadoorie Experimental Station, where they were growing pineapples, apricots, sweet potatoes, pawpaws and many other things on high barren ground that had previously been believed to be incapable of bearing crops.

They lunched at Shatin Heights Hotel, and afterwards went out to sit out on the hillside and drink in the marvellous view. When they had been there a little while Merri remarked:

'I had an airmail letter from Bill this morning.'

'Bill?' repeated Julian vaguely.

'Yes; Bill Urata. The American who was with me the day we met.'

'He's not an American, he's a Japanese,' Julian corrected her.

'Yes, I suppose he is really. But he talks and acts like an American.'

'What had he to say for himself?'

'Oh, that he finds Manila interesting and rather exciting. Apparently the hall porter at his hotel wears a loaded gun in case bandits raid the cash desk, and to take a taxi at night is to risk being run into a garage, knocked on the head and robbed. But he said he'd give anything to be back in Hong Kong, and lots of other nice things.'

'I see.' Julian frowned. 'Then it seems that he must have fallen for you. I suspected as much. But I shouldn't have thought a brash type like that would have interested a girl like you.'

Quickly she sprang to Urata's defence. 'I don't think he's brash. One doesn't expect the sort of polished manners you have in a young American who's just left college. It's natural with them to say what they think and be self-opinionated. I liked his vitality and he does the Twist divinely. Anyway, he was delightfully open about himself and his hopes and prospects. Not like you, a mystery man.'

During their three days together Merri had told Julian quite a lot about herself, but he had kept off the subject of his own background. Giving a faint smile he said, 'So you look on me as a mystery man?'

'What else would you expect, Julian? You are obviously of good family, well educated, have lots of money and seem to have travelled all over the world. When men like you come to Hong Kong they are nearly always entertained at Government House, or anyway have good introductions. Yet you don't seem to know a soul here, and yesterday spoke of lonely evenings spent at your hotel. Perhaps I'm being too curious; but at least you might tell me about your family, and if you're married.'

So far he had not given the least hint that he had fallen in love with her, but if he wanted to persuade her to marry him he would have to tell her the truth about himself sometime; so he decided that it might as well be now. After a moment's silence he replied:

60

'The story of my past is not a very pretty one, Merri; and I've not spoken to anyone about it for years. But you are such a sweet and sympathetic person that I will tell it to you; although I'm afraid you won't think very highly of me afterwards.'

She gave him a sidelong glance. 'Are you . . . are you a crook, then?'

'No, I'm not a crook. But Day is not my real name; it's Fernhurst and I'm an outcast. When I was up at Oxford I met a man named O'Kieff. He was a good bit older than myself and an occultist. I was interested in that sort of thing then, so I became very friendly with him. On coming down I went into the Diplomatic Service and as I was quite a clever chap everyone predicted a great future for me. My first post was in Brussels and it happened that O'Kieff came to live there for a while. We renewed our friendship and under the seal of secrecy he gradually confided to me the source of his great wealth. He was the head of a syndicate of international crooks, run by himself and half a dozen other clever men all of whom were above suspicion. I won't bother you with their names, but they were an English Lord whose mind was even more twisted than his body, a Polish Jew, a German Baron, a Japanese, an Egyptian and an Italian Count. All of them were top-line operators. Between them they controlled an underworld empire for white-slaving, dope running, bullion smuggling and selling military secrets.'

Julian paused, flicked the ash off his cigarette and went on, 'I was young and so incredibly conceited that I thought I was cleverer than O'Kieff. While pretending to be fascinated by his stories of tremendous coups they had brought off I planned to trap this crew of supremely evil men and get them long prison sentences. But I had to have help; so I confided in our First Secretary, a charming man named Carruthers. Diplomats, of course, are not supposed to involve themselves in that sort of

61

thing, so he told me off; but to get those men behind locks and bars seemed so important that I persuaded him to play.

'The Seven were shortly to have one of their periodical conferences in Brussels, and on a pretext that I won't go into now I got O'Kieff to invite Carruthers, as well as myself, to dinner with them. That was just what O'Kieff wanted. He had simply been stringing me along in the hope of catching a much bigger fish. I don't remember much about the dinner, but I was picked up drugged and unconscious from a back-street gutter next morning.'

Merri gave a gasp. 'Oh, Julian, how awful!'

'That wasn't the worst. When I got my senses back I was told how the previous night that unholy crew had accompanied Carruthers back to the Embassy. He had given them drinks, then taken them down to the Chancellery and unlocked the safe with all our secret documents in it. They had taken nothing, but gone through the lot. Carruthers had politely seen them off the premises, then gone cheerfully up to bed. I guessed at once what must have happened. O'Kieff possessed extraordinary hypnotic powers and he must have hypnotized poor Carruthers. He had no memory whatever of what had occurred, but the night porter had been an uneasy witness to the whole affair. When Carruthers realized what he had done he committed suicide.'

'What an appalling story.'

Julian nodded. 'You can imagine how I felt. I had drawn him into it, so was directly responsible for his death. And naturally, although I was found drugged afterwards and there was no actual evidence against me, in view of my friendship with O'Kieff plenty of people came to the conclusion that I had been in with the crooks and had deliberately sold my country's secrets.'

'I'm sure you didn't,' Merri exclaimed impulsively. 'You're not the sort of man who would.'

'Thanks,' Julian smiled wanly. 'All the same, I was kicked out of the diplomatic and have been a wanderer, avoiding my own kind, ever since.'

'Did you ever come across any of those awful men again?' she asked.

'Yes. For several years I was so bitter about the wrecking of my life that I carried on a vendetta against them. I happened to run into O'Kieff in a shipping office in London. He was booking a passage to Egypt, so having plenty of money I booked one too.[1] I didn't get him, but I was able to settle accounts with Zakri Bey in the Libyan desert and a year or two later I shot Count Mondragora during the war in Greece.[2] Lord Gavin Fortescue was already an elderly man and he died very unpleasantly soon after the war. Mazinsky, the Polish Jew, fell a victim to the Nazis. Baron von Hentzen was a pal of Hitler's and, like a lot of the other Nazis, when Germany collapsed succeeded in disappearing. What has happened to him, the Jap or O'Kieff I've no idea. After a time I gave up trying to trace them; but God help any of them should they cross my path again.'

'I can understand how you feel,' Merri murmured. 'And I'm terribly sorry for you. But after all these years you really ought to try to forget this horrid business. You're not too old to start a new life, perhaps in America, where it's very unlikely that you would run across anyone who remembers your connection with this shocking scandal.'

'No. I wouldn't live permanently in the United States for all the tea in China. And I don't fancy Latin America either, or any of the Arab countries. But I've often toyed with the idea of marrying and settling down in some place outside Europe where one could be reasonably secure and life is pleasant; such, for example, as the West Indies or Hong Kong.'

1 See *The Quest of Julian Day*.
2 See *The Sword of Fate*.

'Then why don't you?' she asked, her big grey eyes wide and innocent.

'First I'd have to find the right girl and find out if she would have me,' he replied with a nervous little laugh. But, greatly as he was tempted to do so, he had the wisdom to refrain for the moment from pursuing the subject further.

They stayed on to dine at the Shatin Heights, watched a marvellous sunset over the bay to the north of Castle Peak, then drove back to Hong Kong.

Saturday was race day, and a Mrs. Heng, who was a friend of Merri's, had several horses running. Merri had secured for Julian an invitation to Mrs. Heng's box; so, a little before twelve, in order to be in time for the first race, they drove down through the pass to Happy Valley and Julian was duly presented to his portly hostess.

The box was on the upper tier with a perfect view of the course and the milling crowds in the enclosures below; for the Chinese are inveterate gamblers and therefore enthusiastic racegoers. Dozens of Mrs. Heng's friends were constantly coming in and out of the box to exchange tips while being served by the Chinese boys with drinks, and the box was so commodious that in its rear section lunch had been laid for sixteen. With a few exceptions Mrs. Heng's guests were Chinese or Eurasians: charming, friendly people who made Julian feel more than ever that he would like to make his home in Hong Kong and become one of their circle. Owing to the tips he was given he backed two winners and got three horses for a place; so he ended well up on this most enjoyable day.

That evening he took Merri across to Kowloon to dine in the Mandarin Room at the Miramar. On their way home he asked her to pull the car up just before they entered the pass, so that they could look down on the illuminated warships in the harbour and the myriad lights of Victoria and Kowloon. After they had smoked cigarettes he put his arm gently round her slim shoulders.

As she made no movement to draw away, with his heart hammering in his chest he asked:

'Merri, have you ever been kissed by a man old enough to be your father?'

'No,' she replied in a whisper. 'But, somehow, you don't seem as old as all that.'

Next moment his mouth was pressed gently to hers. Her lips were satin soft and sweetly yielding. She put an arm up round his neck and as their bodies met in an embrace he felt a shudder of passion run through her. When their long kiss ended she gave a little laugh and murmured, 'I've rarely known a younger man who could kiss better.'

The multi-coloured lights forgotten, they spent a wonderful half-hour and, now silent from the aftermath of their emotions, drove on to the Repulse Bay.

Before getting out Julian said, 'Tomorrow of course, my sweet, you'll be off duty. But I'll go mad if I don't at least see you. Can't I call on the excuse of wanting to see your mother's garden?'

She considered for a moment. 'All right, then. I'm afraid I can't ask you to a meal. But I'll tell Mother that you are coming in for a drink about twelve o'clock.'

On that they parted, with Julian feeling on top of the world.

Sunday was again a heavenly day, and in the golden sunshine Julian walked the three-quarters of a mile past the Lido to Merri's home. From its situation, which she had described to him, he could not doubt that this was it, but it was a far finer property than he had expected; for, as Mrs. Sang worked in an office, he had not thought of her as a wealthy woman.

The house stood on a cliff a hundred feet above the shore. Below the drive to it lay three narrow terraces lined with flowering shrubs, rockeries and plants in pots. From the lowest there was a drop of twenty feet to flattish rocks out of which had been hewn an open swimming pool. Beside the front door there was a high trellis covered with creeper from which hung big bells of Golden Trumpet.

An elderly Chinese 'boy' bowed Julian into an airy hall. In an alcove at its end stood a life-size gilded bronze figure of the goddess Kuan-yin. He had never seen a finer, and realized at a glance that it was a real collector's piece. Next moment Merri ran out to welcome him, then led him into a spacious drawing room to introduce him to her mother.

The room held many other beautiful things of porcelain, jade and lacquer; but Julian's gaze was fixed on Mrs. Sang. She was a much bigger woman than her daughter and almost as beautiful, but in quite a different way, for she was blonde and blue-eyed. As Merri was nineteen, Julian knew that her mother must at least be close on forty, but he would have put her down as in her middle thirties. Vaguely her face seemed familiar and, as they shook hands, he said:

'Haven't we met somewhere before?'

She smiled with her mouth but not with her eyes. 'Perhaps; but not unless it was in Australia or Singapore. Merri tells me that you have not been to Hong Kong since the war, and I did not come here to live until 1949.'

He shook his head. 'I've never been to Australia and never stayed in Singapore for any length of time except as a soldier in 1941.'

Mrs. Sang shrugged her fine shoulders. 'You are mistaken, then. I was born in Australia and met my husband there in 1944. He was then a refugee from Singapore. After the war we went to live there, but he died two years later. In '48 I came to Hong Kong on a holiday and I liked the island so much that I decided to make my home here.'

The Chinese 'boy' wheeled in a tray of drinks and Julian chose a gin sling. As it was handed to him he said, 'Merri tells me that you work for the Narcotics Advisory Committee. That must be an interesting job.'

'It is,' she nodded. 'Drugs are a most terrible evil and it has become far worse since the introduction of heroin. People could smoke opium in moderation for years without ill effects; but two or three pipes of heroin are enough for the victim to become an addict. Once he has acquired the vice he will sell anything to get it: his dearest possessions, his wife, his home, until he has beggared himself. In a few months he can reduce himself to a moron and a skeleton.'

'So I have heard. But I gather a lot is now being done to reclaim addicts.'

'Yes, if they will accept treatment or are sent to prison for at least six months. And when they are reclaimed they rarely relapse. But our worst problem is trying to prevent the drug from being smuggled in. Over six thousand ocean-going vessels come into Hong Kong every year and it is next to impossible to search them all thoroughly.'

'I suppose you have agents, though, in other ports who tip you off about suspected vessels?'

Her pale smile came again. 'Oh, yes. Unesco and Interpol are a great help to us. My work consists mainly in collating their reports and we are able to seize many packages of the drug directly the ships put in here. But the smugglers are extraordinarily ingenious and often Customs men trained as engineers have to spend days in engine rooms taking the ships' machinery to pieces.'

For a while they continued to talk of smugglers and their ruses, then Mrs. Sang said, 'But you have come to see my flowers' and, standing up, led the way out through the wide window on to a balcony overhanging the beach. From there they descended a flight of steps to the terraces with their multitude of blossoms. As at the Repulse Bay there were great pots of massed carnations and dahlias in flower at the same time; there were also many species that Julian had seen in other countries but not in Hong Kong, and as a background great masses of jasmine, bougainvillaea and Chinese cracker.

For half an hour Julian exerted all his charm while admiring Mrs. Sang's treasures. He had hoped that she might ask him to stay on for lunch, but she remained cold and distant, and when she had shown him her orchid house did not even invite him in for another drink; so he had no option but to thank her and take his leave, consoling himself with the thought that Merri would be coming to pick him up again the following morning.

On Monday they went over to Kowloon and spent the morning admiring the goods in the hundreds of shops along the splendid highway of Nathan Road and its adjacent streets. They were stocked with every type of tempting merchandise—embroidered satins, pearls, leather goods, cameras, antiques—and as Hong Kong is a Free Port they were on sale at incredibly cheap prices. Radios could be bought cheaper than in Japan, whence they came, and rich silks for a fifth of the price charged in London. Julian did his best to persuade Merri to let him buy her a crocodile-skin bag, but she would not allow him to.

'It's not that I wouldn't love to have it,' she said; 'but I couldn't prevent Mother from seeing it, and she won't allow me to accept presents from men.'

He made a little grimace. 'That's a pity, and I'm afraid your mother didn't take a very good view of me.'

She nodded. 'I felt that too. But it wasn't your fault. She is inclined to be moody and difficult at times, and yesterday was one of her off days.'

For lunch Merri took him to Ng Fong Chari's, a little restaurant in a side street, to eat a Beggar's Chicken that she had ordered by telephone before starting out that morning. A lump of baked clay, nearly as large as a football, was brought to their table by a grinning Chinese waiter, then put on the floor and broken open with a hammer. Inside was the bird, cooked to a turn in its own fat.

In the afternoon they returned to Hong Kong for Julian

to have his sleep. Then in the evening they met again and went over to the Princess Garden night club to dine and dance. But they left early and drew in to the side of the road on the way home for another delightful session of embracing and kissing.

As Merri restarted the car, Julian asked, 'What shall we do tomorrow?'

For a moment she was silent, then she said, 'I'm sorry, Julian. I know you'll be terribly disappointed, and I didn't want to spoil your day by telling you before. But actually you only booked me till the end of last week, and from tomorrow I'll have to keep a previous engagement made before I met you. Bill Urata will have got back tonight from Manila.'

CHAPTER VI

OH! TO BE YOUNG AGAIN

TUESDAY was a black day for Julian. When Merri had spoken of receiving an airmail letter from Bill Urata she had not mentioned that in a few days' time he would be returning to Hong Kong. And she had spoken with considerable warmth about the young Japanese. That did not necessarily mean that she was attracted by him, but it did mean that she saw him with different eyes from Julian's.

Although Urata was a Japanese by blood, in all other respects he could be looked on as an American. Experience had taught Julian that, while travelled Americans can be as cultured and charming as any people in the world, since fewer than one in every hundred have ever been to Europe the average Englishman has much more in common with his Continental neighbours than he has with the average American. They are brought up with an entirely different background, intensely proud of their country's great achievements and inclined to regard everything to do with the Old World as effete; whereas the European finds little to admire in a polyglot people one-third of who have periodically to go into homes for treatment as alcoholics, drug addicts or for other mental disorders, yet who dictate the policy of smaller countries through the power of money, often with no long-term knowledge of the issues at stake, and have not yet even learnt to care for the welfare of their own underprivileged classes.

70

It was, therefore, not unnatural that he should regard the crew-cut, camera-draped, loudly dressed young Urata with faint distaste and think of him as a modern barbarian. But he had youth: splendid carefree youth; he danced the Twist and, no doubt, would be only too ready to swim with Merri however cold the water. That, Julian acknowledged grimly, was ample to account for her liking for him.

Somehow, Julian got through the day. But the evening was far worse. He felt certain that Urata would persuade Merri to dine with him. Probably he liked his food made unrecognizable with lashings of vinegar, mustard and onions and his favourite dish was nearly-raw meat; so he would order two huge steaks. But perhaps Merri liked steaks too. Then they would dance. Not gracefully, but with a wild abandon reminiscent of savages in the Congo. Yet they would be laughing and thoroughly enjoying it.

By eleven o'clock still more tormenting visions seethed in Julian's mind. Merri would have her car and Urata could be counted on to get her to take him for a short drive before dropping him at his hotel. She enjoyed being kissed and was passionate by nature. In Julian's arms she had given ample evidence of her hot Asiatic blood. Excited by the dancing and with a man of her own age, she would be even more disposed to let herself go than she had with him. At half past eleven he finished his last brandy-and-soda and went to bed, now blessing Mrs. Sang for her ruling that Merri must be home by that hour.

Wednesday followed much the same pattern. Such doubts as he had had about marrying a girl so much younger than himself were now utterly dispersed. Attacked by a more violent jealousy than he had experienced for many years, he felt that, come what may, he had to win her. Again he spent a miserable day, and late that evening his vivid imagination conjured up pictures that were almost unbearable; for he had persuaded himself that if she proved unwilling the husky young Japanese might take her by force.

Then on Thursday reason and plausibility got the upper hand in Julian's mind. Merri had told him that most of the people for whom she had acted as guide were rich, generally elderly, American couples; but she had mentioned several men that she had taken round the Colony, some of whom she had liked and dined with. As she was so ravishingly beautiful it was certain that some of them would have made a pass at her; so she would have had ample experience in dealing with such situations. And there was no reason at all to suppose that she liked Urata more than she had several other men. She must regard them all as only birds of passage, and even those who did attract her could mean no more than chaps to have a little fun with. All the odds were that young Urata fell into that category. Anyhow, he was combining a holiday with his business trip; so he must soon return to Japan. That, Julian now realized, gave him the ace. He had no ties. His time was limitless. He had telephoned the office of the Hong Kong Tourist Association first thing on Tuesday morning to say that he wished to engage Miss Sang's services indefinitely as soon as she was again free. He had only to possess his soul in patience until Urata departed and sweet laughing Merri would again become his companion for long happy days.

He had not long to wait. At half past eight on Friday morning the telephone in his bedroom rang, and to his delight Merri's silvery voice came over the line. 'Good morning, Julian. I rang up to tell you that Bill is leaving today for Macao. The office tells me that you've booked me again. So if it's all right with you I'll call for you at half past nine.'

When she arrived in her car she said, 'This is the 1st March and it's the hottest day yet; so unless you've any other plans I thought I might take you to bathe at Sheko.'

Stunned afresh at the sight of her flower-like face and slim body, he was willing to agree to anything; so they drove down to the beach. Quite a few people were already in the water, and when he had hired two tents she said, 'What about skis? You do water-ski, don't you?'

He shook his head. 'I'm afraid not. I've never learnt to.'

She sighed. 'What a pity. It's marvellous fun. Bill and I came here yesterday. He's absolutely first-class and wonderful to watch. But never mind. We'll just go in for a swim.'

Again Julian felt the awful handicap of middle-age that, despite his firm good figure, was creeping upon him. But they enjoyed their bathe and afterwards lunched off a delicious crab omelette and avocado pear salad.

When she asked him if he would like to return to the Repulse Bay for his afternoon nap he suddenly formed a determination to break that habit of the ageing and replied, 'No; let's drive up into the hills and find a place where we can sit and enjoy the heavenly view.'

Half an hour later they had left the car and were sitting side by side several hundred feet up looking out towards Lamtong Island and the ocean that faded into a blue haze beyond it.

It was very peaceful and they were utterly alone there. Putting an arm round her shoulders, he made to draw her to him; but she wriggled free and said abruptly, 'No, Julian, no. It's too hot for that sort of thing.'

He did not press her; yet as he refrained he was suddenly cynically conscious that, heat or no heat, had he been younger he would have laughed at her protest then pulled her to him and kissed her.

All the morning he had been tempted to ask her about Urata. Now he could resist no longer, and enquired, 'What sort of a time did you have with Bill?'

73

Her large grey eyes regarded him with an amused look, and she replied, 'I believe you're jealous.'

'Of course I am,' he admitted with a smile. 'I just hated the thought of your being with him, because I know you like him.'

'I do,' she agreed frankly, 'and we had great fun. We danced every evening and it was heavenly. He's the nicest and most amusing man I've met for a long time.'

'Then you find him nicer than me?' Julian asked with a sinking feeling.

She regarded him gravely for a moment with a little frown. 'No, I wouldn't quite say that. The two of you are so utterly different. Bill is a masterful sort of man. He wants his own way in everything, but all the time he is bubbling with spontaneous gaiety. Whereas you are wonderfully peaceful to be with. And you understand things about life and art that Bill hasn't got a clue about. He is much more exciting; but you have so many things he lacks, and I'd put my trust in you much sooner than I would in him.'

'Thanks for the compliment,' Julian smiled, much comforted; but, wisely, he made no further attempt to kiss her.

That night they dined at the Carlton and on the way home she willingly surrendered again to his kisses.

Over dinner they had planned their next day. Merri had said that one of the most enjoyable outings was to hire a private launch and go round the island, but it was so expensive that usually a group of tourists clubbed together to make the trip. Not the least deterred by that, Julian had asked her to engage one so that they could enjoy a long day together on the sea.

Next morning they left Ferry Pier in a big motor launch with a crew of five: a skipper, an engineer, a deck hand, a cook and a steward. In the forepart of the launch there was a cabin that would seat ten in rough weather, and a small bar; above it the deck, covered with an awning, was furnished with a table and a number of cane armchairs. Below, in the stern, lay the engine room and the galley.

In perfect weather they headed westward, with no more than a gentle breeze to chop the sea slightly and refresh them in the torrid heat. By midday they had come round to Ti Tam Bay and, anchoring, went overboard for a swim. Back on board they were served an excellent lunch, then during the afternoon they rounded Kau Pi Chau Point and headed north. By six o'clock they had entered the Lei U Mun Channel and were about seven miles from Victoria, but opposite Quarry Point the engine broke down.

That did not particularly worry them, as they had planned to make the most of their day on the water and dine on board. However, the trouble proved more than a temporary fault and, after tinkering with the engine for three-quarters of an hour, the Chinese engineer told them apologetically that it might be two or three hours before he could get it going again.

Still not unduly worried, they watched the sun decline in the west crowned by a great aura of orange, salmon and gold, while drinking cocktails then eating a very pleasant meal. By the time they finished it had grown chilly; so they went down into the cabin and, with the aid of a pile of cushions, snuggled up comfortably in a corner there. With the failure of the engine the lights had also failed, so by nine o'clock they were shrouded from the sight of the crew by complete darkness.

Confident that it could not now be long before the repairs to the engine were completed, Merri was in one of her happiest moods. She let Julian kiss her to his heart's content, responded passionately and now and then gave little sighs of pleasure.

He had not meant to force the pace but after a while the temptation was too much for him and he said softly,

'Merri, I love you. I love you desperately. Will you marry me?'

She gave a little gasp, drew away from him and asked, 'Do you . . . do you really mean that?'

'Of course I do,' he assured her. 'You are the loveliest and sweetest thing that God ever put breath into. I've told you all about myself, so you know what you'd be taking on. I've had a rotten life so far; but you said yourself only the other day that I ought to settle down and make a new life for myself. I know I'm much older than you, but I'm still young enough to do that, and I'm sure I could make you happy. My sweet, I beg you to say yes.'

She gave a sudden nervous little laugh. 'I . . . I've had quite a number of proposals; but never before two in one week.'

'Does that mean that Bill proposed to you?' he asked with a frown.

'Yes,' she nodded. 'On his last night here, before he left for Macao. He was terribly set on marrying me; but I couldn't, even if I really loved him enough, and I'm not sure that I do. You see, the Japanese are responsible for a great deal of the dope running that goes on here, and Mother loathes them on that account. She would never consent to my marrying a Japanese.'

'I see. Then that puts Bill Urata out of the running. And, anyway, you're not in love with him.'

'I find him terribly attractive. But that's not the same as being head over heels in love, is it?'

'No. And what about me?'

'I find you terribly attractive too, but you fulfil an entirely different need in me. In some ways Bill is almost a barbarian; whereas you have all the intellect, love of beauty and kindly worldly wisdom that appeal so strongly both to the Chinese and European in me.'

'Such qualities are much more lasting, Merri, than being able to dance the Twist and ride a surf-board with agility. Say "yes"; I implore you to.'

She shook her dark head. 'No, I can't. Please, Julian, don't press me. To be honest, I've let you make love to me partly, at least, to get Bill out of my mind, because that's all over and I want to forget about him. Perhaps to tell you that is unkind, but it wasn't altogether that. I've never been kissed by such an accomplished lover, and I'll admit that your gentle fondling of me sends me into a dream of bliss. But you must be content with that for the moment. To marry you is another thing, and you must give me time to think.'

More than content with her admission that she liked him so much, Julian refrained from urging her further, but again drew her to him and time drifted by unnoticed by them.

When at last she asked the time he looked at his watch and saw that it was after ten. Worried now about getting her home, he went aft and spoke to the engineer, who was working on the engine by the light of a torch. The Chinese assured him glibly that the major trouble had been dealt with but another half-hour went by before the engine began to stutter. Unrealized by them, the current had meanwhile carried the launch several miles down towards Lamtong Island. In consequence it was midnight before they at last landed at Starr Ferry, and they still had to collect the car and drive across the island.

Fearing that Merri's mother might be waiting up for her, Julian insisted that she should drive straight home so that he might support her explanation for her lateness, and afterward he would walk back to his hotel. When they arrived he found that their fears were only too well founded. Mrs. Sang let them into the house herself and her fine face was grim with disapproval.

Merri nervously gabbled out an account of what had happened, but her mother said only, 'You go straight up to bed, child. I want a word with Mr. Day and he shall do the explaining.'

With a crestfallen glance at Julian, Merri went upstairs, while he followed Mrs. Sang into the drawing room. Pushing the door to behind them, she rounded on him and, her eyes hard as agates, said angrily, 'The engine broke down! I don't believe it! That's the oldest story in the world. You fixed things with the crew of the launch so that you could make love to Merri.'

'No, honestly. It's the truth, Mrs. Sang,' he protested.

'You're lying! Her lipstick's all over your face. I shouldn't be surprised if you succeeded in seducing her.'

Julian drew himself up and retorted sharply, 'I did not; and you've no right to suggest such a thing. I admit to kissing her, of course; but she's not a child just out of the school room, so why shouldn't I? And you may as well know that I've asked her to marry me.'

'Marry you!' exclaimed Mrs. Sang, her blue eyes widening.

'Yes. Why not? I'm a bachelor with no entanglements, and I'm sure that I could make her happy.'

For a moment the handsome blonde woman stood there staring at him, then she burst out, 'No! I won't have it! When you were here on Sunday you saw all the valuable things in this house. You realized that I was a wealthy woman and that all this will go to Merri. You're just a fortune hunter, trying to turn the child's head with your knowledge of the world and polished manners.'

'What nonsense!' Julian gave an angry little laugh. 'You haven't the least foundation for making such a charge. I'm probably as rich as and maybe richer than you are. In the United States alone I have enough money safely invested to buy this house and everything in it.'

Mrs. Sang's hands were trembling. 'All right, then!' she snapped. 'If I'm wrong about that there's another reason. You're too old for Merri; much too old. At your age how could you expect to keep pace with a girl of hers? After the first excitement of being married and having her own home had worn off she would become bored with you. How can you expect me to agree to her making a marriage that would be bound to go on the rocks within a few years?'

'I don't agree that it would,' Julian replied stubbornly. 'Merri's great wish is to travel. She is highly intelligent and greatly interested in art and history. In these days there are very few men who're not tied by some business or profession, and wealthy enough to take their wives to live for a while with every comfort in any country they wish to see. I'm in a position to provide her with a whole series of new sights and interests for years to come; so you're quite wrong in supposing that she would become bored if she married me.'

'One can get bored with travelling after a few years. And what sort of a life is it for a girl to live out of a trunk for months on end, even in the very best hotels? The real joy of marriage is to settle down, make a home, have children and live among a circle of friends.'

Julian gave a slight smile. 'I think now, Mrs. Sang, I can guess your real reason for objecting to me as a husband for Merri. As she is your only child and you have very little social life you are most reluctant to lose her. It's only natural that you hoped that when she did marry it would be someone with a good position here in Hong Kong. Well, let me reassure you. I've found Hong Kong to be one of the most delightful places I've ever stayed in, so I am quite prepared to buy a pleasant property on the island. Merri and I would travel only part of the year and make our permanent home here. Does that satisfy you?'

'No, it does not!' Merri's mother flared, her blue eyes blazing. 'Since you drive me to it I'll give you a reason that is final. When you came here on Sunday you thought we had met before. You were right. We had. I recognized you immediately. I was Matilda Cray, the young

Australian V.A.D. who appealed to you for help when the Japanese broke into the temporary hospital at the Jockey Club. If you'd been half a man you would have saved me from rape and worse. I'll not let my daughter marry a coward.'

CHAPTER VII

THE PAST CATCHES UP WITH
JULIAN DAY

MOMENTARILY speechless, Julian stared at the woman who had once been Matilda Cray. Then he had seen her face fully only for those two agonizing minutes when his muscles had seemed near breaking point as he had tried to hoist her up through the skylight; now he realized that she had hardly altered at all. The tall, well-made girl had only put on flesh, acquired a few wrinkles round her eyes and a harder mouth, to become this big, handsome woman.

As he stared at her, she went on furiously, 'I suppose you know that the nurses in that hospital, British and Chinese alike, were raped time after time all Christmas Day and all through the following night, and knocked about and beaten into the bargain? That's what happened to me after you took to your heels to save your skin. But I fared worse than they did; far worse. A Japanese officer took a fancy to me and had me shanghaied to a house on the mainland. He kept me locked up there for weeks while he inflicted every sort of bestial lust on me. Then . . . then when at last he tired of me he sold me into a brothel in . . . in Canton. If you've any imagination, Mr. Day, try to picture the sort of hell that was for a young girl like me. On some nights I had to accept as many as a dozen stinking sweaty coolies one after the other. That lasted a whole year. If I hadn't been as strong as an ox I would have died after a month of it. That's what you let me in for.'

Panting, she paused a second and Julian stammered out, 'But Mrs. Sang, I . . . I——'

With an angry gesture she cut him short. 'That I'm not an old harridan peddling myself on the waterfront for enough rice to keep me alive, or long since dead, is no fault of yours. But I survived. Sang . . . Sang came to that low brothel one night, having been misled into believing it a good-class one. He happened to see me, paid for a whole night with me and after he had had me talked to me for a long while. He was a wealthy merchant and he bought me out. Later, in 1944, he married me. After he died I . . . I saw the red light and got my money out of China. But my family had long since given me up for dead. I couldn't bring myself to return to Australia with little Merri—a half-caste child—and face them; so I came here: a lonely widow with a ruined life. You could have saved me from all those agonies I went through, but you lacked the courage. Now you know why I won't have you as a husband for Merri.'

Holding out both his hands in a helpless gesture, Julian said, 'Yours is a terrible story—terrible. I can't find words to express my . . . well, horror . . . sympathy . . . distress. They're all inadequate. But you are being unjust to me. Remember everything happened very quickly. I saw you only for a moment through the skylight before calling to you, and looking down on you I underestimated your weight. Even so, in normal circumstances I think I could have pulled you up; but I had a wound in one arm, was bruised all over from having escaped capture by rolling down a steep hillside, and was practically all-in from three days of constant marching and fighting. You can't hold me guilty of more than an error of judgment.'

'I do! When you found you couldn't pull me up you could have shot me. In those days my looks had attracted a dozen men who tried to seduce me. But I had been brought up to believe that to keep herself chaste was a woman's first duty; so I was a good girl. I meant to keep myself for some man I'd fall in love with and marry. Rather than be raped by the Japanese I would willingly have died. If I'd known the hell that was in store for me I'd have gladly suffered death ten times over. I implored you to shoot me. But you hadn't the guts. You just crouched up there looking on while one of them blacked my eye and they threw me down on the sofa.'

Helplessly, Julian shook his head. 'I couldn't have shot you. My pistol was empty and I hadn't a round of ammunition left. I appreciate how you must feel, but there was nothing I could possibly do to save you.'

Ignoring his explanation, she retorted bitterly, 'Yes, you could have if you had done as I asked you in the first place. I called up to you to come down and help me barricade the door. If you'd done that, before they could have broken in we would have had time to get out on the roof together and escape them. But you chose to remain up there rather than risk your own safety.'

Julian realized that she must have nursed this grievance against him for years, and that there was no arguing with her. He could only repeat, 'I was half dead on my feet— too exhausted to think clearly. I admit that I did the wrong thing; but anyone might have in the circumstances. I felt ghastly about it for weeks afterwards. But you cannot blame me for more than an error of judgment.'

'And I paid for your error,' she said with sudden calmness. 'Well, we'll let it rest there. But you know now why I wouldn't have you as a son-in-law. No, not if you were the last man on earth.'

Stung to anger by what he felt to be her injustice, Julian retorted, 'Perhaps, then, you'd rather have Merri marry her Japanese?'

Mrs. Sang's blue eyes dilated again and she repeated in a horrified whisper, 'Her Japanese? What . . . what d'you mean by that?'

Julian felt entitled to get a little of his own back, so he

shrugged and said, 'If Merri were not such a dutiful daughter and, knowing your hatred for the Japanese, turned him down on that account, she might quite well by now be engaged to a young man named Urata.'

'You . . . you're lying!' Mrs. Sang burst out. 'I don't believe it.'

'Don't, then, if you prefer to bury your head in the sand. But if you check up with the Tourist Association you'll find that up till a few days ago she was acting as guide to him, and that they spent a week or more together before I arrived on the island. She told me herself, only yesterday, that he'd proposed to her and that she was half in love with him.'

'This is the end; the end!' Mrs. Sang's voice rose to a hysterical note. 'I was always against her becoming a guide. Now I know the sort of people she takes round she shall be one no longer. She is still a minor, so must do as I bid her, like it or not. First thing on Monday morning I'll telephone her office and tell them that she'll not be working for them in future. As for you, I forbid you to see her again or communicate with her in any way. Now get out!'

For a moment Julian stood glowering at the tall angry woman, then he said firmly, 'I still mean to marry Merri if she'll have me, and I'll do as I damn' well please.'

Turning on his heel, he marched from the room and out of the house, slamming the front door behind him.

Next morning he woke to a feeling that some catastrophe had befallen him, then the awful scene that he had had with Mrs. Sang flowed back into his mind. Trying to regard dispassionately all that she had said, he conceded that the ghastly time she had been through might have warped any woman's mind to a point at which she could no longer form a fair assessment of its causes, and it was evident that she had fixed on him as the scapegoat for her sufferings. Throughout the long years since the invasion of Hong Kong, whenever those few terrible minutes

84

in which he had attempted, but failed, to save her had recurred to him, he had again reproached himself for having told her to do the wrong thing. But it had never even occurred to him that she might look on her having become a victim of the Japanese as due to cowardice on his part, and he was fully convinced that any fair-minded person who knew the facts would exonerate him from such a charge.

As Merri must have been born either just before or soon after Mrs. Sang's marriage, it seemed very unlikely that she knew anything about her mother's shocking ordeals, and Julian had no intention of telling her about them. But if he continued his courtship of Merri, as he intended to do, the possibility had to be faced that in a last-ditch attempt to prejudice Merri against him her mother might reveal her real reasons for objecting to him. If that did happen what would Merri's reaction be?

Having considered the matter, Julian decided that it would depend on the degree of trust and affection that he could inspire in his beautiful love. If he could get no further with her than he had up to the present the odds were that she would accept her mother's view of him. Therefore his best hope lay in seeing much more of her; so that if Mrs. Sang did use the past in an attempt to discredit him, Merri would believe his side of the story.

But to see more of Merri, now that her mother would be acting as a watchdog, was going to be far from easy. Deciding to tackle this difficult situation without delay, after Julian had had his bath he rang up her home and asked for her.

A Chinese 'boy' answered the call and lisped, 'Solly, Master. Missie Merri not velly well today. Missie take no telephone calls.'

So that was that. Obviously Mrs. Sang had already given her servants their instructions.

Undeterred, Julian sat down at the writing table and wrote a note that read:

My very dearest Merri,

I understand that your mother intends to forbid you to continue to act as a guide, and I consider her decision most unkind and unreasonable. Obviously she is still living in a bygone age and does not realize that it is now accepted that parents have no right to dictate to their grown-up children.

In view of our friendship I refuse to tolerate this arbitrary attempt to end it; and I hope you will do so too. However you may feel, I positively must see you at least once more, to offer you a little sound advice about how best to overcome her prejudice against your being allowed a reasonable degree of freedom to live your own life as other girls do in these days.

From half past seven this evening I'll be in a car near the entrance to the Lido. As we have not yet had a meal in one of the floating restaurants at Aberdeen Bay, and as it is quite near, if you can join me I suggest that we dine there. But if you can only get out to talk to me in the car for a few minutes that would be better than nothing.

Your devoted Julian

It was because he felt doubtful whether Merri was yet sufficiently attracted to him to invite further trouble by giving him a secret rendezvous that he had taken the line of inciting her to make a fight for her independence and, having read his letter through, he thought there was a good chance of its leading her to defy her mother.

As soon as he had dressed, he walked down past the Lido and reconnoitred the house. From the road he could see only a part of the roof that showed between the trees, and no-one was about except, just inside the gate, a young Chinese whom he took to be a gardener.

Beckoning the man over, Julian produced his letter, together with a ten-dollar note, and asked, 'Do you think you could deliver this letter to Miss Sang without anyone else seeing you give it to her?'

Although poorly clad, the Chinese replied in passable English and appeared to have a quicker intelligence than most of his class. With a broad grin he said, 'Am not allowed in house, Master. Blut it iss fine day, so Missie certain come out. When she do evelyfling O.Klay. I give Missie and no-one see.'

Feeling reasonably confident that the young fellow would succeed in getting the letter to Merri, Julian gave it and the handsome tip to him; then he returned to the Repulse Bay to get through the day with as much patience as he could muster.

At 7.30, with a self-drive car that he had hired through the hotel, he was waiting anxiously outside the Lido. Soon afterwards, to his relief, Merri came hurrying up the road. As she slipped into the car beside him she said a little breathlessly:

'Well, here I am. I'm furious with Mother; absolutely furious. She continues to insist that I must give up my job as a guide; but I find it the greatest fun meeting people from all over the world and taking them round. I'd be bored to tears if, instead, I had to wade through endless reports and file things all day in her dreary old office.'

'Then be your age,' Julian told her abruptly, as he set the car in motion, 'and tell her that as a grown woman you are going to stick to the job you prefer.'

'That won't be easy,' Merri said with a sigh. 'She is a terribly dominating person, and all my life I've been used to doing as she tells me. She has forbidden me to leave the house without her permission and I wouldn't be here now if it hadn't been that I had already accepted an invitation to dine tonight with some people she knows quite well; and she could hardly order me to back out at the last moment.'

The town of Aberdeen lay only a couple of miles away, so Julian decided to reserve until over dinner his arguments to induce her to revolt. As he had fallen silent, Merri asked, 'Where did you find the young Chinese who brought me your letter? He didn't look like a servant from the hotel.'

Julian gave her a look of surprise. 'I thought he was one of your gardeners.'

'No. They don't work on Sundays. When I came out to lie on the hammock he was hiding in the bushes and attracted my attention by giving a low whistle. Then, as I looked in that direction, he beckoned me over, pressed your note into my hand and scuttled away before I had a chance to say anything to him.'

'Then I haven't an idea who he was. I had meant to sneak round to the back door of the house and bribe one of the servants to give it to you when your mother was not about. But I came upon this chap just inside your front drive, and counted myself lucky to have found someone who would do the job without my having to risk being seen.'

'I asked because I thought it funny that you had only folded your letter and not put it into an envelope.'

'But I did. He must have torn it open in order to get at the letter and see what it was about. What an extraordinary thing for a coolie to do. I shouldn't have thought many of them could read—English writing anyhow.'

'Most of the young ones can; and although he was of the working class he wasn't a coolie.'

'Why should he want to read it, though?'

'Just curiosity, I expect. Nearly all the Chinese are insatiably curious and there is nothing they love so much as finding out about other people's private affairs. The very fact that you told him to give it to me in secret would have been quite enough to set him itching to open it.'

'Since he does know what it was about, isn't there a risk that he'll try to earn another tip by spilling the beans to your mother?'

'I don't think he's likely to do that. As a people the Chinese are remarkably honest.'

'Say he did, though; your mama may come chasing after us to get you out of my clutches. Perhaps we had better not dine at Aberdeen, but go somewhere else.'

Merri shook her dark head. 'There's no fear of that. Mother would never make a scene in public.'

A few minutes later they were running into Aberdeen. Some way out from the packed mass of moored sampans, that housed by far the greater part of the population of the place, lay the two floating restaurants. Had they been on land and seen from a distance these great double-decker house-boats might well have been taken for Chinese temples and, although it was only just dusk, they were already gaily lit with many chains of coloured fairy lamps.

Having parked the car, they were met at the landing stage by rival porters, and when they chose the Sea Palace its porter beckoned up a sampan. Its owner and a girl who was little more than a child then poled them across the neck of the bay to the restaurant. Most visitors, on arriving, went straight to the big tank to choose a fat garoupa, or other fish to be netted and cooked as a course in their meal. But Julian was impatient to have his talk with Merri; so as soon as she had telephoned, excusing herself to the friends with whom she had been going to dine, he took her straight to the upper deck. There, after one glance at Julian, the head waiter led them to a table on the landward side from which they could watch the thousand lights come on in the massed sampans along the shore.

Julian liked Chinese food and, while he considered shark's fin soup, birds' nests, fried snake and so-called 'thousand-year-old eggs' much over-rated, he greatly enjoyed Pekin Duck and sucking pig, with their honey-saturated skins roasted to a crisp golden brown. But tonight his mind was on other things, and Merri's too; so having ordered cocktails, they settled for the set dinner. Crab meat with sweet-corn soup was followed by huge fried Prawns with sweet and sour sauce, baked Lobster, diced Chicken sautéed with walnuts and Chow Fan, Young-Chow Style. While they ate these intriguing things, and picked with their chopsticks at the numerous side

89

dishes that accompanied each course, they discussed the situation.

Merri was at first much inclined to accept it, but Julian argued that she would be very foolish to do so. He pointed out that mothers with only one child, like Mrs. Sang, are often apt to become possessive and, although not deliberately, sacrifice their daughters' happiness for their own selfish ends; so that the girl continues as the mother's unpaid companion until, too late, she realizes the trap she has allowed herself to fall into, and is too old to have much choice of a husband. Following up that line, he stressed the fact that Mrs. Sang led a very restricted life; so Merri had little opportunity of meeting eligible bachelors in their own circle, whereas, as she admitted, she had met quite a number since she had been acting as a guide.

To that she agreed, but replied that in any case her mother could, and would, insist on the Tourist Association's dispensing with her services.

'All the more reason,' Julian told her, 'that you should dig in your toes now, and assert your right to take some other job which would bring you into contact with plenty of people, instead of becoming a slave in your mother's office.'

For a while they discussed other jobs that she was qualified to do. But none of them would give her both the opportunity to make many new acquaintances and also enable her to enjoy long days in the sunshine.

At length Julian smiled at her, laid his hand on hers and said, 'There's one way out. Why not make a clean break and marry me?'

She sighed and shook her head, 'No, Julian. I like you. I like you a lot, but I don't love you.'

'Don't put too much weight on that,' he urged her. 'Many marriages which are made solely for convenience, and in which the couple have hardly met one another, turn out the most lasting in the long run. That you like me a lot is enough for the moment. Love will come.'

Then he went on to endeavour to persuade her by saying that he would buy a well-situated house with a good garden in Hong Kong, so that she need not give up her friends, and that they would live there through the best months of the year, but travel during the great heat of summer in France, Italy, Spain and Germany, where he would take her to see the works of the great masters, the châteaux on the Loire, the glories of Seville and the castles on the Rhine. But when dinner ended she still would not commit herself.

'It all sounds heavenly,' she said. 'My favourite dream come true. And I don't suppose I'll ever meet another man with so much knowledge of these lovely things and places, and the time and money needed to show them to me. Perhaps, too, I would fall in love with you if we were constantly together for longer than we have been so far. But I do feel that Mother was right about one thing: the fact that there is such a big difference in our ages. And, as she said, your never having been married before makes that worse instead of better, because men who have lived as bachelors for years often get so set in their habits that when the first excitement of being married has worn off they resent having to lead an entirely different life.'

'I shouldn't, Merri,' he assured her. 'You would be rescuing me from my accursed loneliness, and I'd be happy to do anything to please you.'

She smiled at him. 'You're so kind and gentle and generous, that I believe you would. But I've got to make really certain that I could do my part, and give up lots of things that only young people enjoy, before I can say "Yes". I do promise, though, to think it over very, very seriously during these next few days.'

When they left the Sea Palace they were handed into a sampan poled by a strong-limbed woman and a boy in his early teens. The reflection of the coloured lights of the restaurant danced on the water and in the distance those in the packed sampans looked like a swarm of fireflies; but the night was dark, and it was not until they were about half-way to the shore and close upon her that they noticed a large, unlit launch. Unlike the one in which they had gone round the island, she had no upper deck; but she was as long and, obviously, a sea-going vessel.

She was almost stationary, but as they approached her they could hear her engine purring. Suddenly someone in her switched on a powerful torch and focused it on the sampan. Its beam came to rest on Merri and the man who held it gave a shout. Next moment the launch nosed forward, turned and came alongside them, scraping the side of the sampan and nearly upsetting it. The woman who was poling the boat gave a cry of protest. Then everything seemed to happen at once.

Half blinded by the light from the torch, Julian glimpsed half a dozen men a few feet above him over the counter of the higher vessel. With a long boat-hook one of them gave the woman sampan owner a violent prod in the stomach. Giving a gasp, she fell backwards and overboard. Another man struck at Julian's head with a cudgel. As he dodged the blow, a third flung a big piece of thick material over Merri's head, muffling her cries of alarm. By the time Julian had lurched to his feet in the now dangerously rocking sampan, two of them had leant over, seized Merri by the arms and were dragging her into the launch. What happened to the boy Julian did not see, but his cries, too, had been promptly silenced.

Julian hit out at the face of one of the men who were hauling Merri on board. His fist landed with a thud, The man gave a grunt and let go his hold, but the other had a firm grip on her. Just as Julian was about to seize her round the waist, she kicked out violently. Her right heel caught him in the chest, temporarily throwing him off balance. Before he could recover the man he had hit grabbed Merri again and she was pulled over the side.

Without a second's hesitation Julian scrambled over

92

after her and hit out right and left. A blow to the chin sent one man reeling. Another, who grappled with him, he kneed in the groin. Then one of the others struck him on the side of the head with a bludgeon. Reeling back, he fell against the gunwale of the launch. One of them seized his legs, jerked them up and tipped him over the edge. Under the thrust from his feet as he had followed Merri the sampan had drifted away. As he blacked out his last conscious thought was that he had struck the water and was going under.

CHAPTER VIII

THE MAN WHO CAME UP
FROM THE SEA

No ACTUARY, knowing all the circumstances, would have assessed the chances of Julian's surviving the night at more than a thousand to one against. And had he been thrown unconscious into most other harbours he would certainly have drowned. That he did not was owing to the fact that the Chinese, who live and die in waterborne sampan towns, are taught, even as tiny tots, to keep themselves afloat in case they tumble overboard, and later they all swim like fish.

The strong-limbed woman who had poled the sampan from the restaurant was no exception. Although winded by the jab from the boat-hook, she had soon got back her breath, and it was Julian's luck that he was thrown in within a few feet of her. Diving like a heron, she grabbed him by the hair and brought him to the surface.

Her young son, filled with terror at the totally unexpected and murderous attack, had not waited to see its outcome. Quick as a flash, he had dived overboard. On coming up, his first thought had been for his mother's sole means of livelihood—the precious sampan. A few swift strokes had brought him to its far side. As soon as it had drifted clear of the launch, he scrambled in and seized a paddle. Deftly he turned the boat and, exerting all his young strength, brought it alongside his mother; so that while supporting the unconscious Julian with one arm she could use a hand to cling on to it.

Two minutes later another sampan, taking diners ashore from the Sea Palace, came on the scene. With excited cries its occupants hauled Julian and the woman to safety. Meanwhile the long low launch, with Merri half stifled in its stern, had turned towards the opening to the bay and, with its powerful engine going at full throttle, was heading out to sea.

When Julian came to he was in the Aberdeen hospital. He had not swallowed much water, but a blinding pain, as though his head were on fire, prevented him from thinking clearly; yet episodes from the recent fracas flitted through his mind like flashes from a cinematographic film, and he began to shout deliriously:

'Merri! Save Merri! Save Merri!'

A Chinese nurse, who had him under observation, promptly gave him an injection and in a few minutes he drifted off into unconsciousness again. When he came out of his stupor it was daylight. His head was still throbbing dully, but his mind was capable of re-visualizing the whole ghastly affair in its proper sequence. Seeing that he had woken, a nurse brought a Chinese doctor to him, and Julian said tersely, 'Fetch the police. I must see the police at once.'

The doctor gave him a friendly smile, but shook his head and lisped, 'Not let. They are al'leady doing all that es possible. You are suffeling flom concussion. You must lest. Plesently I'll bling the police to you.' Then he was given a drink and a sedative that sent him off to sleep.

It was not until the Tuesday afternoon that he was allowed to make a statement to the police. A Eurasian officer and a Chinese sergeant came to take it. From them he learned that, while his own identity had been quickly established through an examination of the contents of his pockets, his papers had given no clue to that of his companion. So, although the head waiter at the Sea Palace had said that the kidnapped girl had often brought visitors to have a meal there, and that he thought she was

95

one of the professional guides from the Tourist Association, it was not until some hours after Mrs. Sang had telephoned to report that her daughter was missing that they had put two and two together. When Julian had furnished them with every particular that he could he said miserably:

'You say that so far you have failed to trace the launch. But you must have some idea where these bloody Chinese pirates hang out. Can't a force be sent to raid their dens?'

The Sergeant showed his teeth in a slightly superior smile and the officer replied, 'This is not the work of pirates. Normally they have only junks, and they would never dare come right in to Aberdeen and kidnap the sort of people who patronize the Sea Palace.'

'How do you explain this awful business, then?' Julian demanded angrily.

The officer shrugged. 'As we see it there are two possibilities. It is said that Miss Sang was an exceptionally beautiful girl. Some very rich man may have taken a fancy to her. If she had refused to have anything to do with him it is possible that he may have hired these thugs to carry her off for him. There is also the possibility that she may have been snatched by white-slavers. As with the pirates, such people do not normally molest girls of good standing, because to do so results in too great a hue-and-cry by their relatives. But, despite all our efforts to prevent it, the trade still goes on, and the white-slavers are much cleverer, richer and better organized than the pirates. For a beautiful Eurasian girl they could get a very high price, so it may be that it is they who have abducted Miss Sang.'

Julian groaned. The thought of Merri in the hands of a wealthy unscrupulous sensualist was bad enough; that she might, at that moment, be being beaten into submission in a brothel did not bear thinking about. As he made to sit up, a pain shot through his head. Flopping back he burst out:

'Then why the hell haven't you attempted to find her by raiding all the brothels in Hong Kong?'

'Sir,' the officer replied, 'within the meaning of the Act there are no brothels in Hong Kong. There are many bars in what we now term the Susie Wong quarter that sailors and others frequent. They drink and dance with the hostesses and, if the girls are willing, afterwards accompany them to rooms upstairs. But such places are all under police surveillance and you may rest assured that Miss Sang is not in one of them.'

'Where might they have taken her, then? To a Chinese port?'

'I doubt it, sir. There are still houses of ill fame in every country in the world. But in recent years the Government of Red China has been endeavouring to bring about a much higher standard of morality. It now enforces heavy penalties on people who are caught infringing the new laws. If Miss Sang has been white-slaved it is more probable that she has been taken to Macao or Formosa. But we think it much more likely that she has been abducted by someone who is in love with her, and that she is still in the Colony.'

Julian had been unable to throw any further light on Merri's disappearance, or even provide the police with a possible clue; so, after he had told them that he was prepared to pay ten thousand Hong Kong dollars for information which would lead to her recovery, they left him in a state of such appalling frustration and almost unendurable misery that he developed a high fever. In consequence, it was not until after lunch on the Thursday that he was allowed to return to his hotel.

Meanwhile numerous accounts of the case had been published in the papers with photographs of Merri and the reward being offered. But they failed to bring forward anyone who could throw light on her abduction, and the police had made no progress with their investigations.

Back in his old room at the Repulse Bay, by then nearly numb with grief, Julian went straight to bed. But when he woke on the following morning, with his temperature again normal and feeling physically, at least, somewhat recovered, he decided that he ought to go to see Mrs. Sang.

There was nothing that he could say or do to mitigate her loss and he dreaded an interview with her, since it could lead only to reproaches being heaped on him. But by taking Merri out to dinner in defiance of her mother's expressed wish he felt that he was, in a sense, responsible for the awful thing that had happened; so he owed it to Mrs. Sang at least to give her the opportunity to ease her feelings by abusing him to any extent to which her anger and distress might lead her.

Accordingly, when he had dressed he wrote a brief note:

Dear Mrs. Sang. I am now out of hospital, and if you would like to see me I will call upon you this afternoon. Then he gave it to the hall porter to be sent to her by hand.

Soon after he had lunched he received an even briefer reply: '*Yes, I should like to talk to you. Come to see me at four o'clock. Tilly Sang.*'

Gloomily resigned to submitting to her bitter recriminations, he ordered a car for ten to four and had himself driven down to her house.

When he was shown into the drawing room one glance at Tilly Sang's face confirmed his belief that he had let himself in for a terrible gruelling and that she intended to castigate him unmercifully. Her blue eyes were harder than ever, her thin lips were tightly compressed and the battleship chin, which indicated the powerful will that had brought her through her sufferings, stood out aggressively.

But at the sight of him her expression suddenly changed. His head was still bandaged, forty-eight hours of fever had wasted his cheeks, his eyes were dull and his face drawn. He looked ten years older than when she had last seen him.

Coming to her feet she said, 'I . . . I had no idea that you had been beaten up so badly. Please sit down. It was good of you to offer to come to see me.'

Sinking into a chair, he replied, 'It was the least I could do. Although I can't add anything to what I told the police, which they will have passed on to you. I came only to give you the opportunity of reproaching me, as you have every right to do.'

She nodded. 'I've every cause to call you to account for having persuaded Merri to go out with you in defiance of my orders; and I certainly intended to. But it is obvious that during the last few days you have been through a terrible time; and, as the injury to your head was reported to me as not very serious, it must have been mentally as well as physically. My reproaching you will not get us anywhere. But is there nothing at all that you withheld from the police—no little thing Merri said or did while with you—that might provide us with a new line of enquiry?'

'No, nothing,' Julian assured her despondently. 'Ever since I got my wits back I've been racking my brains for something of the kind, but uselessly. The police told you, of course, about the man in your garden to whom I gave my letter?'

'Yes. And working on the description of him that you gave them, they've been hunting for him high and low. But as well look for a needle in a haystack as a nameless Chinese in Hong Kong. Anyway, all the chances are that having read your letter and let his employer know that you were going to take Merri to dine at Aberdeen that evening, he would have been one of the men in the launch and got away with the rest of them.'

'That's about it,' Julian agreed, 'and the police seem to think that these people made off with Merri either to Macao or Formosa intending to . . . to sell her into a brothel.'

Tilly Sang shook her blonde head. 'No. I'm convinced,

thank God, that's not what has happened to her. She was kidnapped by that Japanese.'

'Japanese?'

'Yes. The young man you told me about. The Tourist Association people confirmed what you said about him, and that his name is Bill Urata.'

'Oh, him.' Julian quickly shook his head. 'No; I don't think that's in the least likely.'

'Why not? You told me yourself that he had proposed to her, and that she liked him enough even to consider accepting him, but refused because she knew that it would make an irreparable breach between her and me if she married a Japanese. Apparently he's a rich young man, the son of a wealthy ship-owner in Osaka; so he'd have both the money and the means to pull off a coup of this kind. He probably arranged for one of his father's ships to be lying off Hong Kong, then sent his spy ashore to try to find out Merri's engagements. When the man got hold of your letter and learnt that you were taking her to Aberdeen that night that provided Urata with the perfect opportunity. All he had to do was to come in with his launch and wait there, scanning with his torch the people who were coming ashore after dining at either the Tai Pak or the Sea Palace until he spotted Merri, then go alongside the sampan and grab her.'

Again Julian shook his head. 'I only wish I could believe you to be right, Mrs. Sang. If that had been the case at least we'd know that Merri's fared no worse than to be abducted by a man she likes and who is in love with her. But I just can't believe that Urata is the sort of chap who would be not only ready to defy the law but, possibly, have his people commit murder to get hold of her.'

'Then you don't know the Japanese.'

'But I do know Urata, whereas you don't. Besides, by upbringing he is an American; and not a gangster, but a man with a respectable background. I admit that your theory is highly plausible, but I'd bet any money that he was not responsible for abducting Merri. He was certainly smitten with her; but he's only a playboy, and playboys don't go in for that sort of thing.'

'Playboy or not, a Japanese is capable of going to any lengths to get what he wants,' Tilly Sang insisted. 'Those little swine are as immoral as alley cats and as unscrupulous as the Devil himself. I ought to know. But speaking of them reminds me that I owe you an apology.'

Julian gave her a look of surprise as she hesitated for a moment, then went on, 'The other day I called you a coward and I was wrong about that. I went down to Aberdeen on Monday and talked to the woman who owns the sampan. She said that when she came up she saw that you had jumped into the launch and were fighting like a tiger against the six murderous toughs in it. Not many men would have had the guts to take on such odds barehanded. And there's another thing. For years, while I was going through hell, I always held it against you that you didn't shoot me rather than let me be raped by those Japs. But it wasn't until you called here that I learned that you couldn't because you had no bullets for your gun. I realize now that I've been unfair to you and that, in the circumstances, you did your best for me.'

He bowed gravely. 'It's good of you to say that, Mrs. Sang; and if anything could comfort me a little at the present time it is to know that you don't think quite so badly of me. I can honestly assure you that if I'd been down there in the room I would at least have hit you on the head with the butt of my pistol before they got the two of us, and that for months afterwards I felt absolutely terrible about having failed to get you up on to the roof.'

For the first time Tilly Sang smiled. 'Let's say no more about it, then. Perhaps you would like some tea, or a drink.'

He accepted and, for a further three-quarters of an hour, while they had tea together, they talked round and round the subject uppermost in both their minds. Mrs.

Sang remained convinced that by then Merri was well on her way to Japan with Urata; but, much as Julian would have liked to agree, he could not overcome his fears that she had been white-slaved. By the time Julian left, their mutual anxiety had drawn them together; so the meeting ended in a manner that an hour earlier he would never have thought possible. They had promised to keep in touch and shook hands as though they had always been friends.

During the two days that followed there were no new developments, and Julian mooned about unhappily, trying to accustom himself to the thought that the odds were now all against his ever seeing his beautiful Merri again. Wherever he went in Hong Kong or Kowloon sights and sounds reminded him that when he had last been in those places they had been made the more delightful by her sunny presence at his side, telling him all sorts of things and bubbling with easy youthful laughter. He had begun to hate the island and longed to leave it, yet he could not bring himself to make plans for his departure without knowing what had happened to her.

Then, just as he was going to bed on Sunday night, the telephone rang. As he put the receiver to his ear a woman's voice said urgently, 'Is that you, Julian?'

He felt almost certain that the voice was that of Mrs. Sang, but doubted for a moment if it could be hers because of the use of his Christian name. 'Yes,' he replied. 'Is that . . . is that Tilly?'

'Yes. I've news. News of Merri. Not very good news; but news. And I can't tell it you over the phone. Can you come over here at once?'

'I'll be with you in under a quarter of an hour,' he replied briskly. Replacing the receiver, he scrambled into his coat, hurriedly left his room and ran down the corridor.

Tilly Sang was waiting for him at the front door of her house. Shutting it quickly behind her, she led him into the drawing room and said, 'She is in Japan. I knew it.'

'What!' Julian exclaimed. 'It was Urata after all, then?'

'I imagine so. But about that I'm uncertain. It may be that he was not in love with her at all but was an agent, just angling for an opportunity to kidnap her. Anyhow, I'm convinced now that he's not at the bottom of it, because they want me to go to Japan.'

'What happened?'

'I was about to go to bed. My room overlooks the bay. Soon after I had put on the light I heard something click against the window. The noise came again. Someone was throwing small stones up at it. I opened it and went out on to the balcony. There was a man below on the upper terrace. When he saw me he called to me to come down and talk to him. The moonlight was sufficient for me to see that beyond the swimming pool, where the rocks shelve sharply to the sea, there was a motor boat with several men in it, and that out in the bay there was what looked like a small tramp steamer. I guessed at once that he had come off from her, and immediately feared that this was an attempt to kidnap me too. So I refused.

'He said then that he had seen a report in the papers about my daughter being abducted. By pure chance he had recognized her from the photograph printed with the article. He knew who had got her and could lead me to her if I'd come to Japan with him. Such a story was much too thin. I told him so, and said that if he were an honest man he would wait there until I could get the police and he could tell them what he knew.

'At first he tried to bluff me by saying that the police must be kept out of it, because they believed him to be a smuggler and might try to pin something on him; but that he had risked coming to me because he wanted to earn the reward. I said he could if he would give me the information which would lead to my getting Merri back. But he wouldn't. Then, seeing that I didn't mean to play, he came clean.

'He admitted that he had been sent by the people who have got her, and said that before they would let her go they wanted to talk to me personally. When I asked him why, he replied, "Because you know many things that could be useful to them. Tell and you can have your daughter back." I tumbled to it then. It's the Japanese dope ring that have got Merri.'

'I thought most of it was smuggled in from China,' Julian interrupted.

'So it is; but a lot of it comes from Japan, and I am the head of the department that is a thorn in the side of the Japanese smugglers. They have their spies and must know that. If they could get hold of me they could make me reveal our methods of getting information in advance about their shipments. But they wouldn't stop at that. They'd kill me.'

'Do you really think so?'

'I'm certain of it. I hold so many strings to the illicit traffic from Japan, and in the past few years must have cost them many thousands of pounds by causing their parcels of dope to be seized. They would never let me return to Hong Kong and resume the fight against them.'

'What did you say to the Japanese, then? I take it he was a Jap?'

'Yes. I again refused to go with him. Then he gave me an ultimatum. He said, "If you won't come to Japan with me now you must come on your own. Either you will be sitting in the lounge of the Miyako Hotel in Kyoto at ten o'clock in the evening a week from today, or we will cut your daughter up into little pieces." '

CHAPTER IX

THE SPRAT TO CATCH THE MACKEREL

FOR a moment Julian stared at Tilly Sang in horror. Then he burst out, 'But you must go! You must! You can't just remain here and let Merri be murdered.'

Staring back at him, she wrung her hands and cried, 'God knows I'd give all I possess to prevent that! I offered to ransom her, but he only laughed at me. And if I do go they'll kill me. I'm certain of it.'

'No!' he said sharply. 'It will need all your courage; but you've got plenty of that. We'll get on to the police. They'll get in touch with the Japanese police, who will protect you and enable us to trap these people.'

She shook her head. 'That's no good. You don't know them. They have spies everywhere; even in the Japanese police force. They would find out that the police were shadowing me; then, like all kidnappers, they would never risk being caught with their victim. They would kill Merri at once and dispose of her body; so that there would be no evidence against them.'

'That's a ghastly thought. But we'll have to risk it. For you to go there under police protection is our only chance. At least we know now that Merri has not been sold into a brothel and is still alive, but she'll be dead within ten days if we make no effort to save her.'

'We can't even be certain that she is still alive. Anyhow, if I did go we've no guarantee that they would release her. They would be afraid that she would tell her story and give the police the evidence to arrest them. Oh God,

I don't know what to do! I feel sure that it's not only information this man wants. If he does get hold of me I'm certain that he'll kill me.'

'This man,' Julian repeated quickly. 'You know who is the head of the ring, then?'

'Yes. At least I . . . I think so. I couldn't swear to it, but I'm as near certain as can be.'

'In that case, why shouldn't we put the police on to him right away? Even if you have only suspicion to go on they would start enquiries and, perhaps, find some excuse to search his premises.'

'I daren't; and I've already told you the reason. He would be tipped off that the police were after him and protect himself by doing away with Merri.'

'If you are not absolutely certain that this particular man is the head of the ring what leads you to believe that he is?'

She made an angry gesture. 'Oh, there are a dozen lines in my files that seem to lead to him. Added together it could hardly be anyone else; but not one of them is strong enough to hang a case on. If we had had any concrete evidence against him we would have asked the Japanese police to pull him in long ago. The trouble is he never leaves Japan, and he's too rich and powerful ever to need to run any risk himself. If I'd had any doubts the man who came up from the sea would have settled them for me when he demanded that I should go to Kyoto. There are a dozen other big cities in Japan, but it is in Kyoto that this human spider lives.'

Julian nodded. 'I see. That certainly adds greatly to the probability that you are right. In addition to being rich and cautious, what sort of a man is he?'

'He must be well over sixty, comes of a good family and has a finger in all sorts of pies. He owns a controlling interest in a radio factory, a coastal shipping line, a silk works, a famous doll shop and . . .'

'A doll shop?' asked Julian with a puzzled frown.

'Yes; not the sort where you'd buy a doll for a child, but one of those that are peculiar to Japan. The dolls are real works of art. They represent mikados, empresses, shoguns, court officials and famous geishas, in gala attire. Everything is correct to the minutest detail and the embroidery on the silk and satin clothes so fine that it has to be examined with a magnifying glass. Some of them cost as much as a hundred pounds sterling, and the rich Japanese collect them as Europeans do Dresden or snuffboxes. Incidentally, he is a great collector of antiques. When the Japanese overran China they looted it of an immense amount of treasure and a great part of the stuff is still in private houses in Japan. He is said to have paid very high prices for many beautiful things.'

For a moment she paused, then hurried on: 'Of course, all these activities are good cover for dope smuggling. They conceal packets of heroin even in miniature radios and in rolls of silk. We have found it, too, buried in the stuffing of quite ordinary dolls. He is not above using antiques for that, either. It comes through in the secret drawers of lacquer cabinets and in the hollow bodies of cheap modern Buddhas faked up for the tourist trade. And, of course, these things are smuggled through as part of the genuine cargoes of his coastal ships.'

'What else do you know about him?' Julian enquired.

She hesitated. 'Not much. He travelled extensively when he was a younger man and, of course, was an officer during the war. He was married but lost his wife some years ago. Like most of these Japanese he was a great lecher, and he used to throw big geisha parties at his house for himself and his friends. Our informants report that he still sends for one of the more expensive ones now and then. But the Japanese tycoons don't mix business with that sort of pleasure so much in these days.'

'How do you mean?'

'In the old days all big business was transacted at geisha parties. Each man had his favourite girl and the host used to be expected to invite her. Over the meal, while the girls waited on them, they talked stocks and shares, contracts and mergers. Afterwards they relaxed, the girls danced and sang for them, and the party ended as one might expect. But now all big business is done on the golf courses. The Japanese have gone mad on golf. It may surprise you to know that the entrance fee to the crack golf club in Tokyo is six hundred pounds sterling.'

'It certainly does.'

Walking over to a trolley in a corner of the room, Tilly Sang mixed herself a stiff whisky-and-soda, then told Julian to help himself if he would like one. When he had done so they sat down and proceeded to hash matters over for the best part of an hour. He continued to insist that she could not possibly just let matters slide; while she, although obviously desperately concerned about Merri, maintained that if she herself went to Kyoto her life would not be worth an hour's purchase.

By one o'clock in the morning they had got no further; so, telling her that he would come to discuss the matter with her again in the morning, he prepared to take his departure. As she accompanied him through the hall to let him out, his glance happened to fall on the magnificent life-sized gilded bronze figure of the goddess Kuan-yin. Pausing in front of it, he said:

'One moment. I have an idea. You say this man is so rich that he wouldn't listen to the offer of a money ransom. But if collecting Chinese antiques is his passion this might tempt him.'

Tilly Sang shook her head and said despondently, 'I don't think it would. I've certainly never seen a finer. But it's me he wants to . . . to eliminate.'

'Yes, I appreciate that.' Julian turned and looked at her. 'But why? Because over the years you have become the leading expert on the methods used to smuggle dope from Japan into Hong Kong. Because your activities have cost him a lot of money. Perhaps even because he thinks that you have now become a menace to him personally. But from what you've told me I judge him too old a hand at the game to fear seriously that you'll catch him out; so I doubt the last. If so it boils down to this being a plot he has hatched to save himself from further loss of revenue. But when men become very rich many of them place other desires before that of simply making more money. They begin to crave for honours, estates and big houses in which they can entertain, political influence or possessions of which they can be proud. It is at least possible that to own your Kuan-yin this dope king would be willing to go on losing a certain amount of money and return Merri to you.'

Again Tilly Sang shook her head. 'I doubt it. Really, I think it's most unlikely.'

'Anyway, it's worth trying,' Julian urged her. 'Do you happen to have a photograph of it?'

'Yes. A few years ago I had photographs taken of all the best pieces in the house, and a book made up of them.'

'Good. We could have had a photograph taken to-morrow, but this will save us a day; and we've got seven days to work in. There is at least one air service to Japan every day, if not two. If it's posted tonight it should be in Kyoto within twenty-four hours. With luck we'd get a reply by Wednesday. And if he turns down the offer that will still leave you three clear days in which to make up your mind to go there yourself under police protection.'

Obviously she had little faith in his idea, but he had judged rightly that she would clutch at any straw to avoid, for the time being, agreeing to go to Japan. Returning to the drawing room, she produced an album from the drawer of a bureau and tore out the page with the photograph of the Kuan-yin, below which was typed a description of the figure. As she did so, Julian said:

'Now write him a covering letter making the offer, then we'll pack the photograph up and I'll take it with me. The airport at Kai Tak is certain to be open all night. When I get back to the hotel I'll make the night porter rouse out a driver and a car for me and take it over to Kowloon myself. Then we'll be sure of getting it on the first plane leaving for Japan in the morning.'

'No,' she replied. 'The letter is going to be a very tricky one to write. I may have to make several drafts before I'm satisfied that I've put things in the most likely way to excite his cupidity. I may even offer, if he'll do a deal, to resign from my job with the Narcotics Advisory Committee as an extra inducement. But I'll have to think about that. You go back to your hotel now. When I've written the letter I'll get my car out and take it to the airport myself.'

With that, for the moment, Julian had to be satisfied; so he said good night to her and walked slowly back to his hotel. On the way there he told himself that he ought to be a little comforted by this new development. At least Merri had not been white-slaved and disappeared for good to suffer as her mother had done in some house of ill fame in Macao or Formosa. He felt, too, that for the present she was in no immediate danger, since for her kidnappers to kill her prematurely would be pointless and by keeping her alive they could put the squeeze on Mrs. Sang by forcing Merri to write a pathetic letter of appeal to her mother. Even so, he knew that the week to come was going to be a desperately anxious time for him.

Since coming out of hospital he had several times thought of going down to Aberdeen to thank the woman sampan owner who had saved his life, but had still been so groggy from his recent fever that he had not felt up to it. By Monday morning he was practically his old self, so he had a car take him to Aberdeen and sought out the woman.

Having through an interpreter expressed his gratitude and admiration for her courage, he asked what he could do

110

for her by way of reward. She replied very humbly that her boat was old and that if he could possibly spare a hundred dollars that would help her to exchange it for a better one. Smiling at the modesty of her request, he had her take him to a boat builders and, to her delighted amazement, ordered the best sampan that money could buy to be made for her; then he gave her five hundred dollars to buy new clothes for herself and her son.

But that had occupied only a morning, and he knew that he had to get through another two or three days of suspense before a reply could be expected from Japan. Thinking it just possible that Tilly Sang might receive a cable, and fearing to be out should she telephone him, he spent the time hanging about the hotel. It was while he was having breakfast on Thursday morning that the anxiously awaited call came through. Hurrying into his clothes, he went down to the house. On his arrival Tilly lost no time in telling him the result of their bid to ransom Merri.

'He's interested,' she said. 'Although he pretends that he knows nothing about Merri's having been kidnapped. But he says that it is impossible to judge from a photograph whether the Kuan-yin is a genuine antique; so I must send it to him on approval.'

'Thank God!' Julian exclaimed. 'We'll get it packed up at once.'

She gave a bitter laugh. 'Yes, I suppose so. But you are an optimist if you expect a man of his kind to give us a fair deal. He'll keep the Kuan-yin. He may even pay me for it. As we'll have proof of delivery he can hardly avoid doing that. But he won't let Merri go. Not unless I go to Japan; and I doubt if he'll do so even then.'

'If he wants the Kuan-yin badly enough he will,' Julian replied promptly. 'And there's no need for you to go there. I'll take the Kuan-yin to Japan and negotiate with him. Either he hands Merri over to me or he doesn't get the goddess.'

'Perhaps you're right. It's certainly a good idea that you should act as my intermediary. I can only pray that you may be successful.'

'If we're on the right track you can be sure I'll leave nothing untried,' Julian assured her. 'But his having denied all knowledge of Merri does make it possible that he is innocent and you've picked on the wrong man.'

Tilly gave an angry snort. 'You wouldn't expect him to be such a fool as to admit his guilt, would you? Of course he'd deny having Merri in order to protect himself.'

'That's true. Still, you had better show me his letter, so that I can see exactly what he said and be better able to judge the form.'

After a moment's hesitation she went to a drawer in her desk, took the letter from it and handed it to him. It was typewritten, in English, and read:

Dear Mrs. Sang,

    The honour of your acquaintance having been denied me and, in fact, never previously having even heard speak of you, I was much surprised at the contents of your letter. And more particularly so as you appear to believe that I am, in some way, connected with the most regrettable disappearance of your daughter. Having disabused your admirable mind of this unworthy suspicion, I send you my condolences on your loss and sincerely trust that the all-seeing gods will devise ways in which your estimable daughter will shortly be returned to you.

    Now with regard to your fortunate possession of the figure of the Queen of Heaven, a photograph of which you enclosed in your letter. It undoubtedly appears to be an exceptionally beautiful portrayal of the goddess and, should it be genuine, I should greatly like to add it to my collection. However, without casting the faintest aspersion on your own unquestionable honesty, I feel sure you will forgive me for remarking that certain skilful, crafty and evilly disposed persons have, at times, succeeded in

112

producing very passable faked reproductions of such valuable antiques.

Since you are agreeable to disposing of the figure, I therefore suggest that you should have it shipped to Japan in order that I may inspect it. Even with my limited knowledge of ancient craftsmanship I might then be able to satisfy myself with regard to its genuineness. If so I should be most happy to ask your acceptance of a suitable return for it.

May the gods prosper all your undertakings, my dear Mrs. Sang. Meanwhile I shall hope to hear further from you shortly; and, I hope, favourably.

With my respectful compliments to your esteemed-person . . .

Julian read it through quickly, looked again at the small letters of the signature—which at first glance were a little difficult to decipher—then gave a gasp.

'What is it?' Tilly Sang asked quickly. 'What's the matter?'

A slow, grim smile spread over Julian's face. 'Inosuke Hayashi,' he murmured. 'Well, you were right about him being our man. I haven't a doubt about that now.'

'You know him, then?' she exclaimed in surprise.

'Yes. It's a small world, isn't it? Although I suppose there are not many really big operators of dope rings in it; and that is the tie-up. Before the war Hayashi spent a lot of his time in Europe. His cover was chief representative of the Shikoko Products Company, who were wholesale exporters of soap; but his real business was distributing narcotics. He was one of a group of super-crooks. They were much too canny ever to risk being caught through doing a job themselves, but employed scores of smaller fry on espionage, bullion thefts, I.D.B., white-slaving and every other filthy racket. I was then a young diplomat. I chanced to find out about them while in my first post, at Brussels, and flattered myself that I was clever enough to land the whole bunch in jail; but they very nearly landed me in jail instead. Anyway, matters ended with a most unsavoury scandal that ruined my career. Later I succeeded in reducing the number of the group and doing it a considerable amount of damage, but that is another story. The last I heard of Hayashi was that he had been sentenced to ten years as a war criminal. Being a good bit older by then I decided, rather than risk my own neck again in an attempt to get even with him, to leave it at that. But now, after the suffering he has caused Merri, I mean to put an end to the little swine if I possibly can.'

Tilly nodded. 'I don't wonder you feel so bitter about him. You are right, too, about his having been given ten years.'

'Why didn't you tell me about that?'

'I . . . well, I didn't think it really necessary. Although I suppose I ought to have because it's probably one of his reasons for wanting to get me into his clutches. You . . . you see . . . Sang, my late husband, was one of the witnesses against him at his trial and gave evidence about the atrocities he committed while in Singapore.'

'I do see; and I no longer wonder that you are so scared that if you go to Japan he'll try to do you in. I suppose the damage you are doing to his dope smuggling would be quite enough for him to want you out of the way. But with the long-term desire to be revenged added to it you have ample grounds for your fears. Still cupidity, if it's strong enough, can overcome vindictiveness, and from his letter it looks to me as if he really means to do a deal.'

She sighed. 'I hope to God you're right. Anyhow, I'll get the Kuan-yin packed up this morning, and arrange for the first ship leaving for Japan to take it. I think, too, I'll get . . . er, Pao Tin-yum, and his wife . . . Pao Ping to go with it as well as you.'

'Who are they?'

'He is a shrewd man and manages all my business affairs. I'm sure you will find him a great help. And if you do succeed in getting Hayashi to hand over Merri the poor child is sure to be in a terrible state of mind; so it would be a good thing to have a woman with you to comfort her and look after her on the journey home.'

'Yes; that's a good idea. When can I meet them?'

'Come back after lunch. I'll have them here and the Kuan-yin packed up by then.'

Having agreed to do as she suggested, Julian took his leave and walked back to the Repulse Bay. On entering his room he saw, to his amazement, Bill Urata sitting there in one of the armchairs. Next moment the stalwart young Japanese had sprung to his feet and was advancing on him with blazing eyes.

CHAPTER X

AN ALLY, OR . . . ?

PAUSING in the doorway, Julian exclaimed, 'What the hell are you doing here?'

'I'm here to see you, of course,' Urata shouted. 'The desk gave me your room number. As it's still early it seemed likely you'd be here. Door was on the latch so I figured you must still be around and decided to wait. But what's become of my honey? You're responsible, damn you! Where have they taken Merri?'

'If I knew I wouldn't be here,' Julian snapped.

'I'll lay you would,' stormed the young Japanese. 'What's she to an old stuffed shirt like you? Just a young Eurasian girl you took on as a guide. I know you British. You think yourselves so mighty superior that anyone with a coloured streak can be treated as dirt.'

Julian had difficulty in controlling his temper, and retorted caustically, 'Before you start talking nonsense about the colour-bar you'd better get back to the States, go south and start going about in public with a negress.'

His yellow face livid, Urata thrust out his arms and in a furious rush attempted to grapple with him.

When young, Julian had been quite a passable boxer. Taking a quick pace back, he feinted at Urata's face and hit him hard in the stomach. With a gasp the Japanese fell backward and collapsed, doubled up on the bed.

'Now!' said Julian, while Urata was still striving to get back his breath. 'Get some sense into your thick head, or clear out. I'm no more responsible for Merri's having been

kidnapped than you would have been had it been you
who had taken her to dine at Aberdeen. And I'm every
bit as concerned about what has happened to her as you
are.'

'You . . . you can't be,' Urata wheezed. 'She . . . she's
my honey. My . . . my fiancée.'

Staring at him, Julian said, 'I don't believe it. I know
you proposed to her. She told me so. But she didn't
accept you.'

'Well . . . well, maybe not one hundred per cent, but
when I left her I was plenty hopeful.'

'Then you will be interested to hear that we are rivals
for the lady's hand. I, too, proposed to her, and she came
very near to accepting me.'

'You're kidding.' Urata struggled to his feet. 'I'll not
wear that one. What'd a girl like Merri see to go for in
an old bastard like you?'

Julian felt like hitting him again, but kept control of
himself and retorted:

'Quite a number of qualities that she wouldn't find in
a half-educated little Japanese whipper-snapper whose
long suit is to ape the manners of an American hobble-
dehoy.'

Urata's black eyes smouldered dangerously. 'You
bloody Limey! You lay off me and Americans too. If it
weren't for the States with Lease-Lend and Dollar Aid
the whole bunch of you would be as old-hat as the Greeks
and Romans by now.'

With a disdainful shrug, Julian said, 'I suppose it's
understandable that people like you should think that
and take no account of the fact that in both wars we
stood up to the Germans for years before America felt
that her own salvation depended on coming to our aid.
But such recriminations get us nowhere. Why did you
come to see me?'

Urata smoothed down his crumpled check suit and
replied, 'When I was in Macao I got an urgent cable from

117

my old man to return to Japan. This past week I got off three airmail letters to Merri. Receiving no reply got me all steamed up, so yesterday I called her office, and they gave. Being crackers about her I hopped the afternoon plane and got in late last night.'

'May I take it that you are already fully informed about this ghastly affair?'

'Yeah. What I want to know is what's being done and who's doing it?'

'The police are doing everything they can, but up till now they haven't got a clue.'

'And you're just sitting on your fanny knocking back champagne and caviare, eh, instead of creating hell to get the search revved up?'

'If I were I'd prefer them to your national delicacies of warm saki and raw fish,' Julian returned icily. 'But what do you expect me to do?'

'Why, for Chris' sake! Get ahold of Mrs. Sang. Squeeze her for the low-down that she might not be willing to give to the cops about other guys besides you and me that Merri's been going places with recently. Maybe it's some lecherous old coot who's snatched her, or maybe someone who had a grouse against her family.'

The young man's distress was so evident and urgent that Julian decided that, in fairness, he should be told what was going on. Sitting down in one of the armchairs, he motioned Urata to another and said:

'If you hadn't been so abusive I would have told you before that that is exactly what I have done. Moreover, I've offered a reward of ten thousand Hong Kong dollars for information which will enable us to get Merri back.' Then he went on to relate the relevant facts that had emerged from his meetings with Tilly Sang and their outcome to date.

When he had finished Urata said, 'Since she's in Japan I'm going right back there, as fast as a plane can take me.'

'You can if you like,' Julian replied. 'But you can't

118

do any good. We can only wait now until the Kuan-yin has been sent there.'

'Be your age, fellow,' Urata retorted. 'This is no job for amateurs but for the cops. Within an hour of touching down I'll have the police in Kyoto on the job. They'll soon flush out this old crook Hayashi and get Merri back.'

'No!' said Julian sharply. 'You'll do nothing of the kind. Hayashi is wealthy, powerful and cunning. Mrs. Sang is convinced that he will have spies among the police. If you start anything prematurely they'll tip him off, and that could lead to his killing Merri in order to save himself from being convicted as a kidnapper.'

Urata shook his crewcut head. 'You're all wrong there. The police in Japan aren't crooked, like plenty of cops in the States. Besides, my old man is a big shot in Osaka, and that's only twenty-five miles from Kyoto. He'll see one of the top boys on this and get his agreement that only his most trusted men are to be put on the job.'

Julian was now considerably alarmed. Knowing about the great network of spies and informers that Hayashi had established in the past, he greatly feared that Mrs. Sang might be right about his now having a similar set-up; so he argued most strongly against the police being called in.

After a while Urata said 'See here; it's going to be all of a week before this goddess thing can be gotten to Kyoto. Just think what that poor kid Merri will be going through all that time. You do what in hell you like, but I'm not going to sit around without lifting a finger to try to locate her. Seeing you're so set against calling in the cops, I'll give way on that and instead employ a private dick. Anyway, I'm going back to Japan tonight to see if I can get a line on this Hayashi. Should I have no luck we'll still have this scheme of yours to ransom her with the idol to fall back upon.'

With a shrug, Julian said, 'Very well, then. I can't

119

stop you. But for God's sake be careful. Remember that Merri's life is at stake and that Hayashi is completely unscrupulous. If you go butting in on the information supplied by some private eye he may well kill her, and you too. Anyhow, if you do find out anything in the next week I'd be terribly grateful if you would let me know.'

'Sure I will. And I'll say now that I was being unfair when I accused you of not caring a cuss what happened to her. Ten thousand dollars, even Hong Kong, is quite a piece of money, and your having offered it for information shows that . . .' Urata paused for a minute, then added handsomely, 'Look, why not come back with me tonight, then I could give you any lowdown I may get on to right away.'

'It's good of you to suggest it,' Julian replied, while thinking quickly. There was nothing more he could do if he remained in Hong Kong for the coming week, and it was many years since he had had even a rudimentary knowledge of Japanese. Probably Mrs. Sang's couple she was sending with the Kuan-yin did not speak it either; so by joining forces with Urata he might receive invaluable help. After a moment he added, 'Yes, I'll come with you. I'm seeing Mrs. Sang this afternoon and I'll tell her that I'm going on ahead.'

Urata said that he felt sure there was an evening plane for Tokyo that dropped passengers off at Osaka and that he would get their flight tickets and telephone a message to the hotel giving the time of the plane's departure. Then he left.

After lunch Julian kept his appointment with Tilly Sang. As they shook hands she said, 'I've found out about sailings. There's a cargo boat leaving tonight, but it looks as though it would be quicker to wait until Sunday morning and use a German liner named the *Lubeck*. I've arranged, too, about packing the Kuan-yin. If I had it crated they might load it by a crane, and we daren't risk an accident; so I'm having a big wicker basket made lined with plenty of packing to contain it. That will make it much lighter, so that it can be carried on board. As it is so valuable, I've booked an extra cabin for it to be locked up in. About Pao Tin-yum, too. He had an important appointment for this afternoon. As we have two days to spare I didn't ask him to cancel it; but he and his wife are coming in tomorrow morning, and you can be here to meet them then.'

'I'm afraid I shan't be able to,' Julian replied. 'But that doesn't particularly matter. They can report to me in Kyoto. I gather that the best hotel there is the Miyako, and if by any chance I'm not there when they arrive I'll have left a message for them.' He then told her about having found Urata in his bedroom and the result of their discussion.

Tilly Sang heard him out in silence; but her face expressed alarm, and when he had done she said angrily:

'Then you told him everything. What in God's name possessed you to do that?'

'Why not?' Julian protested. 'It's obvious that he's head over heels in love with Merri, and just as anxious about her as we are. As he is a Jap with influential connections and knows the city I may find him extremely helpful.'

'Of course he's a Jap. That alone is quite enough to make me distrust him. And all along I've suspected that he may be one of Hayashi's agents. You said that he was in shipping. Hayashi owns a line of coastal traders. What could be more likely than that it's the same line? How could you possibly be such a fool as to trust him?'

'Oh, come! As they already have Merri, what possible reason could Urata have for coming to see me except his anxiety to get her out of her kidnapper's clutches?'

'To find out what measures we are taking to try to get her back. To get in with you, in case you meant to go to Japan and start enquiries there. Hayashi would have felt certain that I'd send the Kuan-yin and probably guessed

121

that I would send someone with it to insist on Merri's being handed over before he received the goddess. Urata's game is to win your confidence, then sabotage any plans you may make to get hold of Merri. Who suggested your going to Japan with him? Did he or did you?'

'He did.'

'There you are, then.'

'No; really, Tilly. I know you've had ample cause to become overwrought during the past week or so. But you are wrong to get the jitters about this. If you had seen the state of mind Urata was in this morning I'm sure you'd agree with me. He couldn't have acted the excitement and distress he showed. I'm convinced that he's on the level.'

She gave a heavy sigh. 'Well, what's done is done. We can't job backwards now. Perhaps you are right about him. If so it's true that he may prove very helpful. But watch him, Julian; watch him like a lynx.'

Then, ten minutes later, as she let him out of the front door, she said sombrely, 'I can't help feeling that the only chance of saving Merri is to go to Kyoto myself and get face to face with Hayashi. We've got it in for one another, and if I could take him by surprise I might come out on top. But I'll only do that as a last resort.'

Back at the Repulse Bay, while Julian was packing a bag, Urata telephoned. He had got seats on the aircraft and it left at six o'clock. Against any unexpected emergency, after paying his bill, Julian changed traveller's cheques for as large a sum as the hotel could let him have, then was driven into Victoria and crossed to Kowloon. At the airport he found Urata waiting for him. There they had a drink together and the young Japanese, apparently wishing to make up for his abuse of Julian that morning, made himself quite pleasant; an attitude to which Julian duly responded. The aircraft took off on time and the flight was uneventful.

When the plane arrived over Osaka the sun was still

shining, but as they descended darkness closed in with surprising rapidity and when they landed it was dark, cold and raining. A Customs Officer made Urata open his suitcase and looked quickly through it, but as Julian was a tourist he gave him a friendly smile and chalked his bag without examining it. A uniformed chauffeur came up to them, bowed gravely to Urata, took their luggage and led them out to one of the family's cars. Owing to the darkness, Julian saw nothing of the city until the car pulled up in front of a big block of modern flats. Five minutes later Bill was introducing Julian to his father, Yutaka Urata.

Urata senior was a plump little man wearing spectacles with heavy lenses. He bowed twice to Julian, his nearly bald head coming down almost to waist level, before shaking hands. Then he said how happy he was to meet Mr. Day, although in such unhappy circumstances, and that a room had been made ready for him in the apartment as Bill had telephoned from Hong Kong that afternoon.

While Urata mixed whiskies-and-sodas for the three of them Julian had a chance to look round the room. It was large and well furnished in a European style that suggested a Germanic influence, but there were no objects in it of special value. When they sat down, Bill proceeded to tell his father all that he had learned from Julian and they then discussed the situation.

Mr. Urata said that he knew Inosuke Hayashi slightly, as their shipping interests had led to them becoming acquainted, and they had, on a few occasions, played a round of golf together. Hayashi, he added, was a very wealthy man, of good family and much respected.

'In spite of his war crimes?' Julian interjected.

Urata looked away uncomfortably. 'During the war many things most regrettable happened. But it was made by the hotheads of the Army. Many of our people had no wish for the war. Myself, many of my friends. It meant the

loss of much business and ruin for many persons who manu-
factured for export. But it was decreed by the Son of
Heaven. There was nothing we could do. Of the atrocities
of which our soldiers were accused we greatly disapproved.
We are a civilized people and horror filled us when we
were told these things. They were committed because the
Japanese lower classes have never known spirit drinking.
On looted whisky they became drunk as not ever before.
It was the soldiers you understand, not the officers; but
the officers were held responsible. The Americans sent
many of them to prison. So was the case of Hayashi.
Many persons say this was unfair. I do not seek to defend.
I only tell what is general feeling. Anyway, many persons
say right or wrong Hayashi much suffering endured, and
it is now all long time ago. Since he leaves prison he leads
life of rectitude. That is why I say that he is much respected. His being suspected of kidnapping a young girl
fills me with amazing. I find most hard to believe it.'

Julian refrained from mentioning the brutal treatment
and semi-starvation that the Japanese officers had
unquestionably inflicted on their prisoners of war; but
he did tell Mr. Urata that he had good reasons for having
no doubt about Hayashi's guilt in the present matter.

After a while the elder Urata said, 'You must be tired,
Mr. Day, from your travel. Bed now I think, with your
permission. I will think much on what to do, and we
make more discussion in the morning, yes?'

Julian found the bedroom to which Bill led him also
comfortably furnished in European fashion, and that the
only outstanding Oriental note in the large apartment
was the lavatory. It had no seat and consisted of an oblong
china trough over which one had to squat. He was soon
in bed and, having had a long day, slept better than he
had on any night since Merri had been kidnapped.

In the morning, with many bows, a diminutive
slant-eyed maid brought him a pot of tea with a minute
saucer-shaped cup and a plate of sweet cakes. As it was

the usual Japanese green tea he found it horrid, but he was to fare better an hour later as she reappeared with a dish of huge prawns cooked in butter and a bowl of big strawberries which tasted like other kinds but were very long and pointed. He had twice had similar strawberries in Hong Kong, and knew that they were sent there from Japan where they ripened very early in spite of the climate because they were grown in greenhouses heated cheaply with the steam from hot springs.

When he had bathed and dressed he made his way to the sitting room. There was nobody there, and it was by then half past nine; so, after waiting for ten minutes, he rang the bell. With surprising speed it was answered by a white-coated houseman who flashed a fearsome row of upper teeth at him then bent almost double, as though offering his head to be cut off. Julian had been searching his memory for a few suitable Japanese words to enquire where the man's master was; but it proved unnecessary to use them. The servant took a pace forward, bowed a second time, grinned again, extracted a piece of paper from a pocket and, bowing yet once more, handed it to Julian.

It was a note from Bill and ran:

Sorry to run out on you but I've some business to see to at the office. Turn on the telly if you want and help yourself to the liquor. I'll be back lunchtime.

The houseman retired as swiftly as he had appeared, leaving Julian standing there far from pleased at being left on his own for the morning. He considered television an admirable medium for witnessing events of importance and, occasionally, watching a version of a good play, but he was far from being a television addict. Nevertheless, he turned it on and found to his surprise that Japan had no fewer than seven home channels running simultaneously. But he could understand hardly a word that was said and none of the subjects being shown interested him particularly; so after playing with it for half an hour, he switched it off and began to look through some magazines that were on a side table. Among them he found a few American ones which, as they were several weeks old, he assumed Bill had bought before setting off on his holiday-cum-business travels. All of them were Hollywood products, mainly featuring film stars and gossip about them, but they kept Julian's mind off Merri until, shortly after midday, Bill arrived.

'How do. It's good to see you here,' the young Japanese said heartily. Then, striding over to the walnut cocktail cabinet, he added, 'I'll mix you a Martini.'

'Thanks,' replied Julian, 'but I'd rather have a gin-and-lime if you've got it.'

'O.K. It's all here, and I'll make it a strong one. You'll maybe need it when I tell you the way things have been moving.'

Julian sat forward quickly. 'You mean you've got news of Merri already?'

'No, worse luck. It's about my old man, and I've a hunch that you won't like it. Last night after you'd tucked up we talked some more. He was dead against our calling in a private eye. Got all het up with the notion that, if the dick turned it in that Hayashi had got Merri at his place in Kyoto, I'd go sticking my neck out to get her and have myself taken for a ride. He was hard sold on it that this was a job for the police. And there's no moving him when he gets that way. First thing this morning he dated the local Chief and had me go down to Headquarters with him, to shoot the whole works.'

126

CHAPTER XI

THE UNPROFESSIONAL GUIDE

JULIAN's eyes went hard and he held Bill Urata's with them as he exclaimed, 'That was contrary to our understanding! You agreed that you would do no more than employ a private detective. If, as a result of this, Hayashi gets wind of it that the police are making enquiries he may do away with Merri rather than let her fall into their hands. If that happens her blood will be on your head.'

The face of the young Japanese went almost grey and he cried, 'For Chris' sake don't say that! I'd no option. Things are different here to what they are in Europe and the States. There, fellers and girls won't stand for being ordered around by their parents any longer. But here the old ways still go on. It's part of the system. I'd sooner jump off a cliff than not do what my old man tells me. He was dead set on going to the police. What the hell could I do but fall into line?'

He could not be held responsible for the age-old customs of his country, and as Julian mentally assessed this new development he decided that it might not be as serious as he had at first feared. While he had accepted Tilly Sang's word for it that Hayashi had spies among the police, in view of his special interests it seemed probable that such spies would be men employed in the Narcotics Prevention Department and so unlikely to learn that his activities were being investigated on a matter that had no connection with it. And at least, Julian felt, the Uratas' having gone to the police proved one thing: they were

127

not in league with Hayashi as Tilly Sang had feared. While in Hong Kong, it had seemed possible that young Urata appeared anxious to go to the police only to support a bluff; his admission now that he had been forced to break his word, and had actually done so, put him in the clear.

After a moment Julian said in a gentler voice, 'Perhaps my judgment was a little hasty; so don't take what I said too seriously. Naturally I was annoyed with you for having gone to the police without first letting me know that you had decided to go back on our understanding. But it's done now. And there is a chance that they may pull our chestnuts out of the fire for us without any harm coming to Merri. Does this mean, though, that we ought to stay here to await the result of their enquiries, or do we go on to Kyoto as we planned?'

'There's nothing to be gained by our staying here,' Urata replied. 'If the cops get wise to anything they'll call us up and give us their hand-out in Kyoto; so I'm all for going there. We'll at least be on the spot then if anything does blow.'

'When do you propose that we should start?'

'After lunch. We've a place there that's been in the family since my grand-dad's time. It's looked after by a skeleton staff, so as we can make use of it at the big festivals. I mean to check in there, and I'd be happy to have you as my house guest, but I doubt your taking kindly to the way of life you'd have to lead. It's traditional Japanese. Almost empty rooms; no beds or chairs and low tables. We sleep on bed-rolls on the floor and eat squatting on our fannies. You'd do better to go to the Miyako. That's American-planned and pretty good with European eats. You'd be more comfortable there.'

Julian nodded. 'Thanks for the invitation, but I agree. As a matter of fact, I was told in Hong Kong that the Miyako is the best hotel in Kyoto, and I told Mrs. Sang to have the Kuan-yin delivered to me there.'

They lunched in the flat and afterwards left in a chauffeur-driven car. When the modern skyscrapers of the big port dropped behind they ran on through seemingly endless streets of two-storey wooden houses interspersed with rows of squalid shacks, so that Julian began to think that this dreary shanty town would never end. Later it transpired that the city did not have any perceptible ending, as two-thirds of the road to Kyoto was a built-up area.

Occasionally there was an open stretch of flat rice fields with hills in the distance, but most of the way was lined with small factories, poor shops, junk yards and one-storey dwellings with paper windows. To make the journey even more depressing it was raining again, the road was full of pot-holes and so narrow that for the greater part of the time they were crawling behind coaches or lorries.

Kyoto had been the capital of Japan for over a thousand years, and the Mikados had resided there, while the Shoguns, who actually ran the country, lived in the eastern capital Yedo, as Tokyo was then called. It had not been until 1868 that the great Emperor Meiji had overthrown the Shogunate and moved his headquarters to Tokyo; so as Kyoto had been the seat of the Emperors for so many centuries Julian had expected to find it a splendid city.

He was sadly disappointed. It had originally been planned as a large rectangle, modelled on the residence of the T'ang Emperors in China, but now it appeared to consist mainly of many square miles of tatty little shops and poor dwellings. As in Osaka, the people in the streets were drab. All the men, other than labourers, were dressed in Western clothes, shoddy cloth suits with flamboyant ties or cheap mackintoshes and caps or trilby hats. All but a few of the women still wore the national costume, but in subdued unattractive colours, and slopped along the pavements in wooden-soled clogs.

Totally unlike the Chinese in Hong Kong, who were always smiling and laughing, they were going drearily about their business, and quite a number of them were wearing thick white pads over their mouths and noses. Out of curiosity Julian asked Urata the reason. The young man promptly produced that which Julian had half expected:

'The folk in my country are very hygiene-conscious. Every Japanese takes a bath at least once a day, mostly in the public bath-houses, and I'd say our clinics here are as good as any in the States. Those pads are worn by people who've gotten colds, as a precaution against spreading infection.'

Not till later was Julian to see Kyoto's more attractive aspects; for in many places not far from the main highway, yet still within the city, there were scores of secluded temple gardens and countrified lanes bordered by tree-surrounded private residences. But only in the city's centre were there a few broad streets with modern blocks and stone buildings. Running through one of these they sped up a hill, leading to the wooded heights to the east of the city, and arrived at the Miyako.

Entering it was like walking into the Ritz after having driven through one of the poorer quarters of Manchester. Porters in spotless uniforms bowed them in, the lofty and spacious entrance hall was filled with well-dressed Japanese, Americans and Europeans. Urata secured a room for Julian, then accompanied him up to it; and, although it was only about a quarter of the size of the one he had had at the Repulse Bay, he saw that it was equipped with every conceivable modern convenience. The air conditioning was perfect, boiling water gushed from the taps in the bathroom at a touch and he had only to press a bell for one of three small neatly dressed maids, all of whom spoke English, to pop in immediately, take his orders to wash or press his clothes and return them in perfect order in an amazingly short time.

As both men were anxious to see the place in which they believed Merri to be held prisoner, as soon as Julian had inspected his quarters Urata looked up Inosuke Hayashi's address in the telephone directory, then they went straight out again.

The car took them through the Shijo Dori, with its big department stores, then north-west till they reached an area where there were few modern buildings and most of the houses stood among trees in private gardens. Hayashi's property proved to be one of the larger of these and formed an irregular island, about two acres in extent, bordered on all sides by leafy lanes. It had big wooden double gates and was surrounded by a tall wall. Leaving the car they walked all round the wall, but the house could be seen only from the front, and then no more than glimpses of its old-style curved roof between the branches of pines and camphor trees.

Having stared at it despondently for a while, and decided that its lay-out offered them no chance of discovering whether Merri was really a prisoner there, they returned to the car, which dropped Urata at his family house, about a mile away, then took Julian back to the Miyako. But they met again an hour later, as Julian had invited the young Japanese to dinner.

When he arrived they went first to the upstairs lounge for drinks, and it was there that Julian saw his rival in a better light. It chanced that at a nearby table there were three men of about Urata's age, two of whom he recognized as having been at school with him before he had gone to live with his uncle in the States. With Julian's consent, he asked the three to join them, and his friends were soon eagerly plying him with questions about his life in America. Julian would have expected him to be superior and boastful, but on the contrary he put on no airs and spoke with great modesty of his success at Berkeley University.

This general conversation proved a pleasant prelude

to dinner and, over it, the two of them continued to talk about America as, although Julian had never lived there for any length of time, the greater part of his fortune was invested in the States and he had visited its principal cities. By the end of the meal they were calling one another by their Christian names; and as they left the big dining room, with its long glass windows that gave a splendid view of the sweep of wooded mountain to the north-west of the city, Bill said:

'There'd be no sense in our sitting around tying ourselves in knots about Merri while we're waiting for the cops to get us the low-down on Hayashi. How say I take you round some of the temples tomorrow?'

'You're right,' Julian agreed. 'We must do our best to keep our minds off her. It's good of you to suggest it.'

'Why, I'd be glad to. I've not been to see these old places myself since I was a young teenager, and there are more here than in any other locality in Japan. I'll pick you up in the auto around ten.'

They went first to the Heian Shrine, a huge building erected only in the nineties to commemorate the eleven hundredth anniversary of the founding of the city. The approach to it lay through an eighty-foot-high scarlet-painted Torri—as the arches with flat tops and up-curved ends, so frequently seen in Japan, are called. In its vast forecourt a number of priests and women wearing white blouses and bright red skirts were strolling about. Bill told Julian that the monks were not Buddhists, as they served only in temples whereas this was a Shinto shrine; and that the women were nuns, although they were allowed to marry.

In the courtyard there were also several large bushes that in the distance looked as if they were smothered in white blossom. But it was a late spring; so few of the trees in Kyoto had yet come out, and when seen from nearer the massed white on the branches turned out to be hundreds of strips of paper tied to them. With a laugh

132

Bill explained that many people came to the Heian Shrine to learn their fortunes. If the paper telling the fortune was favourable they kept it, but if unfavourable they left it tied to a branch.

Having mounted the broad steps to the shrine, they took off their shoes, entered it and tried their luck by shaking one brass rod with Japanese characters on it out of a small hole in the top of a canister that held fifty or more. Bill interpreted: Julian had drawn an unexpected journey to a far country, a good rice crop, no family worries and a disappointment in love. Bill's read success in an undertaking, but later disappointment, only a moderate rice crop, the anger of a parent and success in love.

Julian smiled and shrugged. 'As there can be no earthly reason for me to set off for a far country, and you are on excellent terms with your father, I don't think we need take the predictions about love very seriously.'

In the rear of the shrine there was a big garden with three ornamental lakes, over one of which was a picturesque bridge. From it they fed some fat carp with pieces of bread; but as only a few azalea bushes were in flower, Julian found the garden disappointing.

A three-mile drive brought them to Kinkakuji, the Golden Pavilion, a lovely three-storey building set on the edge of another artificial lake. An artistic creation of great beauty, it had graced the site for five hundred and fifty years then, like so many of Japan's ancient wooden structures, been burnt down; but not until 1950 and not, in this case, by accident: a misanthropic young priest had deliberately set fire to it. His story had been told by Yukio Mishima in a novel that had become a best-seller in the United States, and was said to rival the work of Dostoevsky. However, as a precaution against fires the Japanese kept detailed drawings of all such buildings; so the Golden Pavilion had been re-erected and stood there again in all its pristine glory.

Driving back westward, they ran level with one side of the tall wall that enclosed the Imperial Palace and its many acres of park, then past the fine modern buildings of Kyoto University to Ginkakuji, the Silver Pavilion. Its garden was very similar to that of those they had already visited and, like them, swarming with sightseers, a great part of whom were students and school children. After walking round it the time had come for lunch, and Bill said that Julian must try at least one Japanese meal, adding with a laugh, 'I recall how you ragged me, first time we met, about being an eater of raw fish; so I'll let you off that. But I've laid on lunch at the Kyoboshi *tempura* restaurant, where they give you the whole works.'

The car took them to a narrow side street and pulled up outside what looked like a small private house. A man led them through a very narrow passage, up a flight of stairs and into a low room about fourteen feet square. The walls were painted with landscape scenes in the traditional style and occupying the middle of the room was an eighteen-inch-high table shaped like a flattened horse-shoe. Inside it were the cook's requirements, and round its outer edge there was space enough for half a dozen diners.

A youngish but very fat woman, who proved to be the cook, came in, and with her two maids. Both the girls looked to be only just out of their teens. They were dressed in heavy silk kimonos, their jet-black hair was elaborately piled on their small heads with many combs, flowers and ornaments, and their faces were masks of white paint. After the usual deep bows the cook sat down between a large cauldron of boiling oil, that neither smoked nor smelt, and a bowl of thin rice-flour batter; then one of the maids began to supply her with a succession of bits and pieces.

Bill and Julian had, meanwhile, seated themselves on thin cushions, the former with crossed legs, the latter, after finding it awkward to lean forward in that position, sitting sideways on one hip. The cook took up a small

134

piece of something, dipped it first in the batter then in the oil and laid it on the little dish in front of Julian. Near the dish were several small bowls containing sauces, but he did not risk trying any of them and found no difficulty in using his chopsticks to pop the morsel into his mouth. It was so hot that he could not properly taste it, but he thought it was fish.

Having served Bill with a similar morsel, the cook continued to put other pieces, all of which she had dipped in the batter and oil, on their plates alternately. There seemed no rhyme or reason to the meal. Long peppers, prawns, bits of aubergine, quails' eggs, celery leaves, seaweed and other more mysterious items followed one another and were frequently repeated, although not in the same order.

While they ate, the second maid knelt first beside one then beside the other, filling little shallow cups with warm saki from a small vase-like bottle of eggshell china. The Japanese have poor heads for spirits, and Julian had heard it said that most of them got drunk if they had more than six or eight cups, although each held only a single swallow. He soon decided that he could have drunk half a bucketful without ill effect, but had not the least desire to do so, as the warm, sweet, sticky spirit lacked any definite flavour and cloyed his palate, making him wish for a glass of water. The meal ended with pots of green unsweetened tea, and he was grateful even for that unpleasant beverage. To his great relief, he was at last able to get to his feet, as for the past hour and a half he had suffered agonies shifting from hip to hip. However, being courteous by nature, he thanked his host for the entertainment and said that he had greatly enjoyed it.

Their next visit was to the Tatsumara silk factory, one of the ancient establishments in the western quarter of the city. There, in an almost dark room, several wrinkled old men were weaving with amazing dexterity on wooden hand looms beautifully-patterned brocades, while in another girls were winding silk thread of many colours on to spindles. From a fine display of goods for sale Julian bought a dozen pairs of silk socks for a tenth of the price he would have had to pay in London, then they went out into the garden.

Like all the other gardens, it was beautifully kept and might well have been that of one of the temples; but its lake held a score or more fish the like of which Julian had never before seen. They were almost two feet long and looked like carp, but were many lovely colours, a number of them being gold or silver, and it was these that Julian found so exceptional. They were not like ordinary goldfish but gilded, just as though their scales were made of gold leaf. Bill told him that if he wanted to buy one it would cost him a hundred pounds.

From the silk factory they went to the most famous of all Zen Buddhist temples, Ryoanji. The outstanding feature of the place was its philosophic sand garden. This was an oblong piece of ground, measuring about seventy-five by thirty feet, covered with very fine gravel. The gravel had been raked with the greatest care into lines and curves, and planted in it were half a dozen rocks of varying sizes. Along the whole length of the temple side of the garden there ran two stout wooden steps on which a crowd of people, most of whom were silent, were standing or sitting looking at this unusual form of landscape gardening.

Bill explained that the idea was to aid contemplation, and that if one stared at the sand and rocks for long enough one could imagine them to be islands in the sea, mountains on the moon, or earth as it was originally created. Julian accepted this theory, but thought such a state of mind would be difficult to attain while, as at present, half a hundred Japanese were taking snapshots of others who were only posing as contemplatives for them.

A little after half past five Bill took Julian to the Kanze Noh Hall to see a Noh play. The seats were all stalls and comfortable fauteuils such as one would have found in a first-class European theatre. But the stage was entirely different. Instead of facing the auditorium, it was a canopy-covered structure, with one corner jutting out into it. One of its inner sides was occupied by the orchestra and the other by a seated chorus. When they arrived the play was well advanced, so they saw only the last quarter of an hour of it. That was ample for Julian since, although he found the resemblance to Greek drama interesting, Bill could give him only a vague idea of what was going on; and the actors, dressed in most gorgeous robes, remained entirely silent, doing no more than posture with slow gestures to indicate their distress, joy or anger.

To Julian's relief, Bill had made no arrangements for dinner, so dined again as his guest at the Miyako. Before eating he gratefully put down two large whiskies-and-sodas, regardless of the consideration which would have caused most tourists to make do with one; for in Japan, even in a shop, Scotch whisky cost ten pounds a bottle.

During the day, by tacit consent, neither of them had mentioned Merri, although Julian had frequently thought of her. But it had been a very tiring day; so he went early to bed, and again slept soundly.

Next morning Bill called for him and took him to Nijo Castle, the residence used by the Shoguns in the old days when they came to Kyoto to consult with the Emperors. It in no way resembled a European fortress, but was a large rectangular park enclosed by high walls that sloped inward and were made of big blocks of stone. Inside these there was a smaller area surrounded by a broad moat and similar walls, protecting an inner garden and the Palace.

The building was of the conventional type, made of dark brown, heavily-carved wood. It had a tiled roof that turned up at the corners, supported by short stout plinths and sliding doors the upper part of which consisted of oiled paper; but it was the largest that Julian had yet seen.

The interior also differed from those of the shrines and temples. Inside the outer wooden shell a ten-foot-wide corridor enclosed all the interior rooms. In the felt slippers he had been obliged to exchange for his leather shoes at the entrance of the Palace he began to walk down this long corridor; he noticed at once that, although the floor was even and brilliantly polished, with every step he took it gave a loud squeak.

With a grin, Bill told him the reason. 'Those old Shogun fellers were scared that they might be bumped off by some of the Emperor's boys while they were in his city; so they had these floors constructed round their dwelling quarters. 'Nightingale' floors, they're called. They're laid on thousands of little metal rings that squeak when trodden on. The idea was that their squeaking in the night would give their guards the tip-off that someone was out here gunning for them.'

Having admired the subtle paintings on silk by ancient masters that covered the inner walls, the beautifully decorated ceilings and, in one room, a score of magnificently robed life-sized figures representing a Shogun receiving the homage of his courtiers, Julian asked, 'Can we go now and see the Imperial Palace?'

Bill shook his crewcut head. 'No. The Emperor still comes here at times; so I'd have to get us a permit. Later in the week maybe. Anyway, I could fix it for us to take a stroll round the grounds, and there's acres and acres of them behind that tall wall I indicated to you yesterday. But we'll run out to the Katsura Palace. That's the Crown Prince's place and not all that different, though quite a bit smaller.'

Katsura turned out to be only another large garden, in which the trunks of many of the more precious trees had not yet had removed their winter protective casing of finely plaited straw. In it there were several lakes with a few medium-sized wooden buildings set round them.

It had been drizzling all the morning, but Bill was

anxious to take Julian to see the famous moss garden at the Temple of Saiho-ji. In the woods round it there were said to grow over a hundred different varieties of moss, but Julian found he could hardly distinguish one from another; although he admired the beautiful groves of bamboos, forty-foot high and with glossy trunks as thick round as a man's thigh. They had been there only a quarter of an hour when rain began to come down in torrents; so they beat a hasty retreat to the car.

On the way back into the city Bill said, 'Seeing you enjoyed Japanese eats yesterday, I'm taking you along to a little place called Hyotie's. It's old as the hills. I'd say it was going strong long before those early Yanks threw your chests of tea into Boston harbour. I hope you'll like it.'

With a sinking heart Julian replied nobly, 'I'm sure I shall.'

He had already seen that Kyoto was a city of extraordinary contrasts. Shrines and temples that had flourished for eight hundred years and more were still served by devoted priests who sat before candle-lit altars rhythmically clapping their hands, while in nearby streets bars with blaring juke-box jazz and neon-lit pin-table saloons stood cheek by jowl with shops selling only kimonos or figures of the ancient gods; that a gaudy cinema stood within a hundred yards of the Noh Play Hall, and that, while some of Kyoto's million inhabitants drove about in shiny limousines, others, shod in straw sandals, stood on the pavements clutching staffs and beggars' bowls. In consequence, he was not surprised when, no great distance from the city centre, the car entered a narrow turning that had the appearance of a pretty country lane, and pulled up outside an old-fashioned bungalow.

On entering it and taking off their shoes, they were bowed into a room not more than eight feet square. No cook appeared this time, but a 'Madame' who superintended the meal, and two maids. Julian gave silent heartfelt thanks as he took in the fact that here, although he was to sit on a cushion on the floor, he would at least be able to support his back against a wall.

The meal was served on two low square tables by the two maids, each set in front of one of the guests. It followed the same patternless course, and consisted of much the same tit-bits as that on the previous day; so, although Julian was able to eat it in somewhat greater comfort, he was glad when it was over.

'Now,' said Bill when they had finished, 'I'll take you to see the Daigoji Temple. It's some way out, but has a five-storey pagoda and is one of the high spots of these parts. Then we'll do the Museum.'

'No,' replied Julian firmly. For the time being he had had more than enough of sightseeing in Kyoto during such inclement weather. At the great religious festivals, with their splendid pageantry, or for three weeks in the year when the cherry blossom, azaleas, iris and camellias were all out, the gardens must be a delightful sight, but they were not out yet. And while the trained eye of the Japanese garden lover might appreciate their lay-outs and take pleasure in the fact that, with infinite patience, the gardeners had removed every down-pointing needle from every branch and twig of their pine trees, he felt that to have seen one was to have seen them all. He could not even now remember in which garden he had marvelled at the hundreds-of-years-old pine tree, the lower boughs of which had been trained to give the appearance of a large boat, and in which he had seen the big flat-topped heap of smooth sand on which for centuries priests had stood to take their observations of the stars. 'No,' he repeated, 'I'm used to having a nap in the afternoon; so if you'll forgive me I'd like to go back to the hotel.'

'It's for you to say,' Bill smiled, and added a little pointedly; 'when a feller's getting on into middle age I guess he needs a bit of a let-up now and then. O.K. But there's upwards of four hundred shrines and temples in this town. Plenty of good ones to see yet and keep our

140

minds off Merri. I'll pick you up same time tomorrow; then we'll get going on the round again.'

But Julian was not destined to see any more temples in Kyoto. Next morning, a quarter of an hour before Bill was due to call for him, his telephone rang. It was Bill, and he was speaking from the lobby. He asked Julian to come down at once. When they met five minutes later he took Julian by the arm and piloted him through the crowd in the entrance hall and up a flight of stairs to the tea-lounge, where it was quieter. Then he said:

'My old man's buddy, the Police Chief in Osaka, called me half an hour ago. He says there's no sort of evidence that Hayashi had anything to do with snatching Merri; so getting a warrant to search Hayashi's place is out. But they've traced the ship Merri was brought in on. She's a small tramp called the *Matabura* and I thought we might go see her Captain. Maybe money'll persuade him to give, and we'll pick up some bit of information he didn't turn in to the police. But we'll have to make it snappy. The *Matabura* has been on a run up to Yokohama since she landed Merri, and she's due to sail again at midday.'

Julian readily agreed and they hurried out to the car. As soon as they had settled themselves, Bill gave the gist of the report he had received from the Police Chief. There were always one or two spare cabins on a tramp and it was a recognized custom that their Captains should be allowed to make a little extra money by taking passengers in them when they were not required for other purposes by the owners.

At midnight on the day that Merri had been kidnapped the *Matabura* had been due to sail from Hong Kong to Yokohama, calling in at Osaka on the way. That morning a shipping agent had gone off to the tramp to ask if her Captain could take a Chinese gentleman, named Ling Yee, and his wife and daughter as passengers to Osaka. The daughter, he added, was only just recovering from a serious illness, so would be carried aboard on a stretcher

141

and have to keep to her cabin; but her mother would take her meals to her and Mr. Ling was prepared to pay a bit above the price the Captain would have normally expected to get. The agent produced the money and the Captain had agreed.

That afternoon a coolie had brought off the Lings' luggage and it had been placed in the cabins they were to occupy, but evening came and they did not put in an appearance. The Captain had waited for them with increasing impatience, and even given them a quarter of an hour's leeway; but at 12.15 he had sailed.

Half an hour later, when the *Matabura* had rounded the western end of Hong Kong and was running down the channel between the island and Lamma Island, she had been hailed from a large launch with a number of people in her. The Ling family was among them and Mr. Ling had explained that, owing to his daughter having had a relapse just as they were about to leave their home, the doctor had had to be sent for and their departure had been delayed. As the girl had been declared fit to be moved, and he was still anxious to catch the ship, he had hired a launch in Aberdeen hoping to intercept the *Matabura*.

The girl had been slung aboard in a hammock and taken straight to her cabin. Her parents had proved to be a quiet, respectable couple, but during the voyage none of the ship's company had seen the girl. On arrival at Osaka the Lings had been greatly concerned about their daughter because the previous night she had had another relapse. Mr. Ling had gone ashore and arranged for an ambulance to come down to the wharf and, again slung in a hammock, the girl had been lowered over the side and taken ashore. That was the last the Captain of the *Matabura* had seen of the Lings, but on his return from Yokohama the police had questioned him about his last call at Osaka, and he had told them about the Lings on the chance that the invalid might be the missing girl.

When Julian had heard Bill out he said, 'Since the dates

142

are right I haven't a doubt that the girl was Merri, doped both when she was put on board and landed, and kept under light drugs during the voyage. But whoever handled this job in Hong Kong for Hayashi must be a first-class planner. Of course, after the chap who was watching Mrs. Sang's house had turned in my note, his boss had the best part of a day to work in. His luck was in to find a ship that was sailing that night, but if there hadn't been one he'd have only had to keep Merri hidden somewhere on one of the off-shore islands for a few days then work the same trick. And what a darned clever one. By it he saved himself from having to get forged papers for Merri at short notice, and avoided the possibility of being traced by having gone with her through the Hong Kong immigration people. Merri's kidnapper would have known that we should leave the Sea Palace at least an hour before midnight, and once he'd got hold of her all he had to do was to lie well off the coast in the launch until the *Matabura* came up.'

A good twenty minutes elapsed before they were clear of Kyoto, and they were able to increase their pace only along short stretches farther on. As had been the case when they had driven from Osaka, the narrow road held two streams of traffic that was for a lot of the time moving bumper to bumper, and for a good part of the way they had to crawl behind coaches and heavily loaded lorries. It was, too, another cold, rainy and gusty morning.

Anxiously they kept consulting their watches as the minutes sped by and when they reached the docks the congestion was even worse, so by the time they pulled up on a wharf it was ten minutes to twelve. The *Matabura* was lying some way off and as Bill pointed her out to Julian he saw that she was already flying her Pilot Jack, showing that she was about to leave harbour.

Hastily they secured a motor boat, and promised its owner a handsome sum if he would make all possible speed out to the *Matabura*. Even in the harbour the sea was made

143

choppy by sudden gusts of wind. The sky was overcast and it looked like blowing up for another storm. At the very moment they came alongside, the ship's siren gave three ear-splitting blasts, announcing her departure.

A junior officer had come to the ship's rail and was looking down at them. Bill called up to him in Japanese. He shook his head; but Bill began to shout at him angrily and, with evident reluctance, the officer threw a rope ladder over the side. Bill swarmed up it with Julian after him. As they reached the deck the propellers began to turn. Leaving Julian standing there, Bill ran forward and up the bridge ladder. He was away for a good five minutes. As he came running back, he panted:

'Captain's set against holding her, even for quarter of an hour. But I've fixed it for the pilot to take us off in his boat. Skipper won't leave the bridge. Couldn't expect that while he's getting the old tub out of harbour. We'll have time to frisk Merri's cabin, though. It's not been slept in since. Maybe she managed to hide some sorta tip-off about the people who snatched her, hoping she'd be traced to the *Matabura*. If it linked them with Hayashi we'd be able to get the cops to raid his place. Got to find the steward first, though. He's gotten the key.'

As the vessel had only just sailed, the deck crew were all hard at work; but Bill grabbed one of them by the arm, swung him round and hissed urgent questions at him in sibilant Japanese. The man hissed something back and jerked his head in the direction of the open doorway under the bridge. Bill ran to it and was gone for another five minutes. When he reappeared the ship was clearing the harbour mouth and had begun to roll, but he was holding a key and pointing aft. Julian turned and joined him as he ran on towards a double row of deck cabins in the stern. Fumbling with the key, he got it in the lock of one of the cabins, turned it and jerked the door open.

At the same moment they both moved to enter, and collided. Muttering apologies to one another, they stepped inside. It was a small single-berth cabin and had been tidied up since Merri had occupied it. There was only one cupboard and the bare drab walls offered no place of concealment for any clue she might have left.

Julian pulled open the cupboard, but it was empty. Bill dived at the bunk, snatched off the thin coverlet and began to crush parts of it between his hands, so that had a piece of paper been under the cotton cover it would have rustled. As he did so, he cried to Julian, 'The mattress! That'd be the most likely place she'd hide a letter.'

Tearing the sheets and single blanket away, Julian hauled the canvas-covered mattress from the bunk. Bill produced a penknife and swiftly ripped open one of its ends, then he said, 'Here, you carry on with this. Mustn't let the pilot go off without us. He'll not know we're in here. I'll go tell him and ask how long we got. Be back in a few minutes.'

He dashed from the cabin, swinging to the door behind him. Julian was kneeling on the floor, thrusting his hands in among the mattress's horsehair stuffing. There was nothing in the end Bill had opened, and he had gone off with his penknife; so Julian could not slit open the other end. Frantically, he pulled the horsehair out by the hand-ful. It took him ten or twelve minutes before he was satisfied that no piece of paper had been hidden in it. Quickly he searched the sides of the empty bunk, the top of the cupboard and the ventilator, but with no luck.

Bill had not returned. By then the ship had been under way for at least twenty-five minutes, and was wallowing through a heavy sea. Lurching to the cabin door, Julian grasped the handle and turned it. But the door did not open. He tried it again, again and again. Only then did it suddenly dawn on him that the door must be locked.

At that, chaotic thoughts tumbled through his mind. Only Bill Urata could have locked it. The pilot boat must have put off, within five or ten minutes of passing the harbour mouth. It couldn't live in a sea like this. Bill

145

must have locked him in deliberately and gone off in her. The account of Merri's being brought to Osaka in the *Matabura* had been nothing but a pack of well-thought-out lies. But perhaps she had. This must be one of Urata's ships for them to have let Bill come on board when she was at the actual moment of sailing—or perhaps Hayashi's. It looked now as if that was the same thing. It might well be that the Uratas managed Hayashi's shipping line for him. Tilly Sang had been right. Bill Urata was Hayashi's man and had put on a clever act to win the confidence of his master's enemies, so that he could sabotage any attempt to get Merri back. And he, Julian, had been fool enough to walk into Bill's trap.

Frantically he tried to open the cabin window, but it would not budge; so it was either stuck or had been secured in some way outside. And it was made of heavy plate glass. There was not even a chair in the narrow cabin : nothing with which he could smash it. He pounded on the window with his fists, then on the walls, while shouting to be let out. But a high wind was blowing and spray from the waves now slapping on the deck outside; so he failed to attract anyone's attention.

Heaping the bedclothes and scattered bits of mattress on to the bunk, he sat down on them with his head between his hands. Over an hour drifted past during which he could do nothing but berate himself in abject misery. He was roused by the clatter of a bucket outside. Jumping up, he again shouted and pounded on the window. A seaman heard him, came to the window and stared through it at him with a puzzled look, then unlocked the door.

Angrily Julian demanded to be taken to the Captain, but the man clearly did not understand English. After searching his mind Julian found enough Japanese words to convey his meaning. The man made signs to him to stay where he was and went off along the heaving deck. Five minutes later he returned with a thick-set middle-

146

aged man, in rough but somewhat better clothes. Frowning at Julian he said:

'Me Captain. . . . Kano Dosen. . . . You stowaway.'
Then, pointing at the ruined mattress, he added angrily,
'What for? What for?'

Ignoring the question, Julian indignantly protested that he was not a stowaway but had been locked in.

The Captain tried the handle of the door and said, 'Accident. He go snap, snap.' Forbearing to argue, Julian demanded that the ship should return to Osaka. With a scowl the Captain replied, 'No possible. No possible.'

In vain Julian argued, pleaded, threatened. Then, seeing that his efforts were useless, he asked, 'How soon shall we reach a port?'

The reply he received was shattering. 'Days sixteen. Bad weathers twenty. Make no stop. Ship go Honolulu.'

CHAPTER XII

TRAPPED IN THE *MATABURA*

JULIAN was utterly aghast. At worst he had expected to be carried off to Korea, Formosa or back to Hong Kong; but Honolulu! And to be cooped up for over a fortnight in this miserable little tramp! Again he pleaded with the burly Captain to put the ship about and land him at Osaka, threatened him with an action for kidnapping if he refused, and finally offered him a year's pay to turn in towards the coast and land him anywhere from a boat. Captain Kano Dosen could not be moved.

In his very limited English he maintained that Julian's having been carried off to sea was entirely his own fault. Dosen said that as he had been up on the bridge when the pilot boat put off he had supposed that when young Mr. Urata had left Julian had left with him. The ship, it transpired, was one of the Urata line, otherwise they would not have been allowed to come on board when she was actually on the point of sailing. And Bill had telephoned the previous evening to say that he wished to see one of the cabins before she sailed, but had arrived an hour later than he had said he would. Why Bill Urata should have left without Julian, Dosen could not explain. He could only suggest that it was owing to some misunderstanding between them. Presumably, Urata had expected to find Julian already in the boat, but it had had to leave without him because, owing to the bad weather, to have delayed longer to look for him would have endangered its return to harbour.

Although such an explanation was conceivably possible, Julian did not believe it for one moment. Had that been the case Bill could, on getting ashore, within a very short time have radioed the ship to return to harbour; but he had not. In addition, Dosen denied all knowledge of Mr. and Mrs. Ling and their daughter. His refusal to admit that he had brought such a family from Hong Kong to Osaka convinced Julian more firmly than ever that the Uratas were hand in glove with Hayashi, and had deliberately shanghaied him; so that he would be out of the way when the Kuan-yin arrived and by some trick Hayashi could get possession of it without handing over Merri.

After twenty minutes of futile argument the Captain summoned the steward, whom he ordered to find another mattress to replace the one Julian had ripped to pieces and make him as comfortable as possible with soap, towels and borrowed gear, including oilskins for the voyage. Then he told Julian that he could stay where he was or, if he preferred, accompany him to his quarters.

Julian elected to do the latter, and staggered along the heaving deck to a stuffy day cabin where, having turned on a television set, Dosen left him.

All through the long afternoon the weather worsened. Julian was a good sailor but, after attempting to share the horrid fare of which the Captain's evening meal consisted, he could hold out no longer and a bout of violent seasickness added to his misery. By seven o'clock he was stretched out on the hard mattress in his cabin feeling absolutely ghastly; and, as the small steamer pitched and rolled while battling her way through huge seas that constantly crashed on the deck outside, he had to cling to the side of the bunk to prevent himself from being thrown out.

During the night he was twice sick again, but at last fell asleep. When he woke it was daylight, and, although the ship was still heaving, the sea was much calmer. For a while he lay there again deploring the wretched situation into which Bill Urata had tricked him. All hope of redeeming Merri through the cupidity of Hayashi to possess the Kuan-yin was gone. Her only chance of survival now lay in Tilly Sang's agreeing to come to Kyoto. Since she was so convinced that Hayashi meant to kill her if she did, the chances that she would sacrifice herself for her daughter seemed slender. And, while Julian would willingly have undergone the extreme discomfort and privation that for the next two or three weeks were to be his portion could that have in any way helped Merri, to know that he must face them without its doing so galled him unbearably.

After a time it suddenly impinged on his mind that, although the ship was still lifting and falling, her engines had stopped and she was no longer moving forward. Owing to his parlous state the previous evening, he had ignored the cotton pyjamas that had been found for him and thrown himself down on the bunk fully dressed. Getting up, he went to the door of the cabin, opened it and looked out. To his surprise he saw that the ship was at anchor and lying about a mile off a wooded promontory.

Instantly new hope flared in his mind. The coast off which they were lying could only be Japan. Evidently the previous night's storm had been so severe that Captain Dosen had decided that he must run for shelter to the nearest bay. The morning was fine and the ship still tossing only owing to a heavy swell that was the aftermath of the storm. But now the tempest had subsided it seemed certain that at any moment Dosen would start the ship's engines again and resume his voyage to Honolulu.

For a few minutes Julian's mind was racked with awful indecision. If, as the Captain claimed, he had known nothing of Bill Urata's intention to ship him to Honolulu, he had only to ask for a boat to be got out to put him ashore. But if Dosen was in the plot he would certainly not agree to do that. Instead, Julian realized grimly, directly he made his request he would forcibly be conducted back to his cabin and locked in there. And the only alternative to asking for a boat was to endeavour to swim ashore.

A small harbour off which the *Matabura* lay did not look more than a mile away, but Julian knew that such estimates of distance across water could prove disastrously deceptive. He was a good swimmer, but even a mile when fully dressed would tax his strength to the utmost. Yet to ask the Captain for a boat was to run a very grave risk of his hope of getting back to Kyoto ending in dismal failure, and failure meant not only his having to submit to a wretched voyage to Honolulu, but that Merri's life might be forfeited by it. He knew then that he must risk his own.

Stepping back into the cabin, he took off his shoes, then his coat and wrapped them in it. Tearing strips from a towel he tied the bundle to the small of his back, then stepped out on to the deck. After a quick glance round to make certain that no-one was about, he climbed the rail, hovered there for a moment, took a deep breath and dived overboard.

His dive was a good one; so he hit the water with hardly a splash, but the height from which he had gone in was such that he went down, down, down until he thought he would never stop. By thrusting fiercely against the water he at last began to come up, but by the time he surfaced his lungs were nearly bursting. As he shook the water from his eyes, he could no longer see the shore; but he struck out resolutely with a good steady stroke.

He had been swimming for about five minutes when he heard a shout behind him. Looking back, he saw that a deck hand had spotted him and was gesticulating wildly. Ignoring the man's shouts, he swam on; but when next he looked over his shoulder he saw that several men were clustered about a boat and making ready to lower it. The sight filled him with alarm, as it was evident that they meant to come after him. However, the boat was chocked up inboard and still had its canvas cover on; so he tried to comfort himself with the thought that it would be quite a time before they could get it into the water.

For a quarter of an hour he made steady progress; but each time the swell carried him high enough to glimpse the harbour it seemed no nearer, and the distance he still had to swim more frightening. By then the boat had been lowered and was about to be cast off. Knowing that the crew would soon be rowing all-out in pursuit of him, he was greatly tempted to increase his pace, but resisted the impulse from dread that he would tire more quickly and perhaps drown before either he could reach the shore or the boat could come up with him.

The ten minutes that followed were an agony. Even maintaining a steady pace now caused him to draw each breath with a gasp that seared his lungs. The clothes he was wearing increasingly impeded his movements and the sodden bundle on his back acted as a drag on him. Only one thing served to encourage him. The headland to the south of the little town kept its position; so he knew that no current was sweeping him seaward, and that if he had not greatly overestimated the distance from the ship to the harbour he must by now be well over half-way to it. The awful question was could he continue swimming for long enough to reach land and before the boat caught up with him? He would have given a year's income to be able, by turning on his back and floating for a while, to rest himself. But he dare not. The thought of being captured and carried off again was too unbearable.

A shout from behind told him that the boat could not be far away; but at the moment he heard it the swell carried him up so he saw that the pier of the harbour was now not far off and that well outside it a small fishing junk was just hoisting her concertina sail. If only he could attract the attention of the men in her they might save him from his pursuers.

With aching muscles and pain-pierced lungs he made a

desperate effort and covered the next hundred yards at a slightly increased pace. By then he was swallowing a lot of water and the boat was within ten yards of him; but the sailing junk was coming in his direction and one of the men in her began to shout and wave.

Another agonizing three minutes passed. He was almost at the end of his tether. Then the two boats bore down on him almost simultaneously. A man in the junk threw him a rope. He grabbed it and with his remaining strength endeavoured to haul himself along it. But next moment the boat from the ship was almost on top of him. He was seized by the shoulders and dragged up into her.

Sprawled across one of the thwarts, he was too winded even to make a cry of protest or shout an appeal to the men in the junk to save him. While he fought to get back his breath he savoured all the bitterness of defeat. He had risked drowning in vain and must, after all, make the voyage to Honolulu with the heartbreaking knowledge that little Merri was lost to him forever.

Closing his eyes, he choked up some water. When he opened them again he saw Dosen's rugged face above his own. Bending lower, the Captain hissed at him, 'Great foolish! You mad! Mad; mad! Have you wish drown?'

'Oh, go to hell!' Julian wheezed weakly.

'Hell yes, you near go.' Dosen shook his head. 'I think you sleep. Good time you wakie. See ship make lie up from storm. Say me boat please. I give. Why no? Boat take you shore. To make swim is mad; mad!'

Julian could hardly believe his ears. If he could, the Captain had not been lying to him on the previous afternoon; so he had had his gruelling swim and risked his life quite unnecessarily. Then, as he struggled up into a sitting position, he saw that the little junk was now alongside, her concertina sail lowered and her crew of three men regarding him with evident curiosity.

Perhaps, he thought, that explained Dosen's attitude. The Captain had expected that he would put up a fight rather than be taken unresisting back to the ship. Had he done so the fishermen would have witnessed it and, perhaps, reported the affair or, anyhow, could have been later called as witnesses against him. He might be on the level; but it was equally probable that the arrival of the junk had decided him against risking having to face a charge, that could be proved, of using violence to abduct a British subject.

Either way, all that mattered to Julian was that he had secured his freedom. Dosen, with the usual deep formal bows, made no objection to his transferring to the junk and a quarter of an hour later the fishermen put him ashore in the small harbour.

None of the three spoke a word of English, but as no attempt had been made to deprive Julian of his wallet he still had plenty of money on him. Producing some sodden notes, he rewarded the lean, grinning little men handsomely; then, indicating his sodden clothes, he pointed towards the town. The oldest of the men showed that he understood and led him through the main street to a small hotel.

Its bright-eyed little proprietor, like so many Japanese owing to the Occupation, spoke a strange brand of Americanese, and could not do enough for his unexpected guest. Fortified by a long draught of saki, Julian undressed while a bed-roll was laid out for him on the floor and padded coverlets provided to keep him warm. As he had slept for a good part of the night he felt tired only from his long swim, and that tiredness soon wore off; so he was able to enjoy a hearty breakfast of fresh crabmeat while his clothes were being dried. When he had finished he enquired of the landlord where he was and the quickest means of getting back to Kyoto.

It transpired that the *Matabura* had taken shelter between two small islands that lay just inside the jutting headland west of the entrance to the Gulf of Isewan. The Gulf almost formed an inland lake forty miles long and, in places, twenty broad, that ran up to the great port of Nagoya. Toba was the name of the little town at which Julian had landed, and by rail Kyoto was some seventy miles distant. A local train would take him to the larger town of Tsu, which was twenty miles up the Gulf, and from there he would be able to get a faster train for the longer part of his journey.

Not having realized that he had dived overboard as early as a little before seven o'clock, he was surprised to learn that it was still not yet nine; and a train was due to leave Toba at 9.30. His clothes had been quickly dried, so he decided to catch the train if he could. While he dressed the little landlord obligingly got out his car, then ran him the short distance to the station.

Unlike the expresses, the train was of pre-war vintage and consisted of only three coaches with hard seats; but Julian was so delighted to have regained his freedom that he thought nothing of its discomfort and responded as well as he could with his small stock of Japanese to the smiling advances of his fellow passengers. Although evidently greatly intrigued by this foreigner, who appeared to be rich yet was wearing such sadly crumpled clothes, they politely hid their curiosity while offering him fruit, rice balls and sweets from the packages they had brought with them.

This attitude made it almost impossible to believe that just such people, or their fathers, had, in many cases, behaved with shocking bestiality during the war; but Julian knew that the Japanese troops had shown a bravery in attack unrivalled by any other army, fearlessly dying by the thousand in attempts to storm almost impregnable positions. Allowance, therefore, had to be made for the difference between Western and Eastern mentalities.

The men of the West, when compelled to fight, did so, in most cases with reservations about not getting killed if they could help it and without feeling any positive hatred against their enemies. Whereas those of the East, once committed, were seized with a demoniac fury that caused them to throw their lives away in battle and regard any prisoners they took as evil beings intent on destroying their country and their homes with a fanaticism equalling their own. One thing at least seemed to Julian beyond dispute: in peacetime the vast majority of the people in every country were by instinct kind, hospitable and peace-loving, and the average Japanese as much so as men of any other country.

The little train dawdled on through a pleasant country-side, where men and women in broad-brimmed straw hats were working tirelessly in the rice fields, digging deep trenches to irrigate them, ploughing with hump-backed oxen and making protective fences to shelter their plots with the straw of last year's rice, which would later be laid in the trenches as compost. After frequent stops the train pulled up at Tsu shortly before eleven o'clock and every-one got out.

There Julian found he had over an hour to wait, but at midday a train that had a comfortable first-class coach took him again on his way. It was not an express, and only Japanese food was to be had in the restaurant car, but he made a good meal of the ubiquitous prawns and a big dish of strawberries.

Meanwhile the train carried him away from the Gulf, up through well-wooded mountainous country: very different from the industrial scrap-heap that lay between Osaka and Kyoto. Frequently it ran through groves of huge graceful bamboos and now and then clattered through a densely populated township with many waving children, or past a picturesque curved-roof temple. But unlike the villages in many other countries there were no gaily painted buildings, and the predominant colours of the landscape were a monotonous blend of brown, grey and olive-green.

By two o'clock it was skirting the shore of Lake Biwa, with its resorts from which the population of Kyoto bathed in summer, and by a quarter past it drew in to the fine modern station of the ancient capital. A quarter of an hour later Julian was back in his room at the Miyako.

Thankfully he got out of his crumpled suit, sent it to be cleaned and pressed, had a hot bath and went to bed. At six o'clock he was roused by his telephone ringing. On answering it, he was told that Mr. Yutaka Urata was down in the foyer asking to see him. For a moment he hesitated; then, tight-lipped, he said tersely, 'Very well, send him up.'

That either of the Uratas should have the effrontery to ask him to receive him greatly surprised him, and how they should have known that he was back in Kyoto he could not imagine; but, considerably intrigued to hear what the elder Urata had to say, he got out of bed, sluiced his face, combed his hair and put on his dressing gown. He had only just finished these preparations when there was a knock on the door and, on his calling 'Come in', the small, neat, bespectacled ship-owner presented himself.

He was holding an enormous bunch of chrysan- themums, and bowed not twice but three times, so low that Julian thought he might fall on his face, then diffidently offered the bouquet as he murmured:

'Accept, pliss. I am abased. For what my son did no excuse possible. I am so angry that I could thrash. I tell him he disgrace us. He act like American gangster. Pliss understand, yiss. When I hear I am fill with shame. In Japan we have ancient code of behaviour towards guest. Mr. Day, before you I submit to be revile. I . . .'

It seemed as though he would go on indefinitely, but Julian interrupted curtly. 'Are you trying to tell me that you knew nothing about my being shanghaied on your ship the *Matabura*?'

'Notting. By all gods I swear, notting,' the elderly man assured him with a heavy sigh. 'This morning when I hear I am astound. I face Bill up and he admit. I say you not

157

worthy to be my son. For this our family could disown. Code of all honourable family in Japan made regardless. Shame, shame, shame. To Mr. Day I must now go on knees for you.'

'You say you found out about my having been shipped off to Honolulu this morning,' Julian said coldly. 'May I ask how?'

'The *Matabura* have run into tempest. Her Captain, Kano Dosen, send radio. He say: "Have put into Isewan Channel for shelter, have Englishman Mr. Day on board, have come on board with Mr. Bill Urata at moment of sailing, found locked in cabin, now put ashore at Toba." I then have face to face with Bill and he tell all.'

'I see. And what reason did Bill give for this most reprehensible act?'

Urata shrugged unhappily. 'He say he love this girl Merri Sang very desperate. He say who rescue her from Hayashi get her. You are much to be feared rival. And to you is the Kuan-yin to be delivered. You make bargain with Hayashi and get she free she marry you. His head turned by reading many American gangster books. He decide to act like gangster hisself. Get you out of way, get hold of Kuan-yin, make deal with Hayashi, so earn gratitude of girl and she marry him.'

'So that's the story,' Julian murmured, temporarily reserving his opinion about its veracity. 'How did you know that I had got back here?'

Spreading out his plump hands, Urata replied, 'No difficulty. You had been landed at Toba. What you do but return to Kyoto quick as possible? From Osaka I telephone hotel two hours and half ago and they say you are here.'

'And you mean to tell me that Bill could have had me carried off in the *Matabura* without the knowledge of either the Captain or yourself?'

'Yiss, pliss. Why not? Bill have good brain. He think up good story about *Matabura* bring girl from Hong Kong.

All lies. All lies; but easy to make believe. He know time of sailing. All to do get you there that time. Captain on bridge much occupied to get ship out of harbour. All to do get you on board and lock in cabin. Go off in pilot boat. No-one knows. How should? Most fortunately, storm save you from voyage to Honolulu. For inconvenience caused humble regrets. Yiss, I abase myself. And Bill, how you say, deep contrite. American education good some ways, bad others. This bad part; very bad. Much condemn by all right aspect of Japanese.'

Julian had to admit to himself that the account Urata had given of the affair was a very plausible one. But he still felt disinclined to accept it until his plump little visitor said unhappily:

'This girl, Mr. Day. Bill has shown me photographs of her; many photographs. One must make admission that she has great beauty. But what is she? A guide for the tourists. A person of no consequence. No family; no fortune. For Bill I had great hoping. Our family is very old one. I have no other son. I wish for him good alliance. You are English. In Europe and United States marrying is very different. Pliss understand no offence intended, but in West rich men take for wife actresses, girls who wear dress for model. No background required. Here in Japan iss not so. Good family iss important. I wish for wife of Bill girl who never work and have fine fortune to add to ours. You also wish this girl. I make no disguise. If she made free from Hayashi I do all in my power to prevent that Bill have her for wife. Accept apoligies now, pliss, and this I promise.'

Julian gave a faint smile. From what Urata had said it seemed that he could not be aware that Merri was no little working girl scheming to marry into a rich Japanese family, and that on her mother's death she would herself become a wealthy woman. If that really were so he could not be in league with Hayashi, otherwise he would have known all about the Sangs. Moreover, the little man's

159

anxiety that his son should not marry Merri seemed entirely genuine; and for him to have thought up such an attitude seemed too far-fetched to be likely. This, taken in conjunction with the fact that there was no proof whatever that Captain Dosen had been privy to Bill Urata's plot, decided Julian that it would be unreasonable not to regard his father as innocent.

'Very well,' he said. 'I accept your explanation. But where do we go from here?'

'That iss for you to say, Mr. Day. Against Bill you must have great anger. Perhaps you think to bring against him a charge. For all sakes I am hoping not. To prove that he lock you in cabin and you not miss boat through own fault not easy. But my son I punish myself. He pay you from allowance I make two hundred thousand yen—that iss about two hundred pounds—for inconvenience caused. Also I now forbid to leave Osaka; so that if Miss Sang made free you are only horse in field.'

Julian shook his head. 'Thanks, Mr. Urata, but I wouldn't like Bill to go short of money on account of what he did. After all, we've a saying in England that "all's fair in love and war". I'll admit to having feared that Merri liked him better than she did me, and it seems that he felt that my chances with her were better than his. So I'll not hold his gangster act against him. But I can't afford to risk his making a second attempt to render me incapable of negotiating with Hayashi; so if one way or another you would keep him in Osaka until this affair is settled I'd be grateful.'

'That I will do. And the negotiations you will now perhaps prefer to handle all yourself. I bow myself out. But if there iss still any help I can give, pliss to tell.'

To gain a minute in which to think, Julian got out his case and lit a cigarette. He had been given to understand that in Japan when two collectors wished to make a private bargain over a valuable antique it was customary for the seller to invite the prospective buyer to a dinner, and that only at the end of the meal was the antique casually produced, then discussed. As Urata was acquainted with Hayashi, it had been agreed that the former should invite the latter to a dinner at his house in Kyoto at which both Julian and Bill would be present. Now, if Urata washed his hands of the affair as he suggested, it would fall to Julian to arrange the dinner. But he knew nothing about such functions and to engage suitable geishas to be in attendance might not prove easy. Moreover, seeing what lay behind the meeting, it had seemed preferable to hold it in a private house rather than in an hotel. His conversation with Urata and, above all, the ship-owner's readiness to take no further part in the affair had all but convinced Julian of his honesty. Even so, caution dictated that he should not revive the project of the dinner being held at Urata's house. When he had lit his cigarette he said:

'You could, I am sure, be of great help to me; because to arrange a dinner of the kind we proposed is entirely outside my experience. But I think it would be best to give it in some public place. If you can suggest somewhere suitable, I should also be grateful if you would still issue the invitation on my behalf and attend it, for I feel that everything then would go much more smoothly.'

Urata bowed. 'I am honoured, Mr. Day, by renewal of confidence towards me. Let us hold dinner in first-class geisha house. I recommend if you wish; but better you enquire of management here, choose place and telephone me, then I invite Mr. Hayashi. For this I remain in Kyoto for tonight. This iss Tuesday, the *Lubeck* is due in early Thursday. You will wish no delays; so tomorrow morning I make all arrangements.'

No suggestion could have been fairer; so Julian at once agreed. With many bows, and finally a handshake, Urata then took his departure.

When he had gone Julian rang for one of the little bright-eyed creatures in a brown silk uniform to arrange the mass of chrysanthemums. Then he rang down to the office and made two enquiries: first for the name of the best geisha house in the city, and secondly for a good private enquiry agent who could come in to see him after dinner. A geisha house called the Nest of the Phoenix was recommended and the clerk who answered his enquiries promised, if need be, to trace a good private detective to his home and have him report at the Miyako that evening.

By the time Julian had dressed it was eight o'clock; so as Urata would have got home by then, he put a call through to him. The ship-owner endorsed the commendation of the Phoenix by the hotel and said that he would send a letter by hand right away to Hayashi, inviting him for the Thursday.

Julian dined quietly in the big restaurant. Half-way through the meal a note was brought to him. The management had been successful in engaging for him the best private detective in Kyoto, a Mr. Hidari Rinzai, and he would call at half past nine.

It was through no fault of the management, but bad luck for Julian, that the best private detective in Kyoto happened to be in the employ of Mr. Hayashi's right-hand man Udo Nagi.

CHAPTER XIII

'NONE BUT THE BRAVE
DESERVES THE FAIR'

JULIAN's object in engaging a private detective was to
make a final check-up on Urata. The ship-owner's
explanation had been faultless, his distress at his son's
gangster-like act and concern that he should not marry
Merri had carried conviction. Captain Dosen's attitude
towards Julian fully supported his employer's insistence
that both of them were innocent and, finally, Urata's not
having sought to influence Julian in his choice of a place
to meet Hayashi seemed the clearest possible indication
that they were not working together.

But once bitten twice shy. Having so very narrowly
escaped being forced to make a voyage to Honolulu under
most unpleasant conditions, Julian did not intend, if he
could possibly help it, to expose himself to any more
tricks by the Uratas: either father or son. If the father was
acting honestly, he reasoned, he had left Bill in Osaka and
would take reasonable steps to see that he remained there.
If not the odds were that Bill was back in Kyoto and that,
together, they were by now planning some fresh attempt
to get hold of the Kuan-yin for Hayashi without his either
giving up Merri or having to pay for it.

Julian intended, therefore, that the private detective
should first find out if Bill was at the Urata house in
Kyoto then, if he was not, employ an associate in Osaka
to make certain that Bill was in that city. But while eating
his solitary dinner it occurred to him that when in Hong
Kong he and Bill had first discussed the kidnapping of

163

Merri, it had been agreed that on arriving in Japan they should employ a detective agency to endeavour to find out if Hayashi was holding her as a prisoner in his house.

The project had been abandoned only because the elder Urata had, presumably, insisted on going to the police. Since, according to Bill, the police had failed to trace Merri and ruled that there were no grounds on which to obtain a search warrant of Hayashi's premises, why, thought Julian, should he not put a private detective on the job himself? Whether Hayashi could be tempted into exchanging Merri for the Kuan-yin on the Thursday night remained extremely problematical, and Tilly Sang had been very definitely of the opinion that he would not. Should he refuse, and the private detective find out that he was holding Merri a prisoner, that would provide a second string to Julian's bow. In consequence he decided to make full use of Mr. Hidari Rinzai.

At 9.30 to the minute Mr. Rinzai arrived at the desk in the lofty hall, enquired for Julian and was led over to him. The detective was an inconspicuous little man who might have been any age from forty to seventy, for his dark yellow face was as wizened as a walnut, but Julian thought he was probably not over fifty. When he ceased his obsequious bowing Julian took him up to the bar lounge, which at that hour was almost deserted, and offered him a drink; but he would accept only coffee. Seated in armchairs in a dimly lit corner they then got down to business.

Soon after Merri's disappearance Julian had seen to it that his offer of ten thousand Hong Kong dollars reward for information about her should appear in leading papers in Singapore, Bangkok, Saigon and other cities as far north as Korea and, such matters being Mr. Rinzai's business, he recalled seeing the notice in a Japanese paper; but he showed great surprise when told that Mr. Inosuke Hayashi was suspected in the matter; because Hayashi was reputed to be one of the wealthiest citizens in Kyoto

164

and not at all the sort of man to lend himself to any criminal activity.

However, when Julian had told him as much about the affair as he thought it necessary for him to know, he expressed his willingness to carry out an investigation, then asked a number of shrewd questions. Favourably impressed by his astuteness, Julian gave him a considerable sum so that he would have ample money to endeavour to bribe one of Hayashi's servants for information, as well as immediate expenses; then he asked when he could expect a first report.

Rinzai replied that he should be able to find out by midnight if Bill Urata was in Kyoto; but it would take time to get hold of Hayashi's servants and pump them discreetly, so it might be two or three days before he could ascertain if a young woman answering Merri's description had been brought to Hayashi's house getting on for a fortnight before and was still there.

On that they parted, and Julian settled down to read a suspense story called *Star Raker* by Donald Gordon, which had been recommended to him at the hotel book-stall; and as he found it one of the most exciting tales he had read for a long time it kept his mind off his anxieties until, an hour and a half later, Rinzai rang up.

He reported that Bill Urata was at the apartment in Osaka. This was definite for, using a false name and giving as a pretext a wish to get in touch with his father urgently, Rinzai had actually spoken to him. Well pleased with this first activity of his 'private eye', and still more strongly convinced that Urata senior had no intention of double-crossing him, Julian put out the light and went to sleep.

On the Wednesday morning he awoke early as usual, to realize that somehow he had to get through another day, and now without the lively company of Bill Urata, or any other matter, to distract his thoughts from Merri. Normally he was the sort of man who would have run a mile rather than go on a conducted tour, but to do so would at least provide him with temporary companions, and even to listen to the prattle of a guide seemed better than mooning about for hour after hour on his own; so, after ordering his breakfast, he rang down to the information desk and enquired about sightseeing tours. There were a variety, but mostly in Kyoto, and he wanted to get out of the city; so he booked a seat in a coach that made a day trip to Nara and left at nine o'clock.

His fellow tourists were much as he had expected: more than half of them were middle-aged or elderly Americans —one couple having with them a most horrid little boy whose raucous utterances and rude interruptions of the guide they smiled on indulgently, evidently regarding them as early indications of a forceful personality—a number of middle-class Japanese, two blonde German hikers, an Englishman, who looked as though he might be a professor, with a faded wife and a young couple who were obviously both French and on their honeymoon.

For several miles the cumbersome coach negotiated its way through the narrow streets of Kyoto and its suburbs. Meanwhile the little male guide, constantly flashing his teeth, two of which were aluminium, told them that Nara was one of the oldest cities in Japan and, before Kyoto, had been the capital of the country from A.D. 710 to 784. Gripping his microphone firmly, he went on to tell them about the temples they were to see there and gave a brief account of the religions of Japan, interspersing his talk now and then with some well-rehearsed wisecrack that made Julian groan mentally.

When at last they emerged from the built-up area the pace of the coach increased only over short stretches for, as with the highway between Osaka and Kyoto, the road was in a deplorable condition and so narrow that it could hold only two lanes of traffic. However, at least most of it was free from shoddy little factories, junk yards and back lots, and as they bumped along at twenty miles an hour

166

Julian had ample opportunity to observe the people in the villages and the countryside through which he was passing.

It was mainly flat, with ranges of hills on both sides in the distance, and had little of the beauty of the country Julian had seen on the previous day while making his journey from Tsu by train. The greater part of it consisted of market gardens which supplied Kyoto with vegetables. Every inch was cultivated and there were scores of forcing houses, mostly consisting of semi-circular wooden supports covered with polythene or thick oiled paper, and the care with which the crops in the open had been cultivated testified to the thrift and industry of the Japanese peasants. On the right of the road, too, the guide pointed out a hillock on which was the most famous tea plantation in Japan but, disliking Japanese tea as Julian did, the sight of it left him cold.

It was nearly eleven o'clock before they had accomplished the twenty-six miles to Nara and, somewhat to Julian's surprise, he saw that it had not grown into an industrial centre like Kyoto. Here there were many open or wooded areas, no factories, few shops and the curved roofs of several temples could be seen from a distance. It was, in fact, far more like the picture of Japan that he had envisaged.

Their guide took them first to the Kasuga Shrine, one of the oldest in Japan. It was situated in a huge park about which roamed eight hundred deer. They were believed to be the messengers of the gods and were so tame that they were an active nuisance. Not content with food bought from the many vendors by tourists and thrown to them, they came up and nuzzled in people's pockets then, if disappointed, snapped at their fingers.

The approach to the shrine was through a wood and up broad shallow flights of worn steps. On either side there were innumerable stone lanterns, erected by pious families as memorials to their dead, some of them dating back to the fourteenth century. One night in every year they provide a fairyland scene; for the great majority of Japanese still have a deep regard for ancient customs, so come to the shrine and light a candle or a little oil lamp in their family lantern.

At the top of the rise stood the famous shrine, painted a bright vermilion and with hundreds of lanterns hanging from its curved eaves. It was said to be the oldest wooden building in the world and round it were growing trees of enormous girth. Out of a slice from some of them a table could have been made at which a dozen people could have dined, and the guide declared that the oldest had been planted two hundred years before William the Conqueror invaded England.

Returning to the coach, they drove on to see the Todaiji Temple. This again had a worthy approach along a broad avenue, and on either side of its entrance towered up a terrifying wooden image of a demon king, threatening with raised fists anyone who dared profane the sacred portals. Inside there was a huge seated Buddha. It was fifty-three feet in height, and weighed over four hundred and fifty tons. Aloof and serene it had sat there all through the centuries since before Charlemagne had ruled in France and the Caliph Haroun el Raschid in Baghdad, and neither before nor since had any people ever cast a larger bronze figure.

Looking up at it brought home to Julian more than anything else had yet done the antiquity of Japan's civilization. The temples in Kyoto were no more than delicate buildings with attractively designed roofs, that might have been built in any age; but it was a staggering thought that there should have been craftsmen in Nara capable of designing and casting this colossal figure, that radiated peace and benignancy, when London was no more than a huddle of wooden houses on land retrieved from a swamp.

While admiring this ancient work of art, one thing

detracted from Julian's enjoyment. As at the Kasuga Shrine, and at the shrines and temples he had gone to see with Bill Urata in Kyoto, the whole area swarmed with people. Encouraged by their Government, so he had been told, as an antidote to modern tensions and fears of a nuclear war, the Japanese had developed an absorbing interest in their country's past. Rain or shine, every day, outside every place of major interest could be seen from twenty to fifty parked coaches that had brought numbers of trade guilds, fraternities of housewives, groups of students and other organizations on excursions from distant cities. Black-haired, shiny-faced schoolgirls dressed in neat sailor suits were to be seen by the hundred, and in the milling crowd one could not walk ten paces without having to step aside for some youth, or dapper little man, who was taking a photograph or using a cine-camera.

The coach party were to lunch at the Nara Hotel and, on entering it, became mixed up with the guests about to attend a smart wedding reception. The little bride was almost buried under a traditional head-dress and the women were all dressed in magnificent satin kimonos with enormous bows in the middle of their backs; but the men, in morning coats, lavender waistcoats and carrying 'toppers', would not, if suddenly transported on a magic carpet, have looked at all out of place in the Royal Enclosure at Ascot. The sight typified in Julian's mind the extraordinary way in which the Japanese, in so many ways, appear to have adopted the ways of Western civilization yet at heart maintain their ancient beliefs and customs.

Over a very passable lunch the people seated at Julian's table talked about temples they had seen in Kyoto, and others that they were to visit that afternoon, until he threw a bombshell among them. He had noticed on the folder describing the tour that those who preferred it could be dropped off for two hours at Nara's Disneyland. And he remarked that, as he was thoroughly tired of being jostled by crowds of gaping students, that was what he intended to do.

Most of those present were horrified. They had paid good money to come thousands of miles to see temples, and nothing short of collapse would have prevented them from going to stare at every one that was on their itinerary. But the young Frenchman laughed, looked at his pretty wife and said in French, 'Little one, I think the English gentleman's idea commends itself. Already my mind is confused by the number of temples we have seen in Kyoto, and there are other ways of amusing oneself.'

With a smile, Julian addressed them in French. 'That is just how I feel. Please, Madame, agree; and brighten my afternoon by permitting me to accompany yourself and your husband.'

The girl returned his smile and inclined her head. '*Enchanté, Monsieur. Je vous remercie infiniment.*'

An hour later, some way from the centre of Nara, Julian and the French couple were dropped outside a gaily painted walled city two miles or more in circumference. He had learned that the couple's name was Rimbaud and that they came from Saigon. The husband had been born there and was in the employ of the French Line; the wife had come out two years earlier as governess to the young children of a wealthy official.

The coach had put them off at the bottom of a long slope that led up to the fairytale city, and as they walked up it Julian received a sudden shock. Ahead of them was a small group of people who had been dropped off from another coach. Among them were a tall man who was dressed like an American and, with him, a dark-haired girl. As they paused before going through the turnstile, Julian caught sight of the girl's profile. She obviously had Chinese blood and for a moment he could have sworn that she was Merri. Her height and figure and the bronze lights in her hair all contributed to the illusion. In spite of the improbability of finding Merri there his heart seemed to turn over. But as he drew nearer he saw the girl's face again. She was considerably older and, although very good-looking, nowhere near as beautiful. Then he heard her speak in broad American and put her, and the man with her, down as tourists from San Francisco's Chinatown.

The episode caused him to feel a sudden pang of guilt. For the past hour he had been quite enjoying himself, while poor little Merri must be confined in some dismal room, probably ill-fed and ill-treated and, in any case, eating her heart out with worry about what was to become of her. Desperately he wished that by some magic it could be this time the following day; for by then the Kuan-yin should have arrived and he would be twenty-four hours nearer to making his bid to secure her freedom.

Thoughts of her would have plagued him all the afternoon had it not been for the Rimbauds; but they were young and gay, and it was impossible not to be affected by their enjoyment of the plywood city with its miniature castles, pagodas, dwarf houses in the style of every land, Aladdin's caves and innumerable side shows. They went first in the little train, drawn by the first steam engine ever to be imported into Japan, that ran all round the city's wall, and from it looked down on the stucco jungle inhabited by stuffed animals and primitive hunters, the Indian reservation, the Chinese village and Treasure Island in the middle of a lake. Later they went aboard the pirate ship, down the helter-skelter and on the scenic railway.

At half past three the coach picked them up and made its irritatingly slow journey back to Kyoto. The Rimbauds were staying at an inexpensive hotel, and Julian, dreading another long evening of suspense on his own, pressed them to dine with him at the Miyako. They needed little pressing, as they were far from well-off, and Rimbaud had said that had not the shipping line that employed him

171

given them their passages free they would not have been able to afford to go so far afield for their honeymoon.

Julian was only too happy to give them a good evening with the best of everything, and they particularly enjoyed the French wines he ordered, as the prices in Japan were far too high for them to be able to pay when on their own. Over dinner it emerged that they had spent the first week of their holiday in Hong Kong, so were able to compare with Julian their impressions of the Chinese and Japanese. All three of them thought the Chinese handsomer, better dressed, more amusing and more attractive; but they agreed that the Japanese were an exceptionally clean and more efficient people, and that their politeness and willingness to oblige foreigners were unequalled anywhere.

About in which place they would rather live they unhesitatingly decided for Hong Kong, both on account of its amenities and weather. Central Japan, although twenty degrees nearer the Equator than central England, has an even worse climate. In the summer it could be very hot, but few days passed without rain; in the spring it was chilly, rainy and windy; and in winter it was very cold with frequent blizzards. Madame Rimbaud declared that she thought she would die if she had to live through a winter in one of the little paper-walled houses that so many of the Japanese still dwelt in; and Julian laughingly agreed that she probably would unless she gave up pretty clothes to encase herself in the hideous padded garments and felt boots with which the Japanese protected themselves.

It was after midnight when the Rimbauds left, but when Julian turned in he could not get to sleep for a long time owing to his fears that he might fail to get Merri out of Hayashi's clutches the following night.

While he was breakfasting in his room next morning, the elder Urata rang him up from Osaka with the good news that the *Lubeck* had just docked, and that Hayashi had accepted the invitation to dine at the Nest of the Phoenix that evening in order to inspect the Kuan-yin. He added that important business would detain him in Osaka until well on in the afternoon; so he proposed that Julian should meet him at the Phoenix at eight o'clock, to which Julian agreed.

Knowing that several hours must elapse before Pao Tin-yum and his wife could reach Kyoto with the Kuan-yin, Julian decided to kill time by having another look at Hayashi's house and also finding out exactly where the Phoenix was situated. As soon as he had dressed he hired one of the hotel cars and drove, as he had done with Bill Urata, down to an old quarter of the city. Leaving the car on the corner of a lane, he again walked slowly round Hayashi's property. As on the previous occasion, the high walls and big wooden gates prevented his seeing into the garden; so he had to content himself with staring for a while at the section of long tiled roof that he could see through the pine trees and silently praying that Merri had come to no harm there.

Returning to the car, he told the driver to take him to the Phoenix. It proved to be in the same quarter of the city and only about half a mile away. But unlike Hayashi's house it was not surrounded by a garden. It was a large ancient two-storeyed wooden building on the corner of a street and on both sides of it were rows of shoddy shops.

By eleven o'clock Julian was back at the Miyako sitting in the hall impatiently awaiting the arrival of Pao Tin-yum, his mind going round like a squirrel in a cage about his chances of making a deal with Hayashi. Optimistic as he tried to make himself feel, he could not overcome the belief that those chances were far from good. There could be no doubt that it was Tilly Sang whom Hayashi wanted to get his hands on, and that he had had Merri kidnapped only to force her mother to come to Japan. Could he really be tempted to forgo a chance to eliminate the woman who had done so much harm to his dope trafficking and whose husband had been in part responsible for having him sent to prison for ten years, simply to add another antique to his fine collection? And what if he refused or, clever devil that he was, managed to trick them out of the Kuan-yin, as it seemed almost certain that he would attempt to? If either happened then, Julian realized, his only hope would be in Rinzai. If the wizened little detective secured definite information that Hayashi had Merri in his house it might be possible to get in and rescue her.

It was not until half past twelve that Pao Tin-yum and his wife Pao Ping at last arrived with their precious package. At first sight Julian was by no means favourably impressed by them. The couple were well on in middle age. The man was tall, gaunt and with a fleshy nose. He was sallow-skinned, but his features suggested that he had European blood as well as Chinese. His mouth was cruel and his eyes inclined to be shifty. The woman was squat, fat and had a waddle. Her mouth, too, was hard and her eyes shrewd. She was wearing a well-made dark blue coat and skirt and a rope of good-sized pearls; pinned to the lapel of her coat there was a diamond brooch that must have cost well over three figures in pounds sterling. Her husband's long grey overcoat was also of good quality, and his large feet were encased in well-polished shoes.

They asked at once to be taken to their room, but would not allow the seven-foot-long oval-shaped wicker basket that contained the Kuan-yin to be taken up in the luggage lift. As it was now in the same city as the unscrupulous Hayashi, Julian agreed that it could not be too carefully guarded; so it was placed on end in one of the electric passenger lifts and all three of them went up with it to the double room that Julian had engaged for the Paos in the same corridor as his own. Having seen the Kuan-yin carried into it, he asked them to meet him in the upstairs lounge when they were ready to go in to lunch; then he left them to unpack and have a wash.

Over lunch he found them decidedly taciturn. They had left Mrs. Sang in as good a state as could be expected and had had an uneventful voyage. Pao Tin-yum's grandmother, it transpired, had been a Portuguese and he had been born in Macao, but had lived since the war in Hong Kong. About his business he was somewhat vague. He said that he owned an interest in an amusement parlour and in a small restaurant and that, as he had been a friend of Mrs. Sang's husband, when she had come to live in Hong Kong he had taken over the management of her affairs.

Finding it difficult to extract any further particulars of interest from him, and that Mrs. Pao was even less inclined to be communicative, Julian told them about the arrangements for that evening. He then raised the question of transporting the Kuan-yin to the Phoenix, but learned that the problem could easily be dealt with. Mrs. Sang had realized that it was too large to go in a car, so had cabled a garage in Osaka to have available a small closed van in which it could be taken to Kyoto. Pao, with his wife in the cab, had driven the van himself, and it was now in the hotel garage; so it could be used again to take the Kuan-yin to the Phoenix. It remained only for him to be guided there; so Julian said that he would take a taxi and tell the driver to go at a moderate pace, then Pao would have no difficulty in following him.

To assess the social status of quite well dressed foreigners, particularly when they are Asiatics, is never easy; but Julian had soon decided that the Paos were very far from being the sort of people he had visualized when thinking of them. He had not expected them to be high-caste Chinese but had supposed that Tilly Sang's man of affairs would probably be a sedate lawyer, or at least a business man of some standing who spoke good English. But clearly the Paos, although they appeared to be quite well-off, were not of a type that would have been accepted in such circles, or even reasonably well educated. Both of them at times fumbled with their knives and forks—which showed that they habitually used chopsticks—the man ate voraciously, cramming his food into his mouth, and the woman repeatedly began to suck her teeth, then remembered not to.

When Julian had signed the bill they agreed that they should meet down in the hall at half past seven, have the Kuan-yin loaded into the van and be ready to set off at a quarter to eight. They then went upstairs to spend the afternoon in their respective rooms.

Considerably relieved to be free of his unattractive guests, Julian partially undressed and lay down on his bed. Somehow he had yet to get through another five hours before he could take the first active step in his attempt to secure Merri's freedom. To have gone out into the city would not, he knew, have served to distract his thoughts; so it was better to surrender to them, although they were far from happy ones.

When he had set out from Hong Kong he had counted on having the aid of Bill, his father and a Chinese couple—the man of whom might prove more capable than any of them in bargaining with Hayashi—and a pleasant woman whom, should Hayashi refuse to do a deal, he might possibly be willing to allow to share Merri's captivity and comfort her until her mother could be persuaded to come to Japan. With the assistance of four such people, gathered as had been earlier planned in Urata's house, Julian had even toyed with the idea that, should Hayashi prove obdurate, they might resort to force and detain him there until he agreed to send for Merri.

But now the situation was very different. Bill was out of the running; his father might, conceivably, still be playing some deep game, so could not be relied upon entirely; and, although the Paos had faithfully carried out their mission of bringing the Kuan-yin to Kyoto, Julian instinctively felt that he would not trust either of them further than he could see them.

The more, too, that he thought of the whole business from start to finish the more gloomy he became about his prospects of inducing Hayashi to part with Merri in exchange for the Kuan-yin. For what now seemed an endless time he had buoyed himself up with that hope; but Tilly Sang had never put much faith in his idea, and he himself knew, only too well, that Hayashi was as cunning as a weasel. When offered the Kuan-yin he must have laughed to himself at the thought that his plot was going to bring him a quite unexpected and valuable bonus. Somehow he would manage to trick them out of it. Without acknowledging that Merri was his prisoner he might turn the conversation to women and remark that he was looking for a new concubine, then revert to her disappearance, offer his co-operation in searching for her and ask for the Kuan-yin as the price of his assistance. Faced with some subtle threat of that kind how could they refuse to give it to him? And he would still hold Merri as the bait to bring her mother to Japan.

Minute by minute the long afternoon wore away into evening. At half past six Julian got up to shave and dress. He had only just gone into the bathroom when his telephone rang. It was Hidari Rinzai and he was down in the lobby. Julian told him to come up at once.

As soon as the little man entered the room Julian saw from the grin on his wizened face that he had good news, and two minutes later he had poured it out. He said that with a good part of the money Julian had given him he had succeeded in suborning a maid in Hayashi's house. Merri was there, locked in an upstairs room. No harm had come to her and she was being well looked after; but she was very sad and wept a lot.

Greatly relieved that she was there, and safe and well, Julian sat down at the desk in the window and wrote a cheque for a handsome sum in Rinzai's favour. As he gave this reward to the detective his hand was trembling with excitement at the thought that, now he knew definitely that Merri was in Hayashi's house, he could go to the police and demand that they should search it.

177

A second later his elation ebbed, for his old fear had suddenly recurred to him—that going to the police might ruin everything. Before entering Hayashi's house they would have to get a search warrant from a magistrate, and they might not be able to do that until the following morning. If, as Tilly Sang believed, Hayashi had men among the police whom he paid for information he might be warned, and during the night spirit Merri away to some other hiding place. After a moment's thought Julian asked:

'What chance do you think there is of getting into the house and rescuing Miss Sang?'

Rinzai shrugged. 'Iss possible but would be difficult. Hayashi not often leave house and he have several menservants. But pick time perhaps maybe.'

'I happen to know that he is going out to dinner this evening,' Julian said quickly.

'Ah! Chance good then. Master go, servants also seek amusing. Go too. One stay perhaps and few women. That all.'

'Do you know in which room Miss Sang is locked up?'

'Yes, sir. Corner room on upper floor, south end of house, on right of landing back side of building.'

Julian's pulses were racing again as he asked, 'If I made it very well worth your while, would you be willing to go in with me and help me to get Miss Sang out?'

The detective thrust out his hands. 'No, sir. Pliss excuse. I not break law. If caught I lose licence. No money you give make good for end my business.'

'I appreciate that,' Julian nodded. 'Still, you could lend me a gun, or sell me one. I don't mean to kill anybody, but I may come face to face with the servants and need a weapon to hold them up.'

'No, sir; no!' Rinzai again vehemently declined. 'All pistols numbered, and permit now required to carry in Japan. If found on you traced to me. Big trouble for lending. Not doing, sir. No.'

Feeling that he stood no chance of persuading the little

man to change his mind, Julian thanked him again and quickly got rid of him.

It was by then nearly seven o'clock and he had to make a decision that was all-important. Should he go to the dinner and try to make a deal with Hayashi or use his absence from his house to make an attempt to rescue Merri? His hopes of pulling off a deal had dwindled sadly; so, after a few minutes' thought, he made up his mind to go in and try to get her.

Although, owing to the import of arms now being forbidden in so many countries, he no longer travelled with a pistol in his luggage, he had always retained a short sword cane. It was in the form of a leather-covered swagger stick such as many Army officers carried, and he had bought it during the war. It looked innocent enough, but had been made by the Wilkinson Sword Company and contained a deadly steel blade about fifteen inches long. Getting it from the bottom of a suitcase he tried it, to see that it still drew easily, then put it handy to slide down the inside of his trousers so that it would lie against his left thigh when he went out.

Sitting down again at the writing desk, he wrote two letters. The first was a brief note to Urata, simply saying that he had been unavoidably detained; so not to wait dinner for him, but he hoped to come in later. The second was much longer and to the police. In it he said that he had received information that a Miss Sang, who had been kidnapped in Hong Kong on the 3rd March, was being held prisoner in Mr. Inosuke Hayashi's house and that he was about to attempt to free her. Should they receive the letter they could take it that he had been overcome by the servants and was also being held prisoner there. In that event he would rely on them to take immediate action and come to the assistance of Miss Sang and himself.

By the time he had finished it was a quarter past seven, and to avoid having to give an explanation down in the lobby he decided to tell the Paos at once that he would not be coming with them. Taking his note to Urata with him, he went along to their room.

In answer to his knock Pao cried, 'Who iss there?' and when Julian told him he shouted back, 'Cannot come in. My wife undressed.'

To that Julian replied in a sharp voice. 'Then come to the door. I wish to speak to you urgently.'

After an interval of at least a minute Pao Tin-yum unlocked the door and opened it, but only a couple of inches. His shifty eyes alive with suspicion he said, 'Iss not time yet to go. We not ready. What you wish?'

'To tell you that I shan't be coming to the dinner after all,' Julian replied abruptly. 'Something has occurred that will prevent my doing so; but I will engage a taxi to guide you to the Nest of the Phoenix and when you get there I want you to give this letter to Mr. Urata.'

'Whether you come is no matter,' Pao returned indifferently. 'I am responsible for the Kuan-yin. Mrs. Sang make it clear that it for me to hand over goddess if Hayashi agrees our terms. But will do as you wish.'

Then, having taken the letter, he shut the door.

As Julian walked back to his room he felt more than ever distrustful of the Paos, and even thought it possible that they had been got at by Hayashi. But it was no good worrying about that now and, anyhow, they knew nothing about his own intentions. The important thing for him to decide at the moment was at what time he should make his attempt to get into Hayashi's house.

Hayashi could be counted on to leave it a few minutes before eight, but for how long he would remain away was an unknown factor. Perhaps two hours; but as he was not a personal friend of Urata's their conversation over the meal was unlikely to be more than an exchange of banalities, and if Hayashi proved impatient to see the Kuan-yin the whole business might be concluded in an hour. There then occurred to Julian the possibility that events might move much faster. He felt certain that

Hayashi would have thought up some plan for attempting to get hold of the goddess without making any return for her and if the Paos were in with him they might help him to pull a really fast one. They would not take the Kuan-yin direct to Hayashi's house, as to do so would be plain theft, but if he received it in the Phoenix they could not be accused of that. The dinner would be in a private room and Urata could be given a 'Mickey Finn' which would knock him out within a few moments of his drinking it. If that happened the Paos could also sham having been doped and Hayashi be back in his house with the Kuan-yin under half an hour.

There were quite a lot of snags to such a plan; but Julian knew the man he had to deal with and, although he would greatly have preferred to give the servants plenty of time to go out for the evening, fear that Hayashi might have hatched some plot of that kind decided him to go in soon after eight o'clock.

Having collected his sword stick and the torch he always kept beside his bed, he went downstairs and gave his letter to the police to an under-manager with very clear instructions that only if he were not back by eleven o'clock should the police be called in and the letter given to them. Then he asked for two taxis to be at the door at twenty to eight.

A few minutes later the Paos emerged from one of the lifts and the porters carried the big wicker basket containing the Kuan-yin to a place near the door, where Pao Ping sat down beside it while her husband went to fetch the little van. As soon as he had brought it round from the garage Julian watched the basket being loaded into it, then he gave instructions to the driver of one of the taxis he had ordered to lead the van to the Phoenix. Having given the party ten minutes' start he got into the other taxi and told the man to put him down on the corner of the street in which lay Hayashi's house.

By the time he arrived there it was fully dark and,

181

having paid off his taxi, he walked round to the north wall of the garden. During his reconnaissance of the place that morning he had noticed the branch of a catalpa tree that hung down over the tall wall. After a quick glance to right and left to make certain that no-one was about, he tensed the muscles of his legs and jumped. His outstretched fingers caught the branch and it did not break. For a few seconds he swung there, then he pulled himself hand over hand along it until he was leaning against the top of the wall. Sending up a prayer that he might succeed in rescuing his beautiful Merri, he scrambled over and dropped down into the garden.

CHAPTER XIV

MR. HAYASHI MAKES A PLAN

WHILE Julian had been giving lunch that day to the Paos, Inosuke Hayashi had been in consultation with his Chief of Staff, Udo Nagi.

They were dressed in the rich garments of their country and sat cross-legged opposite each other across a low table of exquisite workmanship. On it were a number of photographs. They were enlargements of films taken that morning through a telescopic lens on a dock in Osaka. Studying one that was of Tilly Sang, Hayashi said with a grim little smile:

'As I felt sure it would be, this woman is Matilda Cray, who later became Madame Lo. She has changed little and is still beautiful. From her body I derived much pleasure. When I tired of her I sold her into a brothel in Macao. I do not recall the name of the man who bought her from me, but about a year later he sold his place to one Lo Kung. He took a fancy to her and made her his mistress. Later, when she had his child, Lo married her and for a while she acted as his "Madame" in the brothel. On Lo's death she employed the man Ti Chang, who is now known in Hong Kong as Mok Kwai, as her manager. By then she was quite a wealthy woman and evidently decided to become respectable. It is true that she is an Australian, but the story you picked up that she met Lo there and married him in Singapore is false. As far as I know she has never been there, but transferred herself direct from Macao to Hong Kong. Brothels, as we well know, can be very profitable concerns and, it seems, she was loath to lose the big income she was making out of girls; so having sold her place in Macao for a handsome sum, she took Ti Chang with her to Hong Kong and set him up in the Moon Garden.'

Hayashi paused, so Nagi put in deferentially, 'May it not be, honourable master, that the woman being already rich had Ti, or Mok as he is known there now, open the Moon Garden mainly for the purpose of obtaining information about Japanese visitors to Hong Kong? My reports show that all the girls there were instructed to show special willingness to oblige such visitors in any way, make them drunk if possible, and question them about their war experiences. Doubtless Mok passed on such information to Madame Lo—or Sang, as she now calls herself—thus enabling her to ensnare such men as visited the Moon Garden and were so foolish as to admit that they had served with the 230th Regiment during its victorious occupation of Hong Kong.'

'Sagacious Nagi, about her method of learning that persons on whom she sought to be revenged were in Hong Kong, you are unquestionably right,' Hayashi conceded. 'But she might have employed other methods, and to secure five victims I could have thought of better ways than running a brothel for some twelve years; so the profit motive must have entered largely into that. However, it is certain that she received her information through her girls and, even if they were not successful in finding out where the men were staying, Mok could have had them followed to their hotels. After that she could have met with few difficulties. What virile Japanese could resist the temptation to pick up a beautiful big blonde woman if he saw her sitting alone in a lounge and she indicated that she was willing to talk to him? On learning that she was not a prostitute but a woman of the world and, as she would have told him, a lonely widow, his urge to overcome such scruples as she showed would have been

irresistible. No doubt she made a great play of her
eputation and not wishing to be seen in Hong Kong with
a Japanese, then made casual mention of her little villa
in Macao, and that she was going there for the week-end.
So, it must have been, that the five men went to their
deaths. But tell me in more detail about her departure
from Hong Kong and arrival in Osaka this morning.'

'The *Lubeck* sailed from Hong Kong on Sunday last,
honourable master. That morning, according to our
agent's report, a Chinese couple collected the Kuan-yin
from the woman's house in a small van, and drove with it
to the dockside in Victoria. As my honourable master will
be aware, Hong Kong being a Free Port there is no
examination of outgoing baggage; so, having shown their
passports at the emigration desk, the couple had the
basket carried straight on board. It was locked up in a
cabin next to the one they were to occupy and remained
there throughout the voyage.'

'And none of your people saw Madame Sang either on
the dock or aboard the ship before it sailed?'

'No, honourable master.'

'Yet she must have been in the ship, for she was seen to
walk off it this morning.'

'Indeed, yes, honourable master. And, most fortunately,
I suspected that she might somehow have smuggled herself
on board, owing to a report I received that on the same
day as the Kuan-yin was taken from her house she had
disappeared from Hong Kong. That was why I went to
the dock myself this morning, with several of our people,
to keep observation.'

'Describe to me exactly the landing of her party.'

'It was a little before eight when the *Lubeck* docked,
honourable master. At about half past the passengers
began to come off; first a few, then in a crowd. Madame
Sang was among the crowd. Immediately I saw her I
ordered that photographs should be taken. She was
carrying only a small suitcase, and she appeared to be

185

with another woman, to whom she spoke once, but only briefly. The woman was, I think, American, and had with her three children and much luggage. They went through the passport office together, but in the Customs shed Madame Sang left her, went out and took a taxi. By then all the passengers had disembarked, the last to do so being the couple with the Kuan-yin. When they came out of the Customs shed a small green van was waiting to meet them. Later I learned that it had been hired by cable. The Kuan-yin was loaded into it. Having given its driver some money and received from him a key, the man and his woman got into the cab and he drove off.'

'You had both the taxi and the van followed, of course?'

'Certainly, honourable master. The taxi took Madame Sang to a small hotel, the Fushimi, in Gojo Street; but she did not book a room, and remained there only half an hour while she had breakfast. When she came out she did not take a taxi. Carrying her small suitcase, she walked about a mile, asking the way several times by showing a slip of paper which must have had an address on it, until she reached Kitaoji Street. In this poor part of the city she looked about until she found a side turning with a row of lock-up garages in it. Meanwhile, it was to the same place that the man had driven the van. Unlocking one of the garages he had run the van inside and shut the door. Madame Sang went into it and also shut the door behind her. Ten minutes later the van came out, the Chinese woman locked the door, joined her husband in the cab and he drove off. About an hour ago they arrived at the Miyako. The couple were met by the Englishman, Day, about whose activities, honourable master, I have reported to you, and the Kuan-yin was taken up to a room he had booked for the couple who brought it.'

'And Madame Sang?'

Nagi spread out his great hands. 'Disappeared, honour-able master. After waiting till the van had been gone half an hour, our people forced the lock of the garage and it was empty.'

'Then Madame Sang must have been inside the van and is now at the Miyako.'

'One cannot doubt that, honourable master. Equally I do not doubt that Madame Sang left Hong Kong in the big wicker basket that we believed to contain the Kuan-yin, and that by the same means she arrived in the room upstairs at the Miyako. The purser and stewards of the *Lubeck* have been questioned. There was no Madame Sang on the passenger list and no person resembling her was seen during the voyage. She must have travelled in the locked cabin reserved for the Kuan-yin. Her couple would have brought her food and if she wished she could have taken exercise on deck late at night with little risk of being challenged. One may be sure that her wicker basket is well lined with much padding, so she would have ex-perienced little discomfort while being carried aboard at Hong Kong. On arriving at Osaka she would, of course, have had to leave it; otherwise she would have been found in it by the Customs. But there were over two hundred passengers in the *Lubeck*, so for a woman they had not previously seen to mingle with them when coming off would have aroused no comment. She attached herself temporarily to the American woman because that woman had a lot of luggage, and some of it would have been taken for hers; but had she had none at all the Customs would have thought that queer. That is why she took a suitcase with her and——'

Hayashi made an impatient gesture. 'Nagi, your deduc-tions are excellent; but having made your point you should not labour it so much. What we have to consider now is why the woman should arrive in Kyoto in this way. For reasons that you well know I have long been set on inducing her to come here; but I expected her to do so openly, in the hope of redeeming her daughter. But no; by subtle means she succeeds in reaching Kyoto in secret, obviously with the intention that I should remain in ignorance of her presence. But why? What can her intentions be?'

Nagi bowed his head almost to the floor. 'Honourable master, for having allowed my stupid tongue to wag idly I abase myself. I should have known that your lightning-like mind would become aware of these assumptions without your humble servant mentioning them.'

Ignoring the apology from his henchman, Hayashi remained silent for a moment; then he said, 'For her to have come in secret there can be only one explanation. She plans to take me by surprise and murder me. Yes. I see her design quite clearly. Tonight I am invited to dine with the ship-owner Yutaka Urata at the Phoenix geisha house, and afterwards to inspect the Kuan-yin. But when the casket is opened it will not contain the Kuan-yin. Madame Sang will be lying in it, and as the lid is raised she will rise up and shoot me.'

'May the gods protect you, honourable master,' murmured Nagi. 'But should she commit such a crime in the Phoenix she could not escape being charged with murder, and executed.'

'She could,' replied Hayashi tersely. 'She would plead justifiable homicide. She would say that I had had her daughter kidnapped and the police would at once search this house. The Englishman, Day, would insist on their doing so. They would find the girl here and she would bear out her mother's story. At the trial it would be pleaded that the mother had believed that to kill me was the only way of obtaining her daughter's release. She might get a year or two in prison, but no more; and Madame Sang, as she now calls herself, would willingly submit to that for the pleasure of having revenged herself on me.'

'One who is warned avoids danger in time,' observed Nagi. 'Honourable master will not then go to this dinner.'

'I must think,' Hayashi replied. 'If I do not she will

remain a menace to my life. If I do I may be able to eliminate her, and so both avenge my son and secure my own future. Yes, I must think.'

Taking up a small silver bell, he tinkled it. Almost instantly a painted panel in the opposite wall was slid back to reveal a young woman, dressed in a rich kimono, waiting there on her knees. Hayashi said only one word. The girl bent swiftly forward until her forehead touched the highly polished floor, then scurried away. Two minutes later she reappeared, still on her knees and carrying a tray with opium pipes and impedimenta on it. Shuffling forward with amazing quickness, she set the tray down on the low table, then bowed her head to the floor twice again. Coming up she swiftly moulded two small pellets of opium paste, spiked them in turn with a long needle and held them over the flame of a small oil lamp, then inserted them in the bowls of the pipes. Having completed her task, throughout which her white-painted face had remained as expressionless as a china mask, she repeated her genuflections, shuffled swiftly backwards on her knees and disappeared.

Hayashi took only three draws on his pipe, then laid it aside. The room was warm owing to a charcoal brazier that burned in its centre. For a while he fanned himself; then snapping closed his fan he said:

'This is what is to be done. You will have another wicker casket made which must closely resemble that in which Mrs. Sang travelled here.'

Giving him an uneasy look, Nagi murmured, 'Honourable master, if it is required for this evening be so gracious as to consider that I have less than six hours in which to produce such an unusual object.'

'No matter,' Hayashi replied, flicking one of the photographs that lay on the low table in front of him. 'In this you have as good a picture to work from as you could require. Use money or whips. It is immaterial which, but it must be ready by half past seven. This afternoon you

189

will go to Ishimuro Joshu, the antique dealer, and buy from him one of the sacred figures that he fakes for export. It does not have to be a Kuan-yin, and can be metal or stone; but it must be between five and six feet in height and approximately the weight of a heavy woman.'

Nagi gave a smiling bow. 'Honourable master's intention is to switch caskets. Oh, very very clever.'

Ignoring the compliment, Hayashi went on, 'We shall need a van. It must be of the same make and colour as that used to bring Madame Sang to Kyoto.'

Nagi ducked again. 'No difficulty, honourable master. That was a green-painted Ford with the insignia of an Osaka florist's shop on the sides. Such vehicles are common. I can procure one within an hour, and by the use of quick-drying paint it will not be noticeable by eight o'clock that the inscription is freshly painted.'

'That is well. Have the Ford, the wicker casket and the image brought here. The switch can only be made between a quarter to eight and eight, when the other van will be on its way from the Miyako to the Nest of the Phoenix. Some means must be devised to hold it up and temporarily remove the Chinese couple from it. When they are released they must find our van where they left the other, and drive it to the Phoenix. The casket in it will be brought upstairs and, after I have dined with Urata, opened. I shall laughingly declare the figure in it to be a fake, then condole with him for the trouble he has been put to for no purpose, and return here.'

'And the other casket, honourable master: that which will have Madame Sang in it?' enquired Nagi softly.

'That will have been brought to this house.' Hayashi's lined old face creased into a diabolical grin. 'Tonight I will avenge the death of my son. Or perhaps not tonight. No. We will first leave Madame Sang shut up in the coffin she has designed for herself for a night and a day, or possibly longer; so that she may sample the pangs of hunger and thirst. But not for too long. I should never forgive myself if I allowed her to die too quickly. When we do open the basket she will be too weak to give us any trouble, and we will have the girl there to provide an hors-d'œuvre to the prolonged banquet by which I will drain away Madame Sang's reason and life.

'I am getting on in years, but not too old to enjoy a fresh young woman; and Madame Sang shall be a witness to my enjoying her daughter. Then, Nagi, you who are still strong and vigorous shall have the girl. Although she will lack the training in the art that makes our geishas so accomplished, we should be compensated for that by her being such a dainty morsel. Afterwards, as part of your reward for having conducted the enquiry into this affair with so much zeal, you may take her to your house and instil into her the little tricks by which she can best please you.'

Nagi's dark eyes glistened. 'Honourable master, you are most generous. She has the bloom of a peach and the perfume of a freshly opened lotus. Had it not been for your express commands I could not have kept my hands off her while bringing her here.'

After a moment he added, 'This switch of the vans containing the two wicker baskets will need much organizing and very careful timing. We have in our favour that to reach the Phoenix the van must pass through several quiet, ill-lit streets bordered only by private houses. Therefore to hold it up will be easy. But, having removed the Chinese couple from its box, to take them out of the street so that they do not see their van driven off, then enable them to return and drive its substitute to the Phoenix, presents a difficult problem. Has my honourable master any ideas on this subject?'

Hayashi remained in thought for a moment, then he replied, 'Did you not tell me that although the couple are using the name of Pao, they are actually Mok Kwai, earlier known as Ti Chang, and his wife?'

191

'That is so, honourable master. Having spoken with Mok at the Moon Garden, I recognized him at once by the scar on his throat, and also recognized his wife.'

'Then as they are brothel keepers we can make use of that. Have two of our people of respectable appearance—Yoshimitsu, perhaps, and another—be in a car at the Miyako a little before the van is due to leave. They will follow the van. You will arrange for a lorry and other vehicles to block the van's passage in whatever quiet street you select. Yoshimitsu will drive up beside it. His story will be that he was about to go into the Miyako when he recognized Mok, just as he was on the point of driving off, as the owner of the Moon Garden; so he gave chase. He will allege that when in Hong Kong he visited the brothel and was robbed of his wallet. By then you will have had a little crowd of our people collect. Yoshimitsu will tell his story to them and incite them to violence. Mok and his wife are to be pulled from the van and hustled round the corner, then some way along another street on the pretext of taking them to the police station. You will have contacted one of our friends in the police who is off duty and pay him well. He will emerge from a darkened doorway and enquire the cause of the trouble. As it will be only Yoshimitsu's word against that of Mok there can be no question of an arrest. The police officer will take down Yoshimitsu's story in his notebook, ask to see Mok's papers, and take his address; the couple will then be released. Meanwhile, his van will have been driven off and yours substituted for it.'

Nagi inclined his head until it touched the low table. 'Admirable, honourable master, admirable. All shall be done as you direct. However, one difficulty remains: the Englishman. It must be assumed that he too will set out for the Phoenix with the van, or accompany it in a taxi. It would not be plausible for Yoshimitsu to charge him with complicity in this robbery, and it is to be doubted if he would willingly accompany the Moks when they are

192

hustled off. Seeing the value of the contents of the van, he would almost certainly remain with it.'

'In that you are right, sagacious Nagi. Somehow he must be got rid of. It is most unlikely that a man of his kind would be willing to ride with the Moks in the cab of a van, or inside it; so he will be in a taxi. You could arrange for it to be run into by a lorry; a bad smash so that he is injured and taken to hospital.'

Lowering his eyes, Nagi replied, 'I do not like it, honourable master. The results of such accidents are always uncertain. At times people escape unharmed from the worst of smashes.'

'Then at the last moment he must be prevented from setting out with the van to the Phoenix. We cannot resort to violence in the Miyako; so we must devise some plan for luring him away.'

'That would be best, honourable master; and perhaps Hidari Rinzai, the private-enquiry agent, could help us there. You will recall my passing on to you yesterday Rinzai's report that the Englishman had engaged him to try to find out if the girl was here in your house.'

Hayashi smiled and tapped Nagi gently on the arm with his closed fan. 'An excellent idea. Instruct Rinzai to go to the Englishman at about seven o'clock. He is to say that he has bribed one of my servants and learned that the girl is here safe and well. He must then put the idea into Day's head of attempting to rescue her tonight by saying that as I am dining out most of my servants will take the opportunity to absent themselves. Day can hardly be such a fool as to think there is any great chance that I would exchange the girl for the Kuan-yin. If Rinzai does his work well, Day will decide to come here instead of going to the Phoenix, then we will trap him.'

'But what then, honourable master? Remember he is a British subject. Immediately we release him he will go to the police and the British Consul. Through the newspapers it is common knowledge that the girl was kidnapped and is being held somewhere against her will. He will quote Rinzai as having found out that she was here. As he is in love with her that will be accepted as excuse enough for his having broken in hoping to rescue her. When we catch him we can pretend that we thought him to be a burglar, but in such a case we should at once hand him over to the police. Instead it is necessary that we detain him, and afterwards that we did not hand him over to the police will need a lot of explaining. You can be certain that he will insist on a full enquiry, and although in the meantime we can remove the girl to another place are you entirely sure that all your servants are to be trusted? I believe them to be reliable, but under police examination one of them may be trapped into an admission that the girl was here. No, honourable master. Once the Englishman has been freed I foresee trouble: bad trouble.'

For several minutes Hayashi remained deep in thought then he said, 'You are right, Nagi; so he must not be freed. Have Rinzai tell him that the girl is locked up in an upstairs room: at the back of the house at its south end. When he breaks in let him go up there and only then surprise him. Afterwards it can be said that you thought he was a burglar, and on being discovered he tried to escape by the window. But you will throw him out. Then go downstairs and break his neck.'

CHAPTER XV

THE FINAL HAND IS PLAYED

WHEN Julian picked himself up from his drop off the wall into Hayashi's garden he looked quickly about him. As he had landed in a shrubbery and the moon was not yet up, he could not see much; but by passing between the bushes he could make out against the night sky a part of the back of the roof of the house and, to his left, the glimmer of lights. Having edged his way through a border of big azaleas, he got a better view.

By Japanese standards the house was a large one. Its two storeys formed a solid rectangular mass topped by a typical incurving roof with eaves that turned up at the corners. At its northern end lay a huddle of one-storey buildings and it was from these that the lights came. They were, Julian felt sure, not only garages and so on, but also the servants' quarters; and he blessed the custom of well-to-do Japanese families whereby, in such old properties as this, they had always been averse to having servants living in the house. No lights could be said to show in the house itself, but from the central windows there came a faint glimmer suggesting that a light had been left on in the main hall.

Although the big building appeared to be deserted, Julian did not approach it direct. He had come in over the north wall and Rinzai had said that the room in which Merri was kept a prisoner was on this side of the house but at its southern end.

From what Julian could see of the garden it was laid

out in the same way as those of most small temples. In the middle was an ornamental lake with, on the side facing the house, a little pavilion in which to hold the tea-drinking ceremony. A belt of trees, that he knew to be mainly pines, ran all round the inner side of the wall, screening the garden from being overlooked by other buildings in the vicinity; while smaller trees, that were probably cherries just coming into bloom, had been planted in carefully chosen positions. There would, he knew, be no flower beds but numerous groups of flowering shrubs.

Turning away from the house, he stepped out on to a stone path and, placing each foot with great care, began to walk along it. As he progressed, he entered a small woodland that lay beyond the end of the lake. There, as he had expected, the path curved in a semi-circle that brought him round until he was approaching the south end of the house.

Suddenly he halted and his heart gave a lurch. Just where the woodland ended, at right-angles to the path, there was a wooden humpback bridge, spanning a few feet of water and leading to the pavilion. On the far side of the bridge, silhouetted against the lighter background above the water of the lake, he had caught sight of a man. His body was hidden by the curve of the bridge, but his head and the wide-brimmed, high-crowned hat that he was wearing stood out above it. He made no sound and was standing quite still; but Julian took him for a night watchman who had been patrolling the garden, had caught the sound of his footsteps and was now listening for his approach.

Thanking his gods that he was standing in deep shadows, Julian remained rigid with apprehension for a good two minutes. But the man did not move. For another two minutes Julian waited, striving to control his breathing and afraid he would give himself away if he moved either forwards or backwards. Then realization came to him. It was not a man but one of the stone lanterns with which the Japanese are so fond of decorating their gardens.

Silently berating himself for his stupidity and needless fit of the jitters, he moved cautiously on. When he reached the south end of the house and looked up, his heart gave another bound; but this time from joy. A pale light showed through the window of the room that Rinzai had said was Merri's. She was there and, as it was only about half past eight, probably reading or sewing to while away yet another lonely and anxious evening. How overjoyed she would be if she knew that he was standing only twenty feet below her and, unless things went radically wrong, would have her out of her prison within the next quarter of an hour.

For a moment he thought of throwing some little pebbles up against the window to attract her attention. But quickly he abandoned the idea. As she was locked in, he would have to go up there to free her; and for them to hold a whispered conversation while he stood outside would be only a waste of time.

Tiptoeing along the side of the house, he came on a door, but it was locked and looked too stout to force; so he turned his attention to the windows. They were, as was usual in old Japanese houses, flimsy affairs that could be slid to and fro. At his first strong sideways pull on a casement the catch gave and the window slid open.

One of the most irritating things he had found in Japan was that whenever he entered a temple, a shrine, a non-European restaurant or a private house, he had had to take off his shoes and, while slopping awkwardly round in the felt slippers provided, get chilly feet. But now he sat down and took off his shoes; not out of consideration for Hayashi's polished floors but as a precaution against making more noise than was inescapable. There was, however, still the unpleasant possibility that while in the house he might be surprised, and it would prove a serious handicap if he were forced to run for it through the garden in his stockinged feet. So he also took off his socks, put his shoes on again and drew the socks over them.

Climbing in through the window, he stepped down on to the floor. It immediately gave a loud squeak. Muttering a curse, he took a step forward and the floor squeaked again. To his consternation he realized that it was another of those 'nightingale' floors, with thousands of small rings underneath it, such as the one it had amused him to walk along in the Shogun's Palace.

For a moment he stood still. No sound broke the silence, so he got out his torch and flashed it about. He had entered the house at the south-west corner and saw that a broad corridor ran in both directions. The rooms enclosed by the corridor would, he guessed, be almost bare of furniture, having nothing in them but a few cushions and mats, a low table and, probably, one or two extremely artistic flower decorations placed so as not to spoil the effect of the paintings on silk of temples, pine trees, dragons, birds, deer and tortoises hung on the walls. But here, in the broad corridor, Hayashi had arrayed his fabulous collection of antiques. Gods and goddesses, beautiful lacquer cabinets and priceless jade carvings lined both sides of the corridor.

After a swift glance round, Julian put out his torch and went forward. The alarming squeaking of the floor continued each time he advanced a foot and put his weight on it, until his forehead was damp with perspiration from fear that if any servants were in the building his presence in it must be heard; and the faint starlight coming through the windows was just enough to have the eerie effect of making the life-size figures of the idols seem to be alive and menacing.

A glimmer of light led him to the main hall. Two oil lamps were burning there in front of ten-foot-high gilded Buddhas seated cross-legged on either side of a broad staircase. He put a foot on the lowest step and found to his relief that it did not creak. Quickly now, he ran up them.

On the landing he turned left and, treading cautiously, advanced down a corridor that was in almost complete darkness. Then, half-way down it, he caught sight of a thin line of light that he felt sure must be coming from under Merri's door.

Hastening now, he ran to it, then flashed his torch down the sides of the panel. There was no lock to be seen, so he swiftly assumed that Hayashi had not troubled to have one fitted; because, without money or friends to aid her, Merri could not have escaped from the house, let alone have got out of Japan, before he had traced and concerted some means to recapture her.

Smiling to himself, Julian slid back the door and stepped into the room, confidently expecting to find Merri there and rejoicing in advance at the thought of how overjoyed she would be to see him. Next moment the smile froze on his lips. By the light of the single electric bulb he saw that, instead of Merri, three knobbly faced Japanese men were sitting in utter silence, cross-legged on the floor. As though set in motion by the pressing of a switch, they came simultaneously to their feet and rushed at him.

At the sight of them it flashed into his mind that as no-one other than Rinzai had known of his intention to break into the house, and Rinzai had said that it was in this particular room that Merri was being kept prisoner, the detective must have double-crossed him.

The rush of the three men upon him was so swift that he had no time to slide the door to before beating a retreat. Tensing himself, he struck out at the middle one of the three and landed a blow on his chin that sent him sprawling. As he jumped back the other two collided in the narrow doorway and, for a moment, were jammed together there. Before they could get through it he had whipped out his sword stick, turned and was running down the passage. Temporarily blinded by having just faced a light, he covered a few paces then pulled up short. A huge, gorilla-like man had crept up behind him and was barring his retreat. It was Udo Nagi, who had been lying in wait for him in a nearby room.

Without hesitation Julian lunged at the big man's stomach. At the same moment Nagi raised a blackjack and brought it down hard, partially knocking aside Julian's blade. But his parry was not quite quick enough. The steel ripped through his side. With a yell of pain and fury, he lurched sideways and, clawing at his wound, fell against the wall. Julian dashed past him, heading for the stairs. But the other men were hard on his heels.

On reaching the broad staircase he pelted down it four steps at a time. He was only half-way down when one of his pursuers, regardless of consequences, leapt on his back. The impact shot him forward, dragging his feet from under him. The two of them crashed on to the stairs and, still clutching one another, rolled to the bottom.

It was Julian's luck that as they rolled to a standstill in the hall he was uppermost and the Japanese, having hit his head on the newel post of the banisters, had been temporarily rendered muzzy. Disengaging himself, Julian scrambled to his feet and made for the front door, with a sudden surge of new hope; for it now seemed certain that if he could get through it he would escape. But a fifth man, attracted by the shouting, had suddenly arrived on the scene from the direction in which lay the servants' quarters. He was old, skinny and grey-haired but, running sideways at Julian, he stuck out his leg and managed to trip him.

As Julian measured his length on the highly polished floor the other two men who had chased him from upstairs flung themselves down upon him, seizing his arms. He struggled to his knees but the old man who had tripped him now kicked him in the stomach. The man who had been momentarily rendered *hors de combat* by hitting his head on the newel post had recovered and came to the aid of the others. Between them they again forced him to the floor, turned him on his back, then stamped on his middle until his eyes were starting from his head and the breath was driven out of his body.

Pulling him to his feet, his three original attackers dragged him towards the stairs. He glimpsed the old man who had prevented him from escaping leering at him with a toothless grin, then turning away to return to his own quarters. Almost exhausted, but fighting still, he was hauled up the stairs. Nagi, still clutching his wound but leaning against the banisters, was shouting curses and encouragement to his henchmen.

On reaching the landing, the three wiry Japanese pulled and kicked Julian back along the corridor until they reached the room outside which, ten minutes earlier, he had felt such elation at the thought that he would find Merri. Groaning, Nagi had limped along after them. As they entered the room, he wheezed out in Japanese of which Julian understood just enough to make out his meaning:

'Out of the window with him! Out of the window! Then help me down to the garden so that I can break his neck.'

Shouting, cursing, kicking, Julian was dragged across the room. His captors thrust him towards the window, then lifted him and pushed his head and shoulders out of it. In the faint light he saw below him a sheer drop of eighteen feet. To fall from such a height on to the path of flat stones meant that he would at best break a leg, or splinter bones that would start an internal haemorrhage, if not land on his head. In vain he strove to cling to the window-sill. They prised free his grip of it, heaved up his legs and threw him out.

Just as when he had been thrown overboard from the launch on the night that Merri had been kidnapped at Aberdeen, by all the laws of the Medes and Persians he should have been dead or dying within the next ten minutes. But as he fell he glimpsed the figure of a man walking quickly round from the front of the house. Hearing the noise above, the man looked up. As he realized that Julian was about to fall on him his mouth opened in a gasp. He made a quick step back. But too late. Julian crashed sideways on him across his face and chest. He went over like a ninepin flat on his back, his head striking the stones of the path hard as he fell.

Half stunned, Julian lay across his inert body for a moment; then he realized that, except for an awful pain all round his right shoulder, he was unhurt. His mind had registered Nagi's intention to come down and finish him off. That spurred him into renewed activity. Although he had wounded Nagi, within a few minutes the others would be down there, and if they caught him his life would be forfeit.

Dragging himself to his feet, he staggered round to the front of the house. There, to his surprise, he saw the van that, when he had last seen it, contained the Kuan-yin and was being driven off to the Nest of the Phoenix by Pao Tin-yum. In the pale light coming from the front door there was no mistaking it, for the same Japanese characters and a spray of chrysanthemums were painted on its side.

Although still half bemused by his fall, it impinged on his mind that, somehow, Hayashi must already have succeeded in getting hold of the van and its precious contents. The man he had fallen upon must have driven it there and been going round to the back of the house to secure assistance in unloading it.

To his right Julian saw that the big gates had been left open. The drive up to the house was a semi-circular one. Scrambling unsteadily into the cab of the van, he pressed the self-starter. As the engine purred, he heard the shouts of the men who had attacked him. They had raced downstairs and were now emerging from the front door of the house, only fifteen feet in front of the van.

For a moment they did not realize that Julian was in the driving seat, then one of them saw the white blob of his face behind the windscreen. Letting out a falsetto screech, he pointed at it. Julian switched on the headlamps, temporarily blinding them; but the other men were directly in his path. Knowing that if he failed to get away they would kill him, he had no scruples about charging them and let in the clutch.

The van began to move. Before it had gained speed one of the men ran at it and flung himself on the bonnet. With a frantic prayer that the engine would not stall Julian pressed on the accelerator. Shooting forward, the van struck one of the men in its path knocking him sideways. The other jumped clear, then as the van ran past him sprang at Julian and grabbed him by the arm.

Meanwhile the man on the bonnet was crouching there, clinging to the windscreen wiper with his left hand and hammering with his right fist on the glass in an attempt to break it. His cropped head, glaring eyes and ferocious yellow face were barely a foot from Julian's. At the same time the other man was clutching Julian's injured arm and had his whole weight on it. Julian was dragged sideways and sickening pain racked his shoulder.

The van had now gathered speed, but he was forced to take his left hand from the wheel. Clenching his fist he drove it sideways and down, with all the force he could muster, into the face of the man who was clinging to his elbow. He felt the bone of the man's nose crunch; the man let out a howl, released his hold and dropped back on to the drive.

At that moment, under the blows of the man on the bonnet, the windscreen shattered. Glass flew into the cab and a piece of it nicked Julian's cheek. Next moment a yellow hand reached in to seize him by the throat. But by then the van was out of control. It left the drive, ploughed through some low bushes, then hit a stone ornament and lurched violently. The eyes and mouth of the man on the bonnet opened wide in terror, then he was thrown off.

Regardless of his injured shoulder, Julian seized the wheel with both hands and applied the brake. The van ran on through another bed of azaleas but, by pulling the wheel right over, he swerved the vehicle back on to the drive. It had almost stopped, but was within a few yards of the open gates. Releasing the brake, he turned the van again and a moment later it was out on the road.

Without any thought of direction he drove it for a quarter of a mile, then pulled up to mop up the blood that was running down his face from the cut on his cheek. He had saved himself and retrieved the Kuan-yin, but that was poor compensation for having failed to rescue Merri.

For some five minutes he sat there, wondering what next to do. It was obvious that he had fallen into a carefully prepared ambush, and again he realized that only Rinzai could have betrayed him. That there would be plenty of time to stop the handsome cheque, drawn on a bank in Hong Kong, that he had given the little wizen-faced detective was some small satisfaction. But that was not going to help Merri. He thought again of appealing to the police to raid Hayashi's house, now on the grounds that there was a gang of men in it who had tried to murder him, but realized that having entered the place illegally would prove a very poor basis for bringing a charge against its inmates.

He then began to speculate on how Hayashi had managed to get away with the Kuan-yin. About that two things seemed certain: he could hardly have done so unless he had had the co-operation of that shifty couple, the Paos; and, with their help, he had stolen it. If so he could, any-how, be charged with theft and, as it was still well before nine o'clock, the odds were that provided he had kept his appointment with Urata, he would still be at the Nest of the Phoenix.

Restarting the engine, Julian turned the van in the direction of the geisha house and, after twice losing his way but soon getting back on to it, drove up near the Phoenix. As he got out from the cab he noticed that he had pulled up just behind another van of the same make and colour as the one he had been driving. Then, as he walked

204

past it, he saw that on its side were painted the same Japanese signs and spray of chrysanthemums. Another moment and the penny dropped. Hayashi must have had another green Ford van painted to appear the twin of the one hired in Osaka by Tilly Sang, and had somehow rung the changes. No doubt the Paos had done that part of the job for him, but what did the van standing in front of the Phoenix contain?

Stepping round to the back of the van, Julian saw that the key was in the lock. Opening one of the doors he saw that the van was empty. Returning to the van he had driven there he got a screwdriver out of the tool-kit under the seat in the cab and with it forced the van's lock. Inside lay the big wicker casket. Satisfied that he really had got the Kuan-yin, he entered the geisha house. A uniformed porter touched his cap to him, but he took no notice of the man. He was staring across the wide low dimly lit hall. Against the wall at the far end of it Pao Tin-yum and his wife were sitting cross-legged, and between them reposed another wicker casket.

Walking over to them, Julian asked Pao Tin-yum what time they had got there.

'Half-past-eight,' the man replied with a surly look. 'On way we have tlouble. Police stop us and insist to see our passports. But makes no matter. The two Japanese upstairs are still eating. You said Kuan-yin not to be shown until dinner finished.'

Julian pointed at the wicker basket and said, 'Are you quite sure the Kuan-yin is still inside that? I've an idea that it may have been removed while you were talking to the police.'

'Then you are wong,' Pao Tin-yum returned. 'If so we tell by weight. Still velly heavy when carried in here.'

'But the Kuan-yin may have been removed and some bricks substituted,' Julian suggested. 'Open it up so that we can find out.'

'No!' retorted Pao, his manner suddenly becoming

205

suspicious and hostile. 'Mrs. Sang's orders. She say to be opened only front of Mr. Hayashi. Me responsible to her. She my boss. She give orders I take. Only from her.'

For a few minutes they argued the matter, but the man proved adamant; so Julian was more than ever inclined to believe that the couple were in the pay of Hayashi and assisting him in some deep-laid plot. Leaving them he went over to the porter and, with his assistance and that of another man he called up, they got the other wicker basket out of the van and carried it into the hall.

At the sight of it both the Paos came to their feet, their eyes round with surprise. When the second basket was set down alongside the first Julian said, 'Now, which of these contains the Kuan-yin? We had better open them both.' But again Pao flatly refused to allow the basket he had brought to be opened.

Meanwhile Pao Ping had been carefully scrutinizing the two baskets. Suddenly she addressed her husband in a spate of Chinese. He bent and examined the fastenings of the one that had just been brought in. Then, turning to Julian, he said angrily, 'My wife right. This one belong us. Why you play dirty trick? How you get hold of?'

Julian shrugged. 'That is nothing to do with you. I am only concerned that the right basket should be carried upstairs when it is sent for.'

'Me too, me too!' declared Pao Tin-yum. 'Mrs. Sang velly old fliend. I never let down; never!'

He spoke with such ardour that Julian suddenly felt that he might have been wrong in believing the couple to be in the pay of Hayashi, and that while their attention had been distracted from the van the casket had been swapped without their knowledge.

'All right,' he said. 'You stay here and in no circumstances let anyone take it from you before I come back. I'm going upstairs to see how things are going there.'

As Julian was still not prepared to trust the Paos, he went over to the porter and gave him a good tip to see that the basket he had helped bring in was not moved; then he had himself shown to the wash place. The cut on his cheek had stopped bleeding and on feeling his shoulder gingerly he decided that it was only very badly bruised. After cleaning himself up as well as he could, he took off his socks and shoes, put his socks on again and, carrying the shoes out to the hall, put them down beside a number of other pairs belonging to people who were dining upstairs. The porter then summoned one of the 'Mesdames' whose duty it was to chaperone the geishas and go in and out of the rooms to see that no improprieties took place during dinners. Having kowtowed to him she took him upstairs, slid back a door in the wall and signed to him to enter.

It was one of the smaller rooms and furnished somewhat differently from the usual Japanese restaurant, as a concession to the richer Westerners who could afford to pay for a proper geisha dinner. Instead of having to sit cross-legged or sideways at the table, those dining could sit on the floor with a backrest for support and could stretch their legs out at full length under it.

Hayashi and Urata, both dressed in the type of short black European coat that goes with striped trousers, were seated opposite one another, with a pretty young geisha kneeling beside each of them. They had evidently finished their dinner, as the geishas were entertaining them with childish games. At the moment all four were in turn passing round a saki vase and letting trickle from it a drop or two into an already nearly full saki cup, the game being to see who could do so last without the cup overflowing.

When Julian appeared they all stood up. Urata bowed and said, 'Mr. Day, I am much regretting that you were detained. Pliss to meet Mr. Hayashi.'

It was twenty-five years since the two men had been face to face, so Julian had very little fear that the Japanese would recognize him as Hugo Julian du Crow Fernhurst; nevertheless, when they had exchanged deep bows he took his eyes quickly from Hayashi's shrewd ones and said to Urata:

'I owe you both a sincere apology; but a private matter suddenly cropped up that had to be attended to, and I could not possibly get here earlier. I see you have finished dinner; so you must not bother about me. I can easily get some supper later at the Miyako. When I arrived here I saw the Paos in the hall, with the Kuan-yin. As you have finished dinner, shall we have it up and get down to business?'

The Madame said something to Urata in Japanese, and he said to Julian, 'Four special girls I have booked to sing, also do ritual dance with fan for us.' Then he looked questioningly at Hayashi.

At that moment Hayashi was not thinking about geishas; he was wondering how Julian had managed to slip through Nagi's fingers. Rinzai had telephoned before Hayashi left his house to say that the Englishman had, without prompting, thought of attempting to rescue the girl. But perhaps when he had arrived outside the house he had got cold feet and decided not to risk going in after all. Yet he had a slight cut on his cheek, his collar was badly crumpled and he had a button off his coat, all of which suggested that he had been in a fight. Perhaps, though, he had got as far as climbing in over the wall then, after prowling round for a while, lacked the courage to break into the house so climbed out again; such activities would be enough to account for the mark on his cheek and his slightly dishevelled appearance.

However, what had happened to Julian during the past hour was of no special importance to Hayashi, because half-way through dinner a note had been brought up to him which said that the vans had been switched successfully and that the Paos, suspecting nothing, were then on their way to the Phoenix with the one that had been substituted for theirs. Had Julian been within sight of the vans when the exchange was carried out it was certain that he would have interfered; but no mention of him had been made in the note. Obviously he must have been somewhere else at the time and knew nothing about the switch; so Hayashi felt that he had nothing to worry about.

As he had not yet signified whether he wished to see the dancers before inspecting the Kuan-yin, Urata repeated to him what Julian had said. Now, he was anxious to have done with them both; so that he could get home and make Tilly Sang squeal by prodding her with a knitting needle thrust through the wickerwork of the basket in which she had concealed herself. So he smiled, shrugged and said:

'Without disparaging the excellent entertainment provided by my honourable host, such creatures do not particularly amuse me. By all means let us delay no longer delighting our eyes with this beautiful representation of the Queen of Heaven.'

With a nod Julian left the room, went downstairs and had the porters carry up the big creaking basket. By the time he got back the Madame and the two young geishas had disappeared. The basket was set down at the end of the low table. Pao and his wife took up positions at either end of it, the porters left the room and Julian, having slid to the door behind them, remained standing near it. With pleasurable anticipation he was watching Hayashi's face to see how he would react when, instead of the pile of bricks he expected the basket to contain, he found that, after all, it held the beautiful Kuan-yin.

Pao and his wife undid the ties of the basket. Having eased the lid, they looked at one another; then in a loud voice Pao Tin-yum cried in Chinese, 'Are you ready?' and, after a long moment's pause, 'Now!'

On that, they both wrenched up the lid and threw it back. Everything then happened very quickly. Like a Jack-in-the-Box the head and shoulders of a woman emerged. Julian was a few feet behind her. He saw only that she had a mass of black hair, and he did not see her jerk up a hand holding a pistol. Next second a shot rang out. Hayashi, his mouth half open, went over backwards. But only for a moment. He had been sitting at the table cross-legged but, with the dexterity of an old Judo expert, he came up in the same position, and he had whipped a small automatic out of his pocket. Flame and noise spat from it. The woman in the basket gave a violent jerk. The black wig she was wearing fell off and Julian saw then that she was Tilly Sang. With a moan she flopped back into the basket.

Urata and Hayashi were now both on their feet. The former's face showed amazement and horror; the latter's fiendish delight. With loud wails the Paos were about to bend over the basket and attempt to aid their mistress; but Hayashi had taken a pace away from the table and, threatening them with his pistol, he hissed:

'Back! Get back both of you. Right back.'

Cowed by his expression, they did as he had ordered. Then he looked at the others and went on quickly, 'The shots. People come. I was showing you my pistol. An accident. You understand. Say otherwise and I will shoot you also.'

He had hardly finished speaking when the door was thrust back and the Madame appeared in it. A moment later she was joined by the porter. They looked round anxiously; but Hayashi smiled at them, toyed with his weapon casually and spoke to them in Japanese. It was clear to Julian that he was telling his story and indicating that no-one in the room had been hurt. Satisfied that no violence was in progress, the Madame and the porter withdrew. Hayashi then looked across at Urata and said:

'Honourable acquaintance, I condole with you that you should have been drawn into this plot to kill me, for your innocence is transparent. You need feel no compassion for the woman. She was already five times a murderess, and her two servants run a brothel for her in Hong Kong. But respected persons like you and I cannot afford to be mixed up in unsavoury scandals, and Mr. Day,' he bowed

210

slightly to Julian, 'will also doubtless see the wisdom of keeping his mouth shut.' After a swift glance down into the basket, he went on, 'The woman is either dead or dying. The coffin she has made for herself is thickly lined, so her blood will not trickle through to betray us. I intend to have her removed in it to my house. There I will take steps to dispose of her body.'

Turning his sharp glance on the Paos, he added:

'You two will accompany the basket to my house. You run an illegal establishment in Hong Kong. Upon your obeying me depends whether I allow you to return there as free persons or whether you go under escort to be handed over to the Hong Kong police. But I do not propose to trust you with the basket. So I am about to telephone my people to come here and escort you back to my house with it.'

Walking forward, he waved his little gun at Julian and said, 'Stand aside from the door please, Mr. Day; I wish to pass through it.'

'No!' snapped Julian. 'I'm not going to let you get away with this. I mean to send for the police.'

'You are being very foolish, Mr. Day, because it would involve us all in a great deal of trouble. Please to stand aside. Otherwise there will be another accident. This time a real one. You will force me to disclose this plot of Mrs. Sang's. I shot her, you attacked me; so I was compelled to fire at you in self-defence and, most unfortunately, the bullet went through your heart.'

'No!' Julian repeated firmly. 'I mean to have the police make a full enquiry. If you want to know why, it's because you are holding Merri Sang a prisoner and they will find her in your house.'

Hayashi shrugged. 'I see; and you are in love with her. I had temporarily forgotten that. Very well. She has served her purpose. I have no further use for her. If you will assist me to draw a veil over this affair of Mrs. Sang I will return the girl to you.'

'No,' said Julian for the third time. 'That is not enough. I want you dead, or your dope racket broken up and you doing another long stretch in prison for that and for having kidnapped Merri. I've left a letter at my hotel that is to be given to the police at eleven o'clock should I fail to return. If you kill me they will know that it was no accident and you will be executed for it. I don't value my life, so I'm willing to give it in order to get you.'

Giving him a puzzled look, Hayashi said, 'The girl has come to no harm, Mr. Day, and I have ample proof that her mother was a murderess; so I do not understand this intense bitterness you show towards me.'

A grim smile twitched Julian's lips. 'You wouldn't; because you failed to recognize me. My real name is Fernhurst. It was you, O'Kieff and the rest of your devilish gang who ruined my career years ago in Brussels, and caused my friend Carruthers to commit suicide. That's why I am determined to make you pay.'

Hayashi's cruel mouth fell open. At that moment Julian sprang. His right arm was almost useless, but with his left hand he grasped Hayashi's hand that held the gun, forcing it upwards. For half a minute they swayed backwards and forwards in a violent struggle for the weapon. It went off and a bullet smacked into the ceiling. The crack of the pistol was followed almost instantly by two more shots. Hayashi had advanced far enough towards the door for the wicker basket to be behind him. With her last reserve of strength, Tilly Sang had risen up in it again and put two shots through his back. With a long loud groan he sank to the floor dead.

The Madame and the porter arrived on the scene again, followed by the proprietor of the establishment. The police were sent for and depositions taken. Forty minutes later the whole party piled into cars and drove to Hayashi's house. The place was a shambles. Many of the fine statues had been thrown down, the priceless vases

212

smashed and the beautiful paintings in silk ripped to pieces. Nagi, it transpired, had earlier been sent to hospital with a nasty wound that would keep him there for some weeks. The male staff of the household had all been badly beaten up. The head 'boy', his face sadly battered, told the police that soon after nine o'clock a band of hooligans had broken in and wrecked the place.

Julian and Urata searched the house from attic to cellar, and all the outhouses, for Merri; but no trace of her could be found. At half past eleven Julian returned to the Miyako. Any satisfaction he felt at Hayashi's death was more than discounted by the fact that Merri was still missing and there was now no clue to her whereabouts. But when he got to his room the telephone was ringing. Picking up the receiver, he heard Urata's voice:

'Mr. Day, I have good news for you. I am most angry with Bill, but my heart finds it impossible not to forgive. He is desperate for this Merri. Knowing that Hayashi would be taking the dinner with us tonight he came back from Osaka. Here he collect many old school friends. They have many drinks, then with him they invade house. They not find Merri there, but with woman who guard her in small pavilion on lake. She iss now very happy and safe here with us.'

'Thanks. Please give her my love,' Julian replied tonelessly, and replaced the receiver.

So Bill had beaten him to it, and Merri had all the time been in that little pavilion at the end of the lake, near which he had stood for close on five minutes mistakenly fearful that a stone lantern was a night watchman. Had he only known during those minutes, he could have gone in and got her. But fate had been unkind to him.

As he turned away from the telephone he caught sight of his reflection in the mirror on the dressing table. He saw a face that looked every day of fifty. The strain of the past fortnight had aged him a lot. The hair at his temples that had been grey was now white, and his face was deeply lined. What, he wondered sadly, had he really got to offer Merri, except a certain amount of money and a knowledge of the world that could not really weigh very much against other assets that a girl not yet twenty would consider far more desirable?

Next day he lunched at the Uratas' house. After the meal he went out with Merri alone into the garden. She could not have been sweeter as she laid her hand on his, and said softly:

'I do hope you won't feel too badly about things, Julian. It's not that it was Bill who actually got me out of that awful man's clutches. I've been told all you did and I'm terribly grateful. But while I was a prisoner I had a lot of time to think, and I knew then that it was Bill that I loved. Mr. Urata is being terribly kind, and now poor Mother is dead there is no longer a bar to my marrying a Japanese.'

Julian nodded. 'I understand, and I hope you and Bill will be tremendously happy.'

'We will,' she replied confidently. 'But I'm worried about you. Couldn't you possibly bring yourself to go back to England and take up your inheritance? You've paid for your youthful folly a thousand times over, and I'm sure that even those few people who haven't forgotten about that will now be ready to accept your word that you were not really to blame.'

He smiled at her. 'Perhaps you're right, Merri. Anyhow, I'll think it over.'

This book
designed by William B. Taylor
is a production of
Heron Books, London

Printed in England by
Hazell Watson and Viney Limited
Aylesbury, Bucks